WIND RIVER

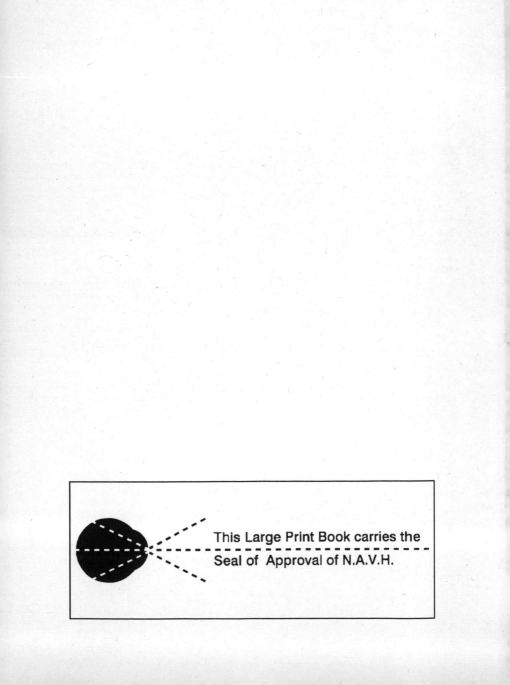

This Large Print Book carries the
Seal of Approval of N.A.V.H.

WIND RIVER SERIES

WIND RIVER

JAMES REASONER
L.J. WASHBURN

THORNDIKE PRESS

A part of Gale, Cengage Learning

GALE
CENGAGE Learning·

Farmington Hills, Mich • San Francisco • New York • Waterville, Maine
Meriden, Conn • Mason, Ohio • Chicago

GALE
CENGAGE Learning·

Copyright © 1994 by James M. Reasoner and L. J. Washburn.
Wind River Series #1.
Thorndike Press, a part of Gale, Cengage Learning.

LIBRARY OF CONGRESS CATALOGING-IN-PUBLICATION DATA

Reasoner, James.
     Wind river / by James Reasoner and L. J. Washburn. — Large print edition.
        pages ; cm. — (Thorndike Press large print western) (Wind river series ; #1)
     ISBN 978-1-4104-7012-6 (hardcover) — ISBN 1-4104-7012-1 (hardcover)
     1. Large type books. I. Washburn, L. J. II. Title.
  PS3568.E2685W56 2014
  813'.54—dc23   2014018444

Published in 2014 by arrangement with James Reasoner and L. J. Washburn

Printed in Mexico
1 2 3 4 5 6 7 18 17 16 15 14

For Barbara Puechner

CHAPTER 1

With the train rocking and swaying beneath his booted feet, Cole Tyler lounged in the open doorway of the boxcar and watched the rugged landscape of Wyoming Territory roll past. He was looking south, toward Big Buffalo Wash and the arid flats beyond that long gouge in the earth. Far in the distance, a nameless range of hills made a faint blue line on the horizon.

By turning his head, Cole could look through the open door on the other side of the car and see the peaks of the Wind River Mountains far to the north, almost lost in the haze of distance. More than once he had ridden through the Wind River range and enjoyed the harsh but beautiful landscape. If there had been time, he might have gone up there again. . . .

But there was work to be done: a railroad to be built, a continent to be bridged. His part in this was a small one, sure, but he had never been the sort to neglect a job once he had taken it on.

A sharp whinny from one of the stalls in the converted baggage car drew his attention, and he turned away from the door to go to the big golden sorrel.

Cole reached over the gate of the makeshift stall and rubbed the horse's nose. "Don't worry, Ulysses," he assured the animal. "You'll be able to stretch your legs soon. We'll be getting to the railhead in a little while, and then you'll get a chance to run."

The sorrel tossed his head impatiently, and Cole smiled. He understood how Ulysses felt. He was getting a little restless himself.

A well-built man of medium height, Cole had gray-green eyes that were accustomed to looking out over long distances. Since the end of the War Between the States a little over three years earlier, he had wandered over a good chunk of the country west of the Mississippi, scouting for the army, guiding wagon trains, and doing a little buffalo hunting. That was his job now — helping to provide meat for the thousands of workers laying the rails that stretched ever farther to the west.

He wore buckskins and high-topped black

boots, and a brown hat with a broad brim and a round crown hung on the back of his neck from its chin-strap. Thick brown hair that had been hacked off squarely fell to his shoulders. He was clean shaven, his features regular and deeply tanned. The Colt conversion revolver holstered on his right hip and the Winchester '66 snugged in his saddle-boot were both .44s, using the metallic cartridges stored in the loops of the shell belt around his waist. A heavy-bladed Green River knife, one of the few legacies of his mountain-man father, was sheathed on his left hip. Wrapped up in oilcloth in the pile of gear next to the stall was the massive Sharps .50 caliber he used for hunting buffalo.

As Cole resumed looking out the door of the railroad car, the stock tender came up behind him and commented, "Mighty ugly country, ain't it?"

Cole looked around in surprise. "Ugly?" he echoed. "Not so's you'd notice."

The hostler frowned and gestured at the semi-arid terrain. "But there's nothin' out there."

"Not much," Cole agreed. "But that doesn't make a place ugly."

It was true there wasn't much to be seen here in southern Wyoming except miles and

9

miles of open country bordered here and there by rugged mountains that seemed to fling themselves up from the plains.

Indians lived here, of course; the Sioux and the Shoshone had been in these parts for a long time. And there were a few ranchers moving in, cattlemen who were either brave enough or foolhardy enough to think they could make a go of a spread in this nearly desolate wilderness.

Forts were scattered across the territory, a reminder that the Oregon Trail ran through here and soldiers had been needed in the past to protect what had seemed like an endless stream of settlers in Conestoga wagons, bound for what sounded like the Promised Land.

There weren't many wagon trains these days, and treaties had been signed between the Indians and the politicos in Washington City — not that either side really abided by those treaties all the time or had ever intended to. Wyoming Territory was still pretty wild country most of the time.

The railroad aimed to change that. The Union Pacific was moving inevitably westward, just as the Central Pacific had started on the West Coast and was coming east. Somewhere, sooner or later, they would meet, and east and west would be finally, permanently joined, ensuring the spread of civilization.

Or at least that was the plan, Cole mused with a faint smile as he watched the landscape roll past. But civilization might have finally met its match in Wyoming.

He turned his head and asked the stock tender, "Didn't you say there's a town already set up at the railhead?"

"That's what I've heard," the young man answered. "A real live, gen-u-ine town with a name and everything." He pointed through the other door at the far-off peaks to the north. "Named it after those mountains. They're calling the place Wind River."

"I tell you, my dear, this is the biggest day in the history of Wind River!"

"Of course, Andrew," Simone McKay agreed. She couldn't resist pointing out the obvious, however. "But the town has been here less than a month, hasn't it?"

Her husband ignored the question and leaned out to peer down the railroad tracks toward the east. The double line of steel ran straight as an arrow for several miles before vanishing in a bend around a ridge that jutted up from the south. Andrew McKay followed the rails with his eyes, and as he did he could almost see the riches coming his

11

way along with the first train.

His partner, William Durand, slapped him on the back. "Getting anxious, eh, Andrew?" boomed Durand. "History will be here soon enough, my friend. And that's what this is, you know — history. Yes, indeed, the first train to arrive in Wind River is quite a historic occasion."

The two men were a study in contrasts, McKay tall and lean, clean-shaven and somewhat austere, Durand much shorter and beefier with a closely trimmed dark beard shot through with gray. They had been partners for over a year, because that was how long it had taken to prepare for this day. Without them, the settlement of Wind River would not even exist.

The railroad station where they waited, a spanking-new building of timber and stone, was the centerpiece of the town, which spread out on both sides of the Union Pacific rails.

To the north was what Durand and McKay intended as the industrial district, with warehouses and cattle pens just waiting for use.

South of the tracks was the rest of the settlement, including the business-lined main street known as Grenville Avenue and the cross streets where residences were already springing up. The impressive homes of Durand and Andrew and Simone McKay were at opposite ends of one of those cross streets at the western edge of town, far enough away from the train station and the cattle pens so that Mrs. McKay was unlikely to be offended by any less-than-pleasant odors.

Durand grimaced as the band waiting on the platform began practicing with their instruments. The musicians should have been better, he thought. They had been given their instruments only a week earlier and had not had enough time to practice. It was such small details that drove Durand mad when they weren't attended to properly. The Union Pacific deserved a proper welcome from the community when the first train arrived in Wind River.

Nothing but handcars had reached the settlement so far; in fact, the final rails had been laid only the day before. But as soon as those spikes were driven, the word had gone back up the line: the UP had a new railhead! It was cause for celebration, and that was exactly what McKay and Durand intended to provide for both the town and the railroad.

As for Simone McKay, she sighed and wished this was over so that she could go home. Summers in Wyoming, in this high, dry air, were not as hot as those in Philadelphia, but today was unusually warm and Simone missed the coolness of her parlor.

She glanced around at the crowd waiting on the platform for the train's arrival. Many of them were Union Pacific workers, given the day off so that they could witness the official moving of the railhead, but most of the citizens of Wind River were here, too.

Standing a few feet beyond Simone's husband was Judson Kent, the tall, bearded Englishman who served as the new community's doctor, and beside Kent was Michael Hatfield, the editor of the *Wind River Sentinel.* Like nearly everything else in town, the newspaper was owned by McKay and Durand, but neither one of them had any journalistic experience. The sandy-haired young Hatfield had been brought in to run the paper, and what he lacked in practical experience he had been making up for with sheer enthusiasm. At the moment he had his arm around his wife, who was holding their two-and-a-half-year-old daughter and looking tired.

Simone sympathized with Delia Hatfield. Wyoming was no place to be raising a toddler, let alone to be expecting yet another child.

14

Someone jostled her, and Simone looked around angrily. One of the UP track layers stood there, a contrite expression on his broad Irish face. "I'd be beggin' yer pardon, ma'am," he said quickly as he tugged off his battered black hat. "I didn't mean t' bump into ye."

"That's all right," Simone told him, her anger evaporating in the heat. "It's rather crowded here on the platform."

"Yes, ma'am, it's all o' that! Ever'body's ready fer th' train t' get here, I reckon. Hell on wheels, they call it!"

Simone smiled tolerantly at his exuberance. "Yes, I've heard that expression myself," she said over the bleating and blatting of the nearby band. "I'm sure it's deserved."

Before the track layer could say anything else, another man shouldered him roughly aside. "Out of the way, you damned mick," the newcomer growled. He was tall and lean, wearing a stained white hat with a tightly rolled brim, a leather vest, a work shirt, and denim pants. A blond mustache drooped over his wide mouth and his hair hung long over the back of his neck. The well-worn walnut grips of a six-gun jutted up from his holster.

Simone's mouth tightened as she recognized him. His name was Deke Strawhorn, and he had been hanging around Wind River for the last week. He was a hardcase, an outlaw, some said, and he had about half a dozen men of the same stripe with him. They moved up behind him now, and the UP worker, who had started to make an angry reply to Strawhorn's gibe, saw the other men and closed his mouth. His face dark with resentment and a little shame at being run off, he moved down the platform to look for another vantage point.

Simone tried not to breathe a sigh of relief. For a moment she had been afraid that a fight would break out right there beside her.

Strawhorn glanced at her, his eyes bold and a faint smile on his mouth, and Simone looked away quickly, turning her attention back to her husband. Suddenly she saw Andrew stiffen, and he lifted a hand to point down the track to the east.

"By God, I think that's it," he said excitedly. "Yes, I'm sure of it. Here it comes!"

In spite of her normal reserve, Simone felt a surge of emotion grip her. She clutched Andrew's arm and leaned forward beside him, craning her neck so that she could see past the other people waiting anxiously on the platform.

She peered along the tracks and at first

saw nothing except empty Wyoming prairie land. Then her eyes found the tiny black dot that came closer and closer as she watched, growing until she could make out the stack at the front of the locomotive with clouds of white smoke billowing up from it.

What was it the UP track layer had called it? Simone caught her bottom lip between even white teeth as she remembered the answer.

Hell on wheels.

Cole braced himself with a hand on the side of the boxcar doorway as the train slowed to a stop. Over the hiss of the steam and the squeal of the brakes, he heard the tinny notes of what sounded like a brass band playing loudly but not particularly well. The town of Wind River was putting on some sort of fandango to welcome the train, he saw as he looked out and took note of the crowd on the platform.

Some of the UP bosses were riding in the first car behind the coal tender, and with practiced ease the engineer brought the locomotive to a stop so that it was next to the platform. Behind it stretched the rest of the train, three more passenger cars and nearly a dozen boxcars. All of them were full, too.

The previous railhead had been Laramie, some eighty miles to the east. Some of the settlement had remained intact, but all the tent saloons had been taken down and the canvas structures stored on the train, ready to be set up again here in Wind River. Along with the tents had come their owners, the saloonkeepers who knew that the Irish work gangs would gladly spend all of their wages on cheap whiskey, games of chance, and gaudily painted women. Those things the saloon owners provided in abundance.

They began pouring off the train once it had come to a full stop. The saloonkeepers, the gamblers, the soiled doves . . . banjo-plinking musicians, faro dealers, singers and dancers, swampers . . . all the men and women whose business was entertaining the laborers — and taking their money in the process. And if some of the Irishmen got robbed or even murdered along the way, well, that was just one of the risks of building a railroad through a wilderness, just like Indian attacks and rock slides and cyclones.

Cole hopped down lithely from the boxcar. It would be a little while before the ramps were put in place so that the horses stabled inside could be unloaded. Since he couldn't collect Ulysses right away, he thought he would take a look around Wind

River. He might even stay a few days before riding out to scout up more buffalo. Towns weren't his favorite places, but every so often it made a nice change to eat a meal in a cafe and sleep in a bed. Made a man appreciate the rest of his life that much more.

From what Cole could see, there was more to Wind River than most of these railhead settlements. Quite a few permanent buildings had already been constructed, although there was still plenty of room along the streets for the tents that had been brought from Laramie. Some of the buildings appeared to be quite substantial, too, not just the clapboard-and-tin shanties that were sometimes thrown up behind elaborate false fronts. He saw a stone structure that was three stories tall, probably a hotel, and several other buildings along the main street had been built to last. Whoever was responsible for Wind River must have had visions of the settlement growing into another Chicago or St. Louis.

Cole paid little attention to the ceremony on the platform as he walked alongside the train. The band had stopped playing, and now somebody was making a speech. Cole glanced at him, saw a tall, dark-haired man in a fancy suit and a top hat. Standing next to him was a shorter, heavier man with a beard, also well dressed, and just behind them was a woman who caught more of Cole's attention. She wore a gown of blue silk and a feathered hat to match, and her hair was dark and thick and glossy. She was as pretty a woman as Cole had seen in a long time, but judging from her expensive outfit and the way she stood with one hand on the arm of the gent making the speech, Cole figured her for the man's wife.

He turned his eyes away from the dignitaries and started to veer around the station. From the looks of things, there would be a saloon or two already open in Wind River, and a cold beer would go down nice, he decided. Just being this close to a bunch of speechifying made him thirsty.

That was when all hell broke loose.

A man yelled a curse, and a second later a woman screamed. Fists thudded against flesh as people began yelling. Cole hesitated, not sure if he wanted to turn around and look or not. This fracas was none of his business, after all.

"Watch it, mister!"

Cole ducked instinctively and twisted around in time to see a man come flying off the platform at him. The man was yelling and pinwheeling his arms and legs, but there was nothing for him to grab onto except thin air. He sailed past Cole and crashed headfirst into the ground.

Somebody had thrown the man off the platform, not caring where he landed. But Cole cared, because the man had almost crashed down on top of him. He looked up and saw a couple of roughly dressed men standing at the edge of the platform, laughing raucously.

Cole felt a red haze spreading through his brain. He walked toward the platform, calling up to the two men, "Think that's mighty funny, do you?"

"Well, you sure jumped, mister," one of them replied. "Didn't really mean to throw that Irish ape at you, but I reckon it turned out a mite humorous."

Cole glanced over his shoulder. The man who had landed on the ground was still lying there motionless, out cold. There was no telling how badly he was really hurt. And the two hardcases on the platform were still laughing about it.

"Yeah," Cole grunted as he reached up without warning and grasped their shirts. "Damned hilarious."

He pulled hard, and the struggling crowd behind the men gave him a hand by surging toward him. The two men plunged off the platform and sprawled in the dust on either side of Cole.

One of them rolled over and came up reaching for a gun, but by that time Cole had turned around himself. The heel of his boot crashed into the man's jaw and sent him sprawling again, this time with a moan of pain. The other man scrambled to his feet, grated a curse, and swung a wild punch at Cole's head.

Cole pivoted in time to block the blow with an up flung left arm. With his right, he hooked a hard punch to the man's stomach as he stepped in closer. A left cross caught the man on the jaw and jerked his head around. Cole dropped him with an uppercut.

There was no time to relish victory, though, because in the next instant somebody landed on his back, staggering him. An arm looped around his throat from behind and tightened brutally, cutting off his air.

Cole drove an elbow back into the belly of his new opponent and smelled whiskey on the breath that gusted past his face in response to the blow. The arm around his neck didn't loosen, though, until Cole lashed backward with his foot and felt his boot heel dig into the man's shin. The grasp weakened then and Cole was able to twist out of it, spinning around to club a blow across the man's face.

Everything around him was chaos now. Men shouted and cursed, women screamed. From what he could see on the platform, the fight had started between some of the railroad workers and a group of hard-faced men in range clothes, but it had spread out to involve everyone in the railroad station and spill off the platform.

The musicians from the brass band were clubbing opponents over the head with trombones, which, Cole thought fleetingly, was a better use for the instruments. Then one of the Irishmen from the UP was running at him, face distorted with anger, fists up and swinging.

Cole ducked aside and shouted, "Hold it, Dooley! It's me, damn it! We're on the same side!"

Dooley wasn't in any mood to listen to reason. He flailed at Cole until the buffalo hunter had no choice but to pound a couple of punches into his midsection and then knock him down with a hard overhand blow. Cole looked around, hoping no one else would jump him, especially not somebody who was supposed to be his friend.

The brawl was still going on, and Cole wondered where the law was, assuming

Wind River *had* any law. The town was so new that the citizens might not have gotten around to electing a sheriff or hiring a marshal. Some of the railroad superintendents were wading into the melee, however, swinging clubs, and Cole knew it was only a matter of time before they restored order.

A gunshot cracked, a thin, wicked sound against the uproar of the crowd, and Cole heard a woman cry out, "Andrew!" His jaw tightening, he vaulted onto the platform and began trying to force his way through the mob toward the source of the shot.

That single report was the only time a gun had gone off during this chaos, but Cole had a bad feeling about it anyway. He palmed out his Colt, taking a calculated risk that more gunfire wouldn't just make things worse, and triggered off three shots into the awning that overhung the station platform. The explosions were deafening in these close quarters.

They worked, though, freezing men with fists upraised to strike. Eyes jerked around and looked toward Cole, who stood with the revolver in his hand, smoke still drifting from its barrel in thin tendrils. He heard sobbing that came from beyond several men who had been struggling to beat each other half to death only seconds earlier.

Cole shoved the men aside, not sure why he was involving himself so deeply in this. It was a question that could wait until later. Right now he wanted to know what had happened here.

Grim lines appeared on his face as he saw the man's body huddled on the platform, blood pooling on the planks beneath him. It was the tall, sleekly handsome man who had been making a speech earlier, Cole saw, but he wasn't so handsome now. One side of his face was pressed against the platform. The features that were visible were contorted in a grimace of agony. His eyes were glassy in death.

Kneeling beside him, lying half on top of him as her back heaved from the wretched sobs that shook her, was the woman Cole had seen with the dead man, the woman he had taken to be the man's wife. The thickset, bearded man was looking down at them, his face pale and stunned.

Another bearded man, this one wearing a dusty black suit and a bowler hat, held the dead man's wrist for a moment before placing it gently on the platform. "I'm quite sorry, Mrs. McKay," he said in a clipped British accent, "but I'm afraid there's not a dashed thing I can do."

The woman looked up, tears streaking her

face. "Did . . . did anyone see who shot him?" she demanded. "Did anyone see who had the gun?"

A young man with sandy hair pointed suddenly at Cole. "He's got a gun!" the young man said excitedly.

Cole tensed again as every eye in the crowd swung toward him. He realized that by butting into this he might have put himself in danger. It all depended on how worked up these folks were and if they were willing to listen to reason.

He jammed the Colt back into its holster and said in a loud voice, "Yeah, I've got a gun. So do most of the men in this station. All I did was fire a couple of rounds into the roof to make everybody stop fighting."

The Englishman, who had been acting like a doctor as he checked for a pulse in the dead man's wrist, straightened to an impressive height and said, "I believe this gentleman is telling the truth. I heard the first shot distinctly, and it did not come from a gun of such a heavy caliber."

"Maybe he's got two guns," suggested one of the onlookers.

"That first shot came from a thirty-two," Cole snapped. "Maybe even a gun smaller than that. I'm not carrying anything but this forty-four, and any damn fool can see that."

26

The heavyset man gestured at the corpse and asked, "But who would have shot Andrew? My God, this is awful!"

"Just a stray bullet, I reckon," contributed a lean man with a blond mustache. He shrugged. "Mighty bad luck."

"Keep your mouth shut, Strawhorn," the heavy-set man said angrily. "We don't need any comments from the likes of you."

The eyes of the man called Strawhorn narrowed, and he took a step toward the thick-waisted man. The prickling feel of impending violence was suddenly in the air again.

"Stop it!" The shrill cry came from the woman who still knelt beside her husband's body. "Stop it, all of you! Andrew's dead, and all you can do is argue!"

A young redheaded woman who was carrying a toddler thrust the child into the arms of the man who had pointed out that Cole was carrying a gun. She hurried forward and bent to put her arms around the shoulders of the distraught woman. "Come with me, Mrs. McKay," she said softly. "There's nothing you can do now. Dr. Kent will tend to things." She looked up at the tall English medico. "Won't you, Dr. Kent?"

"Of course," Kent said briskly. "Mrs. Hatfield is right. Go along with her and the other ladies, Mrs. McKay . . . Simone. I'll be 'round to see you shortly, and I'll give you something to help you sleep."

"I . . . I don't want to sleep," Simone McKay said, choking the words out. "My God, he's dead! Andrew's dead!"

Cole's mouth was a taut line as he watched the young redhead, assisted by several other women, leading the widow away from the platform and through the station to the street. He looked around and saw that the platform, packed so tightly with humanity only a short time before, was half-empty now. Many of the men involved in the brawl had bolted when the shooting started, and most of the others were beginning to drift away now. This little celebration had been blown all to hell, all right.

The doctor looked coolly at Cole and asked, "Do you mind if I inquire as to just who you are, sir?"

"Nobody," Cole said. "Just a fella who wanted to know what was going on."

The Englishman's mouth twisted in a grimace. "Well, you've seen it, haven't you?"

Cole nodded curtly. He was being dismissed, and he knew it. That was all right with him. This killing, and the brawl that had preceded it, were no concern of his.

He turned on his heel and strode to the

steps at the end of the platform, descending them to circle the building and start down the street. Behind him, he could hear the sounds of the train being unloaded. By nightfall, the tents would be set up again. Whiskey would be flowing in the saloons, cards would be shuffled and dealt — sometimes fairly, sometimes not — roulette wheels would spin, and painted women would laugh gaily as they led their customers into the alcoves where the cots were set up. Business as usual, Cole thought.

And not even death could stop it.

CHAPTER 2

Kermit Sawyer brought his horse to a stop, hipped around in the saddle, and looked behind him. Two thousand head of Texas longhorns kicked up one hell of a lot of dust, he thought as he took off his hat and sleeved sweat from his blunt, lined face. To a cattleman, those clouds of dust billowing up were a pretty sight . . . but Sawyer was just as glad that he owned those longhorns and didn't have to ride drag anymore. The air was a lot cleaner up here at the point.

He had always been the sort of hombre to be out front, Sawyer thought proudly. Hell, hadn't he been the first rancher west of the Balcones?

He stretched, old bones creaking a little as he shifted in the saddle. He was a solidly built man in his fifties, with a shock of snow-white hair above features tanned by years of the Texas sun to a shade that almost matched his saddle leather. He favored black clothes, right down to the bandanna around his neck. The only splashes of lightness about him were his hair and the specially made ivory grips of the heavy Colt he wore.

Texas was a long way behind him now. Texas, and the memories the place held. Memories of the wife who had stood by him for nigh onto thirty years, helping him fight off Comanche and drought and wideloopers, the woman who had been able to stir a cookpot with one hand and reload a rifle with the other, the mother of his children, only one of whom had survived infancy. Six months earlier he had put her in the ground, there on the hilltop overlooking the creek, right next to the four smaller graves. She'd wore out at last, Sawyer supposed, just an old pioneer woman gone to meet her Maker.

Her name had been Amelia, and Sawyer could whisper that name now, could remember the way she looked without feeling like somebody was stabbing a knife in his chest. But he'd had to leave Texas and come hundreds of miles up here to Wyoming Territory to escape that pain.

One of the waddies who had come with him on the trek galloped up next to him and asked, "You all right, boss? The herd's comin' up fast, and you don't want 'em trompin' right over you."

"Who the hell're you to tell me what I want?" Sawyer growled, all those memories immediately banished to the corner of his mind where he kept them. "They're my damn longhorns, and if I want to sit here and let 'em walk right over me, it's my own damn business!"

The cowboy swallowed hard. "Well, sure, Mr. Sawyer, if that's what you want . . ."

Sawyer jerked a thumb at the approaching herd. "Get on back there and watch out for strays. That's what I pay you good wages for, ain't it?"

"Yes, sir!" The youngster wheeled his horse and galloped back toward the longhorns.

Sawyer faced front again, squared his shoulders, heeled the big chestnut gelding under him into a trot. He wanted to catch up to the chuck wagon and make sure young Lon had chosen a good spot to make camp.

If Soogans Malone had come along on this drive as coosie, Sawyer wouldn't have worried, but Soogans was too ancient for such a long, arduous trip. Malone was almost as old as Sawyer himself. He'd stayed behind on the home ranch, but he had promised Sawyer that his helper, Lon

Rogers, could handle the chuck wagon. And the boy had jumped at the chance.

Lon wasn't much good at cowboying, but he knew his way around a campfire and a grub wagon. This was new country to him, just like it was to all of Sawyer's riders.

Each day when the old cattleman sent the chuck wagon on ahead of the herd, there was no way of knowing what the boy would run into. Sawyer spurred his horse to a faster gait, eager now to make sure Rogers was all right and had picked a suitable spot for night camp.

It wasn't long before the herd was out of sight, although the dust haze was still visible in the air a few miles behind Sawyer. Like West Texas, this Wyoming country was a land where a man could see for a long way. Hills rose in the distance to the right and left, and up ahead to the north, mountains bulked on the horizon.

That might be the Wind River range, Sawyer thought as he squinted at the far-off peaks. He had been told that the railroad was coming through this area, south of the mountains, and he knew it wouldn't be long now before he found the place where he would establish his new ranch. There was supposed to be good graze in the foothills, and with the railroad close by, it would be easy to

33

ship his cattle to market back east. Wyoming Territory was going to be prime ranching country, and just as he had done thirty years earlier in Texas, Kermit Sawyer intended to be one of the first to take advantage of the opportunity.

He rode to the top of a ridge and reined in abruptly. Up ahead on the prairie, about a mile in front of him, he saw the chuck wagon. It had come to a stop out in the open, with no stream of any sort around it that Sawyer could see. He frowned in disapproval. Even a relative greenhorn like Lon Rogers knew that a herd had to have water. What had the boy been thinking?

Sawyer stiffened as he spotted movement around the wagon. He squinted harder until he could make out the mounted figures. A couple of them had feathered headdresses trailing down their backs, he realized, as a cold chill went down his own spine.

The chuck wagon was surrounded by Indians.

"Son of a bitch," Sawyer breathed as he reached for his saddlebags and dug out the spyglass he kept there. He pulled the glass out to its full length and lifted it to his eye.

He needed a few seconds to find what he was looking for, and then the scene came into focus. There were about a dozen Indians, he estimated.

They weren't attacking. They were just riding slowly around the wagon, looking it over curiously as if they had never seen such a thing before. Sawyer shifted the glass a little and saw Lon Rogers sitting on the wagon seat. The youngster was still alive, and Sawyer was thankful for that much. He couldn't see Lon's face, but he could tell from the stiff way the boy was sitting that he was plenty scared.

With good cause, Sawyer thought as he closed the spyglass and stowed it away in the saddlebags. Those were probably Sioux warriors, and although there was supposed to be a treaty with the Sioux, Sawyer didn't trust the savages for one minute. The Comanch' down in Texas had signed treaties, too, then gone right on with their raiding and murdering.

Sawyer turned and looked back toward the herd. It would take him at least half an hour to reach his men and return to this spot with them. In that time the Sioux could get tired of examining the chuck wagon and decide to have some fun with Lon by torturing him.

Sawyer's blue eyes narrowed. Damned if he was going to stand by and let that happen. Especially not to Lon. He'd promised

Lon's mother that he'd look after the boy. . . .

He spurred down the ridge, galloping toward the wagon.

The Sioux must have seen him coming. It would have been difficult not to see him in that expanse of open country. When he was still half a mile from the wagon, the warriors moved between him and the vehicle and drew their ponies into a line. They sat there waiting as Sawyer rode toward them.

He didn't rein his horse to a stop until only twenty feet separated him from the Sioux. Sawyer regarded them steadily as he leaned forward in the saddle, resting his hands on the horn. His estimate had been accurate, he saw. There were twelve of them, just as he had thought.

Beyond the Indians, Lon Rogers had twisted around on the wagon seat so that he could see what they were doing, and when he saw his employer, he exclaimed, "Mr. Sawyer! Lordy, am I glad to see you!"

"Don't be," Sawyer snapped. "What the hell were you thinking, boy, driving our chuck wagon right into the midst of a bunch of savages like this? Don't you have the sense God gave a jackrabbit?"

Lon swallowed and looked confused. "I . . . I'm sorry, Mr. Sawyer. I don't know where they came from. It was like they grew right up out of the ground. One minute they weren't there, and then the next minute they were."

Sawyer lifted a hand and leisurely waved off the explanation without ever taking his eyes away from the Sioux. "Never mind about that. They give you any idea what they want?"

Before Lon could answer, one of the warriors spoke up. "Want whiskey," he demanded in a guttural voice. "Want baccy. More whiskey."

"I don't have any whiskey for the likes of you," Sawyer told him, ignoring the look of alarm on Lon's face. "Nor any tobacco, either. You can drink coyote piss and smoke buffalo turds for all I care."

A couple of the Sioux looked startled by his reply, including the one who had demanded whiskey and tobacco. The others probably didn't speak English, Sawyer decided.

He didn't give them time to be offended. He reached for the butt of the Winchester socketed into a saddle boot under his right thigh and pulled the rifle free. Laying it over the cantle of the saddle, he went on, "This is a Winchester Model 1866. Holds fifteen shots. That means I can kill ever' damn one of you redskins and have three bullets left over. That's what I'll have to do unless you vamoose out of here."

Several of the Indians were holding single-shot carbines. They started to lift the weapons, and the others reached for arrows in the quivers strapped to their backs. The one who had spoken before gestured curtly, however, motioning for them to wait before they killed this crazy old white man. He met Sawyer's cold stare and asked, "Who are you to talk to Sioux this way?"

"My name's Kermit Sawyer," the cattleman replied, "and I've killed a few dozen of your heathen cousins the Comanche down Texas way. I don't mind killin' a few Sioux if I have to, neither."

Vaguely, he was aware that Lon Rogers was ashen-faced and watching the confrontation with an occasional warning shake of his head. Sawyer ignored the youngster. He wasn't going to let a boy tell him how to deal with Indians.

A few seconds of tense silence went by, then Sawyer lifted one hand and pointed back where he had come from. He knew the dust from the herd would be plainly visible to these keen-eyed savages. "There's two thousand head of prime Texas beef coming up that trail," he declared. "*My* cattle. I've got forty proddy young cowboys driving 'em, and every one of those lads is as quick to kill a redskin as I am. But I'll tell you bucks what I'll do."

The one who spoke passable English laughed harshly. "Tell us, old man," he said.

Sawyer pretended he hadn't heard the laughter or the gibe. "I'll trade you five of those cattle to take back to your village and feed your families, in return for not having to bother with you heathens while we're passing through these parts."

"Many buffalo," the Sioux warrior said scornfully, waving a hand at the plains around them. "Not need white man's skinny cattle."

Sawyer's mouth was getting a little dry, but he managed to chuckle. "Well, longhorn's not the best eatin' in the world, I'll give you that. And some of 'em in my herd are probably damned near as wild as any buffalo you got around here. So I'll throw in a couple of ponies." The horses in his remuda were what the Indians would really be after if they attacked the herd, he knew.

The warrior held up a clenched fist, opened and closed it twice. "Ten ponies," he said.

Sawyer shook his head emphatically. "Three," he countered.

"Eight ponies," the Sioux said angrily.

Sawyer worked the Winchester's lever, jacking a shell into the chamber. "Five, and that's as high as I'll go, you thievin' son of a bitch."

The warrior glared at him for a few seconds, then turned his head abruptly and spoke to the others. While the conversation was going on Sawyer stole a glance at Lon Rogers. If the boy commenced to sweat any more, he'd be sitting in a puddle before long, thought Sawyer.

The spokesman looked at Sawyer again and grunted. "Five ponies and five of these longhorns. It is good."

Sawyer nodded and pointed at the chuck wagon. "And you'll leave my chuck wagon, my riders, and my herd alone?"

"You be safe on Sioux land . . . for while. Not stay long."

"We'll be out of here as soon as we can," Sawyer promised. He slid the rifle back in its sheath and swung down out of the saddle. "Lon," he called to the cook, "come get this horse and ride back to the herd. Tell Frenchy to cut five good ponies out of the remuda and bring 'em up here along with five head of stock. Make sure some of the boys come back with you." Lon hesitated, and Sawyer added, "Well, come on!"

Lon jumped down from the seat of the chuck wagon and hurried toward his boss. The line of Indians parted to let him through, and as the youngster came up to him Sawyer put his horse's reins in the boy's hands. "Don't waste any time gettin' there and back," he said quietly.

"What're you going to do, Mr. Sawyer?"

"I'll stay here with the chuck wagon and keep an eye on it. Don't want to tempt those bucks too much."

"But . . . but what about the Sioux?"

"They won't bother me. We've made a deal. I traded with the Comanch' down in Texas, and they kept their word most of the time when it was a private deal, not a government treaty. I reckon these heathens'll do the same."

Lon licked dry lips and looked at him. "What if they don't? What if we come back and they've killed you?"

"Well, then, son . . . don't give 'em the ponies."

The boy's eyes widened, and Sawyer knew Lon thought he was crazy. That was all right. Sometimes the smartest thing a man could do was to act a little crazy.

"Go on," Sawyer urged. "Get the job done, Lon."

The cook nodded and mounted Sawyer's

horse, wheeling it and kicking it into a gallop.

In less than an hour, Frenchy and half a dozen of the boys would come boiling back over that ridge, and if the Sioux hadn't kept their part of the bargain, those Texas lads would track them clear to Canada if they had to in order to even the score. Sawyer was certain of that.

He watched until Lon had disappeared over the rise, then turned and strode toward the chuck wagon. One of the Indians shifted his horse a little to get in Sawyer's way.

Sawyer just looked coldly up at the warrior until he moved the animal again. As he walked on to the wagon Sawyer thought that Amelia would have understood what he had done. A man didn't back down, didn't turn and run. He stood up to trouble when it came and met it head-on.

But that was a mite easier to do, Sawyer reckoned, when the person you loved most in the world had gone and died, leaving you behind. Life had lost some of its sweetness, some of the reason to keep on clinging to it the way most folks did.

Sawyer stepped up to the wagon seat and settled down on it to wait. The Sioux walked their horses around so that they were facing him again, and he motioned to the spokesman. "What's your name?" Sawyer asked.

"In your tongue, called Eagle Feather."

"Well, tell me, Eagle Feather, are those the Wind River Mountains?" The old cattleman pointed to the peaks rising hazily to the north.

"Wind River," Eagle Feather repeated with a nod. "Sioux land, too."

Maybe so, Sawyer mused, but if the railroad was really coming through the way people said it was, the days of the Sioux's dominion over this territory were numbered. Eagle Feather might not know it, but he was probably already a dying breed.

Sort of like Kermit Sawyer himself . . .

CHAPTER 3

The knock at the door of Cole's hotel room came just as he was about to go downstairs again and look for some place to get a meal. He had washed off some of the dust of the past weeks in a big wooden tub filled with hot water brought up by the clerk, then pulled a clean buckskin shirt over his head and put on a pair of denim pants. Not expecting any visitors, he reached for the coiled shell belt and holster on the bed when the knock sounded.

He slid the Colt from the holster and went over to the door, standing to one side out of habit as he called, "Who is it?"

"I'd like to talk to you, Mr. Tyler," replied a voice that was vaguely familiar. "My name is William Durand."

Cole didn't know any William Durand and was about to say so when the man went on, "It's very important, and it could prove to be profitable for you, Mr. Tyler."

Cole had never been one to object to an honest profit, but he wasn't greedy enough to let the promise of a payoff make him careless, either. He twisted the key in the lock and stepped back quickly, keeping the revolver trained on the doorway. "It's open," he called. "Come on in."

The knob turned and the door swung slowly open. The man standing there blinked in surprise at the sight of the gun pointed at him and said, "Oh, dear." Cole recognized him as the thickset, bearded individual who had been on the platform that afternoon with Andrew McKay.

William Durand wasn't alone, either. Cole saw the British doctor standing beside him, and the sandy-haired young man from the platform — what was his name? Hatfield? — was also with him. The doctor stepped into the room first, casting a scornful glance at the gun, and said to Cole, "You don't need that, my good man. We're here on business."

Cole smiled thinly. "Out here on the frontier, some folks do business with a gun in their hand."

"Yes, but you're not a desperado, and neither are we."

Cole inclined his head slightly in acknowledgment of the point, then slipped his

45

thumb off the hammer of the Colt and slid the revolver back into the holster. He buckled the shell belt around his waist, however, and thonged down the holster.

"I don't know what brought you here, gents," he said, "but I'm hungry, so get on with it."

The heavyset man stepped forward, obviously more at ease now that Cole had put up his gun.

The man extended a hand and said, "I'm William Durand. I was Andrew McKay's business partner."

Cole looked at his hand but didn't take it, said, "I figured as much."

Durand dropped the hand, not seeming to be offended. "This is Dr. Judson Kent."

"Pleased to meet you," the medico said dryly.

"And Michael Hatfield, the editor of the *Wind River Sentinel,*" Durand continued. "We're here as a sort of unofficial town council, as it were."

"I'm honored, I reckon," Cole said. "But what the hell do you want with me?"

"You *are* Cole Tyler? That's how you signed the register downstairs."

Cole felt a brief surge of irritation that they had checked the register. "That's right," he said.

46

"You are presently employed as a buffalo hunter, providing fresh meat for the workers of the Union Pacific?"

Cole nodded but didn't say anything.

Michael Hatfield spoke up, saying eagerly, "You rode with Colonel Jeb Stuart during the Civil War, didn't you?"

"What if I did?" Cole asked.

"But even though you were a Confederate, you signed up as a scout for the army after the war."

Cole shrugged. "The war was over. I didn't see any need to keep on fighting it."

"And you have also guided several wagon trains to Oregon, is that correct?" Kent asked.

Cole looked at the Englishman and said, "You gents have been studying up on me. Why?"

"We're told that you are an honest man and a tough man," Durand stated. "We need someone like that, Mr. Tyler."

"What for?"

"To be the marshal of Wind River."

Cole just stared at them for a long moment, his gaze going from Durand to Kent to Hatfield and back to Durand. He opened his mouth, hesitated again, then finally said, "What the hell are you talking about? Are you asking *me* to be your marshal?"

"That is precisely what we are doing," Kent said in his clipped tones.

Cole looked over at the young newspaper editor. "Hell, this afternoon you practically accused me of killing that fella McKay!"

Hatfield flushed slightly and looked uncomfortable. "I didn't say that. I just said you had a gun. And I know now I overreacted."

"A mite," Cole agreed wryly. "I thought for a second I was going to wind up being lynched. McKay seemed to be a mighty important man."

"He and I built this town, Mr. Tyler," Durand said. "Now Andrew is gone, and we must carry on without him. We must put a stop to lawless displays like the one that took his life, and to do that, we need law and order!"

Cole rubbed his freshly shaven jaw. "Still don't see why you came to me."

"We think you're the best man for the job," Hatfield said. "We've had a constable, but he hasn't been able to maintain order. We need a real marshal."

"I've never carried a badge in my life."

"No reason why you can't start now, eh?" Kent put in.

Cole shook his head curtly. "Sorry. I'm riding out in a day or two to get back to buffalo hunting. I just took a few days off while they moved the railhead."

"We'll pay you more than you make shooting buffalo," Durand said.

"It's not a question of money. I'm not a lawman." Cole stepped past them, went to the door, and put his hand on the knob. "Good night, gentlemen."

Judson Kent faced him. "Are you certain we can't convince you otherwise?"

"There's bound to be plenty of men around here who are handy with their fists and handy with a gun," Cole told them. "Hire one of them." He opened the door.

Durand sighed heavily. "We're very disappointed, Mr. Tyler."

"Well, that's not my problem, is it?" Cole crossed his arms and leaned against the wall beside the door until they had filed out, then closed the door with his foot. He sighed and shook his head. Of all the crazy things . . .

The hotel didn't have a dining room, but there was a hash house down the block. Cole ate his fill, then stood in the street for a moment and listened to the laughter and music coming from the tent saloons clustered at the other end of the avenue.

He'd had a drink earlier, before getting Ulysses settled for the night in a nearby stable, and while he was still a little thirsty, he decided against visiting any of the saloons. The mood in the settlement was still tense. If any fights broke out, he wanted no part of them. He turned toward the hotel instead.

The clerk wasn't behind the desk as Cole crossed the lobby. It was almost like being in a hotel back in Kansas City or St. Louis. There was a rug on the floor and a couple of plants in pots, curtains over the windows, and armchairs and settees scattered around the room. *Mighty fancy for Wyoming Territory,* Cole thought. But it was obvious from everything he had seen that Durand and McKay intended the best for their town.

Unfortunately, they hadn't seemed to count on the riffraff that the railroad brought in with it. As long as it was a railhead, Wind River was going to be wide open and roaring.

Cole went upstairs and down the lantern-lit hallway to his room. He hadn't locked the door when he left, so he didn't think anything of it when the knob turned easily under his hand. But he *had* blown out the candle on the little table next to the bed, and it was lit again now. As soon as he saw that, he froze on the threshold and his hand dropped quickly to the butt of his gun.

"You won't need that, Mr. Tyler," a woman's voice said.

He saw her then, sitting stiffly in the single ladderback chair beside the bed. She wore a black dress and a veil, the mourning clothes of a widow, and even if her voice hadn't been slightly familiar, her garb would have told him who she was.

"What are you doing here, Mrs. McKay?" he asked as he moved his hand away from his gun and stepped on into the room. He didn't close the door behind him.

"My . . . late husband's partner, Mr. Durand, told me that he and Dr. Kent and Michael Hatfield came to see you earlier this evening. They made you an offer."

"And I turned it down," Cole said. He could see her eyes behind the veil, large and dark and luminous. Grief had not dimmed her beauty.

"If it's a question of money . . ."

Cole shook his head. "That's not it. I'm just not a lawman. Never have been."

"But you've guided wagon trains. You've occupied a position of authority."

"That's not like packing a badge as town marshal." Obviously she had come to plead the same case as his other visitors, and that made Cole uncomfortable. Turning down a job offer was one thing, but if this widow woman started pleading with him . . .

"I won't beg you to accept the offer, Mr. Tyler," Simone McKay said, as if reading his mind. "But I will tell you that we need your help. Wind River was growing rapidly even before the railroad arrived. Now that the Union Pacific is here, people will pour into this town from all over the Wyoming Territory. From all over the West, in fact."

"Yes, ma'am, I'd say you're right about that."

"You saw some of the ruffians who are already here. They started that fight with the workers from the railroad. There were all kinds of people on that station platform — gamblers, prostitutes, horse thieves, miscreants of every stripe."

If she was expecting him to ask her what "miscreants" meant, he disappointed her. "You're right," he said. "Your husband and Mr. Durand should have made some provision for law enforcement when they started the town. No offense, but they should have known that all hell was going to break loose."

Simone lifted her chin. "Since we're both speaking plainly, Mr. Tyler, I agree with you. Andrew and William sometimes got caught up in how much money they were going to make and lost sight of some of the practical problems. But we still have the problem." Her mouth twisted under the veil. "I was wrong. I *am* going to beg you to take the job, Mr. Tyler. Help us put a stop to the sort of mob violence that took my husband's life."

Cole sighed. He wanted to tell Simone McKay to go to hell, but it wasn't in him to do that. He liked his job with the railroad. It ensured that he didn't have to stay in one place for too long.

And yet there was nothing saying that the marshal's job here in Wind River had to be permanent. He could draw their pay for a couple of months, tamp down the lid a little on the boiling pot, and then ride on. It was as simple as that.

Oh, hell, he thought. He was talking himself into it, just because some pretty woman in widow's weeds asked him. The smart thing to do would be to go get Ulysses from the stable and ride out of Wind River right now, tonight.

But a man couldn't always do the smart thing, he supposed.

"All right," he said. "You've got yourself a marshal."

Simone McKay stood up and clasped her black-gloved hands together. "Thank you,

Mr. Tyler. You don't know what this means to us."

Maybe not, but Cole knew what it meant to him. It meant sleeping with a roof over his head instead of the western stars, it meant answering to authority, it meant being tied down.

He hoped he wasn't making the worst mistake of his life.

They had a badge for him and everything, Cole discovered the next morning when he walked into the office of the McKay and Durand Land Development Company, which was the closest thing Wind River had to a town hall. Mrs. McKay had obviously spread the word of his acceptance, because there was a sizable crowd waiting for him, including Durand, Dr. Kent, and the young editor Hatfield. Everybody shook his hand, and Kent pinned the badge — a five-pointed star — to his buckskin shirt.

Cole hoped to God they didn't expect him to make some sort of speech.

Evidently they didn't, because Durand took care of that, going on about how glad the entire community was that Cole had taken the job of bringing law and order to Wind River. Cole let him finish, then asked, "What's this chore pay?"

"Fifty dollars a month, plus a free room in the boardinghouse," Durand replied magnanimously.

Those were good wages, Cole had to admit. He nodded and shook hands again with everybody, and as the citizens began to file out, Durand went on, "Your deputy can show you around town and help you get to know everyone."

"Deputy?" Cole repeated with a frown.

"That's right. He was our constable, as I believe we mentioned yesterday, and now he's going to serve as your deputy." Durand turned and motioned to a man Cole hadn't noticed in the crowd until then.

The man shuffled forward, stuck out a hand, and grinned at Cole. "Glad to meet you. Marshal," he said. "Name's Billy Casebolt, and I'm right proud to be your deputy."

Cole shook hands, still frowning. Billy Casebolt was around fifty, he guessed, lean almost to the point of gauntness, with iron-gray hair and the sunburn and permanent squint of a man who had spent most of his life outdoors. He wore a battered old hat, a wool work shirt with the sleeves rolled up to reveal the faded red sleeves of a set of long underwear, denim pants, and rundown boots. A shell belt was strapped around his skinny hips, and an old Griswold and Gunnison Confederate revolver rode in the holster.

Billy Casebolt was a pretty unimpressive-looking specimen, and Cole could see why the old man hadn't been very successful as Wind River's first lawman.

Durand clapped Cole on the back and said, "You two go ahead and take a turn around the town, get acquainted with it and each other. You can use the front room here as your office if you have need of one, Cole."

This was all going a little fast, but Cole supposed there was no real reason for delay. He nodded and said, "Thanks. Come on, Mr. Casebolt."

"Ah, hell, call me Billy. Ever'body does. I'll show you around. This here's a fine town, Marshal Tyler, a fine town. . . ."

Cole let Billy Casebolt lead him out of the office, and they began their tour of the town.

Cole's town, at least for now.

Wind River had almost everything a frontier community needed to function. Timber and stone for the buildings had been carted down from the mountains to the north, and freight wagons had brought in the inventories for the local stores and saloons.

As Cole and Billy walked along Grenville

Avenue they passed an apothecary, a saddle-and-tack shop, a gunsmith, and the huge, block-long Wind River General Store — Andrew McKay and William Durand, Proprietors, according to the sign on the front of the building — where virtually anything the citizens needed could be purchased. Cole already knew about the livery stable, where Ulysses was being cared for, and he saw now that there was a blacksmith's shop next door.

"There's Jeremiah," Billy said, pointing to the smithy. "Come on, I'll introduce you."

Cole heard the ringing of hammer on anvil as they approached the squat, sturdy building that housed the smithy. Heat from the furnace came out the open double doors and made Cole wince slightly. In the red-lit shadows inside the building, he saw a massive shape, saw the man's arm rise and fall as he hammered out what appeared to be some sort of harness fitting.

"Howdy, Jeremiah!" Billy called over the noise of the hammer. "Want you to meet the new marshal!"

The blacksmith stopped hammering and turned to face his visitors. He wore a heavy apron to protect his body from sparks. His moon face under thinning pale hair was flushed from the heat. He regarded Cole and Billy solemnly and stuck out a hand the size of a small ham.

"Pleased to meet you," he rumbled. "Name's Jeremiah Newton."

Cole took the smith's hand, expecting a crushing grip, but instead he got a quick, perfunctory shake. "Cole Tyler," he said. "Glad to meet you, Mr. Newton."

"Call me Jeremiah."

"Jeremiah here's been holdin' services the past couple o' weeks," Billy said. "Reckon he's the closest thing Wind River's got to a preacher."

"We're all charged with spreading the Gospel wherever we can," Jeremiah said. "A man's soul is more important than the shoes on the hooves of his horses."

Cole glanced at Billy, then said, "I reckon I can't argue with that. Hadn't really thought about it until now, but Wind River doesn't have a church, does it?"

"Not yet," the blacksmith replied. "I'm going to build one."

From the looks of him, Jeremiah Newton could build just about anything he wanted, Cole thought. He nodded and said, "Let me know if you need a hand."

"I'll do that, brother."

"We'd best be movin' on," Billy put in. "I'm showin' Marshal Tyler around town."

Jeremiah nodded. "God be with you," he said to Cole. "Smite the wicked." He turned back to his anvil and lifted the hammer again, brought it down with a ringing crash.

As they left the smithy Cole said in a low voice, "Looks like that big fella could do some pretty good smiting himself."

"Naw, Jeremiah's a peaceable sort. Just don't go to arguin' the Bible with him. He can be pretty stubborn 'bout the Good Book."

"I'll try to avoid any theological discussions," Cole said dryly. He pointed with a thumb toward the other end of the street, where the already established saloons had been joined by the hell-on-wheels tents brought over from Laramie. "I imagine Brother Newton's not real fond of that part of town."

Billy chuckled. "Lots of sinnin' goin' on down yonder, that's for sure. But Jeremiah tends to leave those folks alone, long as they leave him alone."

Cole nodded, but he resolved to keep an eye on Jeremiah Newton anyway. He had read enough history to know that religion had caused just as many violent disagreements as politics, and he didn't want any holy wars breaking out in Wind River while he was the marshal.

59

The two lawmen moved on, and as they passed what seemed to be a vacant building across the street, a woman driving a team of mules brought a wagon to a stop in front of the structure. She handled the mules easily, but that wasn't what caught Cole's eye. His attention was drawn by the thick, strawberry-blond curls cascading out from under the woman's bonnet, and the peaches-and-cream complexion of her strong-featured but attractive face. She glanced toward Cole and Billy, and even at a distance, the new marshal could tell that her eyes were a startling green.

Cole paused and nudged Billy in the ribs with an elbow. "Who's that?" he asked, jerking his chin toward the woman. She had gotten down from the wagon and was going over to the door of the building. When she got there, she took a key from her bag, unlocked it, and went inside. The door closed behind her.

"Don't know," Billy admitted. "Can't say as I've ever seen her before. Quite a looker, though, ain't she?"

"Yeah," mused Cole. "I wonder what she's doing in Wind River."

"Well, you're the marshal. Go on over there and ask her."

Cole shook his head. "This badge doesn't

give me the right to poke into people's business as long as they're not causing trouble. If she stays around town, I reckon I'll get to know her." He turned his gaze away from the building where the woman had disappeared. "Let's go."

They walked on down the street, and as they ambled along Cole asked idly, "How'd you get to be the constable here, anyway?"

"Mr. Durand and Mr. McKay wanted somebody who knew their way around the frontier. Reckon I fit the bill. I been wanderin' around out here since the spring of thirty-eight. Did some fur trappin' up in the mountains and got in on the last of the old-time rendezvouses. Went to work for the army after that. Civilian scout."

"I did the same thing for a while."

Proudly, Billy said, "There ain't hardly a place 'twixt the Rio Grande and the Canadian border where I ain't set foot. I've fought the Injuns and lived with 'em, too. Been to see the elephant more'n once, let me tell you. No, sir, there just ain't a more seasoned frontiersman than ol' Billy Casebolt." He sighed. "I guess that don't mean as much these days as it used to, though. This town livin' ain't like gettin' along out in the wilderness. I reckon that's why Mr. Durand and them others decided I wasn't cut out to be anything but a deputy."

"Well, you know these folks and the country hereabouts," Cole told him. "I'll be relying on you for a lot of help, Billy."

At least partially he was just trying to make the old man feel better. It was too soon to tell if Billy Casebolt would be any help as a deputy or if he would just make Cole's job more difficult. But for now, there was no point in being too hard on the old-timer. Cole felt a sense of satisfaction as Billy nodded emphatically and said, "You can count on me, Marshal."

They swung around and headed back toward the other end of town, Billy reminiscing about some of his adventures as an army scout as they walked. Cole was only half paying attention to the yarns, so he spotted the trouble right away when a man came flying out through the canvas flaps over the entrance to one of the tent saloons.

The man's strident yell was cut off abruptly as he slammed into the ground and rolled over.

Cole tensed as he remembered the man tossed off the railroad station platform the day before. That had been the beginning of quite a brawl, and this incident might signal the same thing.

"Come on," he snapped, breaking into a

trot as he interrupted Casebolt's story. "There may be trouble up here."

Billy hurried after him, and by the time they were within fifty yards of the big tent, they could both hear the cursing and yelling and thudding of fists coming from within. A crash that was probably a poker table collapsing under a man's weight sounded clearly.

Cole reached the entrance and thrust the canvas aside, plunging into the melee within the tent. It was yesterday's brawl all over again, he saw immediately. Workers from the railroad were slugging it out with hard-faced men wearing range clothes. The painted ladies in their spangled dresses and the gamblers in their expensive suits had moved to the sides of the tent to give the fighters more room and to stay out of harm's way. That was an option Cole no longer had, not since he had put on the badge.

The long bar running down the right side of the tent was made of wide, thick planks placed atop whiskey barrels. A man was standing on top of the bar, holding a bung-starter and using it to club any of the combatants who came within reach of him. He was shouting curses at them, ordering them out of his place, and he seemed equally angry at both sides in the skirmish. Cole recognized him right away. Hank Parker was hard to miss. He was a hulking, broad-shouldered man with heavy dark eyebrows and not another strand of hair on his head. His left arm was gone, amputated above the elbow, a grisly souvenir of the battle at the Shiloh meetinghouse during the war.

Before Parker had brought it to Wind River, this tent saloon had been set up in Laramie, the latest in a series of railhead settlements where he had done business. Cole had had a few run-ins with the man before, and neither of them had much use for the other.

But that was in the past, and it was Cole's duty now to break up this fight before Parker's saloon was destroyed. He reached for his revolver, intending to squeeze off a couple of shots to bring the men back to their senses as he had done at the railroad station, but just as his hand closed around the butt of the Colt, something slammed into his back and drove him forward off his feet.

Cole landed on the hard-packed dirt floor and rolled over, and as he did so several booted feet thudded against his ribs. He couldn't tell if the kicks were deliberate or accidental, but it didn't really matter. Pain shot through him as he gasped for air to replace what had been knocked out of his lungs. He managed to get his hands and knees under him, then surged up onto his feet just in time to run into a punch.

He staggered back, his vision blurring, but he still caught a glimpse of the man who had hit him. He saw a tall man with a drooping mustache and longish blond hair. The man still held a chair leg in his left hand, and Cole knew the blow that had felled him had been that chair crashing against his back. The man came after him, whipping the chair leg back and forth.

Cole ducked, feeling the chair leg brush his hair as it slashed just above his head. He drove forward with his legs, barreling into the man and hooking a couple of punches to his body.

In these close quarters, the chair leg wasn't as effective a weapon as it might have been otherwise, so Cole pressed his advantage, rocking his opponent again and again with blows to the midsection.

In desperation, the man thrust a boot between Cole's calves, throwing him off balance. Cole fell forward, knocking both of them down. The blond man twisted and somehow managed to land on top. He had lost the chair leg, but that just gave him both hands free to lock around Cole's neck.

Luckily, Cole had grabbed a breath of air just before the man's long fingers closed cruelly around his windpipe. But that air wouldn't last long, and he was already feeling the first stirrings of panic. He brought up cupped hands and slapped them against the man's ears, drawing a howl of pain and a loosening of the grip on his neck. A knee sharply jabbed into the blond man's groin finished the job. He groaned and let go of Cole's neck.

Cole thrust him aside and rolled over. He was on top now, and he struck again and again, smashing his fists into the man's face. The badge he wore was forgotten, his duties as marshal washed into insignificance by the tide of anger flooding through him. It was only after long seconds of battering the man beneath him that Cole realized what he was doing.

He shoved himself to his feet, looking down at the bruised and bloody features of the man, who was only half-conscious and gasping for breath through smashed lips. The brawl was still going on all around him, Cole saw as he glanced around. He had to put a stop to the fracas before he did anything else.

A few yards away Billy Casebolt was struggling in the grip of one of the hardcases while another man slugged him, rocking his head back and forth.

Cole went to his deputy's aid, slipping out his revolver and bringing the barrel down on the head of the man who was handing out the beating. The man sagged, his legs folding up under him.

With that respite, Billy was able to pull free from the other man's grip, and he whirled around and slammed a blow to the man's jaw with surprising speed and strength.

Figuring that Billy could handle himself all right now that the odds were even, Cole pushed past the struggling men and reached the bar. As he started to vault onto the planks Hank Parker turned toward him and lifted the bungstarter to strike him back down. Cole reached up and caught Parker's wrist even as the blow started to fall, stopping the bungstarter abruptly.

"Hold it!" Cole bellowed.

"Tyler!" Parker exclaimed. "What the hell are you doing here?"

Cole nodded to the badge on his chest. "I'm the law in Wind River now," he told the saloonkeeper, shouting over the bedlam inside the tent. "Put down that bungstarter!"

"If you're the law," Parker shot back, "stop these bastards! They're tearing up my place!"

"That's just what I intend to do," Cole said grimly. He lifted his pistol and triggered off two shots.

The tactic worked just as effectively as it had the day before. A shocked silence fell over the saloon, a quiet that was broken a few seconds later by Hank Parker growling, "You just put two holes in my tent, Tyler. You'll pay for patching them."

Cole gave him an icy glance, then shouted to the crowd, "The next man who throws a punch will spend the night in jail!"

Billy Casebolt spoke up, saying hesitantly, "Uh, Marshal, Wind River ain't got a jail yet."

Cole swallowed his impatience and snapped, "I saw a smokehouse down the street. That'll do for locking up any troublemakers." Now that he had their attention, he lowered the gun but didn't holster it. He went on, "You boys may not know it, but Wind River's got law and order now. There won't be any more of these brawls, understand? Now somebody pass a hat. I want all of you men to chip in and pay for the damages you've done here."

"You can go to hell!" an angry voice shot back, the words sounding a little thick and strained. Cole looked down and saw the blond man who had taken the brunt of his rage a few minutes earlier. The man was on his feet again, if somewhat shaky, standing between two of his friends.

"You're not a damned judge," the man continued, "and you can't make us pay one red cent."

Cole saw his point, but he wasn't going to back down. He said, "You're right, I'm not a judge. But if you don't want to pay up, I reckon I'll just have to look the other way while Parker here takes the costs out of your hide."

A little surprisingly, there were shouts of agreement with Cole's decision. The railroad workers began tossing coins into a cap produced by one of them. The blond man looked around and must have sensed that the mood in the saloon wouldn't allow him to do anything except cooperate.

"All right, damn it," he grated, reaching into his pocket and producing a coin that he tossed into the cap. He motioned for his friends to do the same, demonstrating that he was the leader of this bunch of hardcases. Then he glared up at Cole and said, "I ain't going to forget this, Marshal. You'll be sorry you crossed Deke Strawhorn."

"I already am," Cole shot back. "Now get out of here and find someplace else to do your drinking for a while. Don't let me catch you causing trouble there, either."

Somebody handed Strawhorn a white hat with a tightly rolled brim. He winced as he settled it on his head. "You won't catch me, Marshal," he said. "You won't even see me comin'."

With that, he turned and stalked out, his men following him.

Billy Casebolt let out a low whistle as Cole climbed down from the bar. "Sounded to me like that Strawhorn fella was threatenin' you, Marshal. You best watch your back from here on out."

"I intend to, Billy," Cole said with a nod as he took the cap full of money and handed it to Hank Parker, who accepted it with poor grace. He had been wearing a badge less than two hours, Cole suddenly realized, and already it seemed like he had more enemies than friends here in Wind River. "I sure intend to."

CHAPTER 4

Rose Foster heard the gunfire as she was sweeping out the building. She had opened the front door to let the dust out, and the pair of shots sounded clearly. Even though the explosions came from down the street and were nowhere near the building where she was working, Rose's head lifted sharply and her eyes widened. Her full lips compressed as she tightened them and her nostrils flared with the deep breath she took. She hated guns, absolutely hated them.

Which was yet another reason she sometimes asked herself why in heaven's name she had come to such a wild place as Wyoming Territory to open a cafe.

There were no more shots, and after a few seconds Rose relaxed slightly. She had tied a strip of cloth around her thick reddish-gold hair before starting to work, but a few strands had escaped and fallen down over her forehead and eyes. She pushed them back and retied the cloth.

She had taken off her jacket before starting to work, too. Her long gray skirt and white blouse were not fancy, and they showed signs of long wear. But they were clean and well mended. A woman without an abundance of worldly possessions, Rose knew how to care for what she did have.

As she leaned on the broom, taking an extra moment before she went back to work, she looked around at the place and saw all of its possibilities.

There was plenty of space here in this front room for tables and chairs, and she could have a counter built along the back wall so that customers could sit there on stools if they wanted. There were two rooms in the rear, one of them plenty big for the kitchen, the other handy for storage. She would make some red-and-white-checked cloths for the tables and curtains to match for the windows — something to cheer things up a little.

The building was less than a month old and solidly constructed, made to last. It was a trifle dusty inside because dust had a tendency to get in everywhere in this country, no matter how tightly closed up it was, and it didn't take long, either. But all in all, Rose was pleased with her choice. She could make the cafe a success; she was sure of it.

A smile appeared on her face. The past was behind her, and all she had to do now was look toward the future.

There was a step outside, and a voice said heartily from the doorway, "Ah, Mrs. Foster, there you are."

Rose jumped a little. She had been daydreaming, she supposed, and the man had startled her. "Mr. Durand!" she exclaimed.

William Durand stepped into the building. If he had noticed the way she reacted, he didn't say anything about it, and Rose was grateful for that. He took off his derby, gestured around him with it, and said, "I hope you're satisfied with the place."

"Oh, yes, very much so," Rose said quickly. "It'll do just fine. I ought to be open for business in a week or so, as soon as I can have some tables and chairs and a counter made."

"Well, you'll find no shortage of skilled carpenters here in Wind River. I'm sure you'll have no trouble getting the work done, Mrs. Foster."

Rose hated to take a chance on offending him by reminding him of his mistake, but she didn't want him to keep on making it, either. She said, "Perhaps you've forgotten, Mr. Durand, but it's *Miss* Foster."

"Oh, yes, that's right. You're not married, are you?" Durand smiled. "Forgive me, my dear. I suppose that when I see a young woman as lovely as yourself, my natural assumption is that some lucky man has already snatched her up for himself."

"That's all right, Mr. Durand."

He came a step closer to her and motioned toward the broom in her hands. "Could I send someone over to help you?" he asked.

"No, that's not necessary. I don't mind, really. It's just a little sweeping out."

Durand sighed. "Yes, the dust is rather persistent around here, isn't it? Well, I suppose I should be going. . . ." He hesitated, then said, "I hope that you won't mind if I'm one of your first customers when you open for business. I'd like to think that my late partner and I helped contribute to your success by leasing this building to you."

"Certainly, and your first meal will be on the house," Rose said magnanimously. It never hurt to stay on the landlord's good side. Suddenly the implications of something Durand had said soaked in on her, and she asked with a frown, "Did you say your *late* partner?"

A shadow of grief crossed Durand's face. "You mean you haven't heard about poor Andrew?"

"I got into town with my wagon late last night and went straight to the boarding-house you recommended. What happened?"

Grimly, Durand replied, "Mr. McKay was killed yesterday in an accident. A shooting."

Rose's grip on the broom loosened and it clattered to the floor. One hand went to her mouth, muffling the exclamation that came from her. Her fair skin turned even more pallid and her eyes widened in horror. She swayed like a sapling in a blue norther.

Durand stepped forward hurriedly and grasped her arm. "Miss Foster!" he said. "What's wrong?"

She forced herself to answer him. "I . . . I don't like guns," she choked out. "When you told me about . . . about poor Mr. McKay . . . I . . . I can't stand to think about it!"

Durand looked around the room, which was bare at the moment, not even a chair on which the distraught woman could sit. He kept his grip on her arm and used his other hand to pat her awkwardly on the shoulder as he muttered, "There, there."

Rose took a deep breath and struggled to bring her rioting emotions under control. There was no logical reason why she should be reacting this strongly to the news of Andrew McKay's death, she told herself.

She had barely known the man, and their association had been strictly business. They were landlord and tenant, nothing else.

Yet the revelation that McKay had been shot to death — and only the day before at that — made her sick to her stomach and sent fingers of ice tickling along her nerves. This was the sort of town she had come to, a part of her brain screamed. A place where one of the leading citizens, one of the founders, could be gunned down with impunity.

An accident, Durand had called it.

Perhaps she was leaping to conclusions. She made herself ask, "Did . . . did he shoot himself? While he was cleaning a gun, perhaps?"

"I'm afraid not," Durand answered reluctantly, as if worried that his reply would set off a round of hysterics. "There was a brawl at the railroad depot yesterday when the first train arrived, and someone fired a shot. Andrew was struck by the stray bullet."

"Dear God," breathed Rose. "He was married, wasn't he?"

"Indeed he was." Durand nodded. "His wife is grieving terribly, of course. But we've taken steps to see that such a tragedy doesn't occur again. The town has hired a marshal."

The businessman's words reminded Rose of the two men she had seen looking at her earlier as she drove up to the vacant building. She remembered now that one of them, the younger man with the long brown hair and the hat hanging on his back by its chin-strap, had been wearing a badge of some sort. He had looked competent enough, from the brief glimpse Rose had gotten of him, and she hoped he would be able to bring law and order to Wind River.

"I'm sorry, Mr. Durand," she said shakily as she managed to summon up a faint, apologetic smile. "I didn't mean to fall all to pieces like that."

"That's quite all right, my dear." Durand still had his hand on her shoulder, and Rose became more aware now of its weight and the slight caressing motions his fingers were making against her flesh. He went on, "Don't trouble yourself about such matters. Just concentrate on opening your cafe and making a success of it." He paused, then added, "If there's anything I can do to help, please feel free to call on me anytime, day or night."

She thought he placed a slight emphasis on "night," but she couldn't be sure. At any rate, she couldn't afford to act insulted, even if he *was* being a bit too forward. After all, with Andrew McKay dead, William Durand was her landlord now; it was stretching things only a little to say that he held her fate in his hands.

"Thank you, Mr. Durand." She smiled. "I'll remember that. But right now I have to get back to sweeping or I'll never get all this dust out of here."

"You're sure you're all right?"

"I'm sure."

"Very well." He released her and stepped back, picked up the derby he had dropped on the floor when she had looked as if she was about to faint, and placed it on his head again. "I wish you the very best of luck, Miss Foster, and I'll be checking on you, just to make sure there's nothing you need."

"That's very kind, but not necessary. I'll be all right."

"It's no trouble. I insist." Durand took her hand, and for a second Rose thought he was actually going to kiss it. But he settled for a brief clasp and then turned to the door. Rose didn't relax until he was gone. Then she picked up the broom once again.

She wasn't completely at ease even now. The shot she had heard earlier, the news of Andrew McKay's death, the uncomfortable feelings Durand had stirred in her . . . they all combined to make her doubt the wisdom of coming here to Wind River.

But she hadn't really had any choice in the matter. For better or for worse, Wind River was her home now.

She hoped that lawman Durand had mentioned knew how to do his job — but not *too* well. . . .

Cole Tyler and Billy Casebolt were walking down Grenville Avenue after leaving Hank Parker's tent saloon when Cole heard footsteps rapidly approaching behind them. Deke Strawhorn's not-so-veiled threat was fresh in his memory, so Cole turned quickly, the .44 sliding smoothly from its holster as he drew it. His thumb went naturally over the hammer, ready to cock and fire.

Michael Hatfield stopped short and then stepped back quickly, eyes bugging out in surprise. "Don't shoot, Marshal Tyler!" he said. "It's just me!"

The young newspaperman was wearing town shoes, brown twill pants and matching vest, and a white shirt. A string tie was looped around his neck. He had a pad of paper in his left hand and a stubby pencil in his right.

Cole sighed in exasperation. "Not a good idea to come running up behind a man," he advised. "What do you want?"

"I'm told that you just performed your first official duty as Wind River's new marshal. Would you care to comment on that?"

Billy Casebolt jerked a thumb at Parker's tent. "You mean breakin' up that little fracas in yonder? Shoot, boy, there weren't nothin' to that. Just had to pound a little sense into some stubborn skulls."

Michael looked at Casebolt and saw the bruises and scratches on the deputy's face. "Looks like it was quite a fight," he said. "What about it, Marshal?"

Cole shrugged and said, "The town pays me to keep the peace, not to talk about it. A saloon fight's not news."

"No offense, sir, but don't you think that I'd be a better judge of what's newsworthy than you? After all, I *am* the editor of the *Sentinel.*"

For a moment Cole just looked at him without saying anything, then asked curiously, "How old are you, son?"

Michael flushed. "I don't see as how that has anything to do with it, but I'm twenty-four."

Cole nodded and looked at Casebolt. "Twenty-four, he says."

"I heard him," Casebolt said with a chuckle.

80

The reddish tinge in Michael's features deepened. "Now see here, I'm a journalist. I've got a job to do, Marshal, just like you do. If you don't want to answer my questions, you don't have to, but I might just see fit to include your reticence in my forthcoming editorial on the coming of law and order to Wind River."

Cole folded his arms across his chest and regarded the young man stonily. "You might see fit to do that, eh?"

Michael swallowed hard, opened his mouth a couple of times, then finally managed to say, "If you think you can intimidate the press —"

"Ease up, Hatfield," Cole cut in. "I reckon you're right."

Michael blinked stupidly, as if he couldn't quite comprehend what he had just heard. "You mean . . . ?"

"I mean I'll answer your questions," Cole told him, "within reason. Come on."

He and Casebolt started down the street again, and Michael fell in step beside them. "What about that fight?" the newspaperman asked.

"Just a typical brawl between the railroad workers and some of the drifters that always follow the railroad. It didn't amount to much, and the boys passed a hat to pay for the damages when it was over."

"Who instigated the disturbance?"

"Instigated," Casebolt drawled. "I like that un."

Cole ignored the comment. "I don't know who started it. Doesn't really matter, does it?"

"There have been quite a few fights lately, the one yesterday at the railroad station, for example," Michael said. "I just wondered if it was your opinion that one element in the community is responsible for the trouble."

"There's probably more'n enough blame to go around," Cole said. "Everybody needs to behave while they're in town, or they'll wind up in jail — as soon as we get one built," he added with a glance at Casebolt to forestall another explanation of Wind River's lack of a lockup.

"Do you think there will be more trouble?"

"Trouble's never in short supply, most places. I'd be surprised if Wind River was any different. But Deputy Casebolt and I intend to see that anybody who raises too much of a ruckus will regret it."

Michael was scribbling furiously on his pad as he hurried along beside the two lawmen. "I want to make sure I quote you accurately in the paper," he explained.

"Take this newspapering mighty serious, don't you?" Cole asked.

That question brought Michael to an abrupt stop. He stared at Cole and said, "Of course I do. It's my job. More than that, it's my calling. Don't you feel the same about what you do?"

"Not so's you'd notice," Cole replied.

But that wasn't strictly true, he thought. He had understood the importance of scouting for the army and guiding wagon trains to Oregon. In his small way, he was doing his part to help civilization spread across the continent. Now, whether or not that was a good thing, Cole couldn't have said. He remembered the times when he had topped some ridge and looked out over a beautiful valley where maybe few white men had ever passed. If enough settlers came out here, then one day places like that would be no more. That would be a day of regret for men like himself, who had known this land when it was wild and free.

But would he think of what he had done in the past, or what he was doing now, as a calling? Michael Hatfield made newspaper work sound like some sort of divine calling. Cole wouldn't dignify packing a badge in a railhead town by using such high-flown terms.

Before Michael could ask anything else, Cole said, "How about if I ask you a question or two?"

"Well . . . sure, I suppose. If you want to."

"Did Mr. Andrew McKay own the newspaper?"

"As a matter of fact, he did," Michael replied. "How did you know?"

"Just a guess." Cole shrugged. "He and his partner seem to own just about everything around here, either separately or together. The hotel, the livery stable, the general store — all owned by McKay and Durand, right?"

Michael nodded. "And most of the buildings where the other businesses are located are leased from their company. What's wrong with that?"

"Didn't say anything was wrong with it," Cole answered mildly. "The paper's owned by the widow now, is that right?"

"Mrs. McKay inherited the newspaper, yes. And she's made it clear to me that she wants me to continue editing the paper and supervising its day-to-day operation, just as I did when her husband was still alive. It's quite a vote of confidence, you know."

"Where are you from?"

"Cincinnati, Ohio," Michael answered proudly. "My wife Delia and I were both

84

raised there."

"Coming out here to Wind River was your first trip west?"

"That's right." Michael frowned. "Say, you're asking all the questions now. That's not fair."

Casebolt laughed. "Pretty slick, though. The marshal kept you from pryin' too much into what ain't your business."

Michael paid no attention to the mild rebuke. "I'd like to know more about you, Marshal Tyler," he said. "Your background, where you came from, what you've done in the past."

"Those aren't always considered polite questions out here," Cole pointed out. "In fact, they can get a slug put through you pretty quick like, happen you start asking them of the wrong man."

"I suppose I have a lot to learn yet," Michael admitted. "Please, Marshal, don't let my wife hear you saying things like that. She already thinks we should have stayed back in Cincinnati. Delia says it's a much safer place in which to raise a family."

"I don't know that I can disagree with her," Cole said.

"And I already had a job on one of the papers there."

"Doin' what?" asked Casebolt. "Was you

the editor there, too?"

Michael muttered something, and Case-bolt leaned closer to him, cupping a hand behind his ear. "Speak up, boy. I couldn't quite hear you."

"I was a printer's devil," Michael said miserably.

"Well, you've come up in the world con-siderably," Cole told him dryly. "Sorry to hear your missus doesn't like living out here. Billy and I will do our best to bring some law and order to Wind River and make it a more civilized place. Just don't hold your breath waiting for it to happen."

Michael nodded and headed along the street toward the *Sentinel* office, saying that he had enough material in his notes for a story on the brawl at Parker's saloon. When he was gone, Casebolt asked Cole, "You reckon we picked on him too much?"

"Nope. The sooner he learns he's not in Cincinnati anymore, the better off he'll be."

Casebolt looked around at the bustling community and asked, "Just how far off you reckon that civilization is, Marshal?"

"A ways yet, Billy," Cole said. "A ways."

Cole spent the rest of the day walking around the town, getting more familiar with Wind River and its inhabitants, while Billy

Casebolt hurried off to tend to an idea that had occurred to him.

The deputy kept quiet about what he was up to, so it came as a surprise to Cole when he went back to the offices of the land development company late that afternoon and found Casebolt standing proudly under a new sign that hung from the awning over the plank boardwalk.

The sign was made from a thick length of wood in which letters had been burned. Casebolt pointed up at it with his thumb and grinned. "Whatdaya think, Marshal?" he asked, pride in his voice.

" 'Wind Riwer Marshels Office,' " Cole read aloud. "Thanks, Billy. It looks mighty nice." He didn't say anything about the spelling on the sign.

"Figured now that we had an honest-to-Pete marshal here in town, folks ought to know where to find him. I asked Mr. Durand about it and sort of let him think it was your idea. Anyway, he said it was fine, so I went over to Jeremiah's and had him heat up an iron so's I could burn the letters in myself."

"You did a fine job," Cole told him. "Why don't you go get something to eat, and I'll stay here in case somebody comes looking for me."

"That's a good idea, a mighty good idea. I'll be back in a spell."

"No need to hurry."

Cole went into the building's front room, the one Durand had said he could use as an office. There wasn't much in the way of furnishings: an old desk with a scarred top, a couple of straight-backed chairs with covers made from a buffalo hide, a small cabinet, and a spittoon. It wasn't elegant, but it would do, Cole decided.

The door leading to the other offices was in the back of the room, and it opened as Cole came in. Simone McKay came out, followed closely by Durand. Simone was in either the same mourning dress and veil she had worn the night before or another outfit just like it. She stopped when she saw Cole and nodded to him, but she didn't say anything.

"Hello, Marshal," Durand greeted him effusively. "How was your first day on the job? I heard something about a skirmish with that fellow Strawhorn. . . ."

"Didn't amount to anything," Cole said shortly, not bothering to mention the hard feelings Strawhorn had expressed when he was kicked out of Parker's place. He nodded solemnly to the widow. "Anything I can do for you, Mrs. McKay?"

"No, thank you, Marshal," she said quietly. "Just do your job well, and I will consider that part of my late husband's legacy to the town."

"Yes, ma'am. I intend to try."

"I'll take you back to the hotel, Simone," Durand said. "Or were you looking for me, Marshal Tyler?"

Cole shook his head. "Nope. Just getting comfortable with the office. Hope you don't mind the sign Billy put up outside."

Durand smiled. "Not at all. I do wish Deputy Casebolt had checked with me on the spelling first, however. But since Wind River doesn't even have a school yet, we can't be too worried about such things just now."

He put his hat on and led Mrs. McKay out of the office, and Cole went behind the desk and sat down. Even with the buffalo-hide cover, the chair wasn't particularly comfortable. He propped his boots on the desk and leaned back anyway.

Wind River didn't have a school or a church, but there were businesses aplenty, he reflected. That told him something about the thinking of Andrew McKay and William Durand as they went about establishing the town. Simone McKay had told him the night before that her husband and his partner had sometimes gotten carried away with their planning and neglected practical considerations while they devoted their attention to money-making enterprises.

They weren't that much different from the other town builders Cole had encountered out here in the West. Most men came just to make their fortunes, but if they brought their wives and families with them, sooner or later they realized that the settlements had to be decent places to live, too, not just somewhere to rake in a profit. That was when the schools and the churches — not to mention the law — showed up. Wind River was just following a pattern that had been played out many times before.

Billy Casebolt came back to the office a little later, and Cole went to the hash house to get his supper. The food wasn't particularly good, but the big Swede who ran the place had his wife cooking and his four daughters waiting tables, so the service was fast.

After he'd eaten, Cole went back to the office and got Casebolt, and the two of them took another turn around town. There was plenty of noise coming from the saloons, but it was the friendly kind tonight. No fights were breaking out, and there hadn't been any shooting since the fracas in Hank

90

Parker's tent saloon earlier in the day. For his first day on the job, Cole was pretty satisfied.

"Durand said a room in the boarding-house came with this badge, but I haven't moved my gear over there yet," he told Billy when they got back to the office. "I reckon I'll spend one more night at the hotel and move in the morning. You can find me there if you need me."

The middle-aged deputy nodded. "Sure thing, Marshal. Maybe it'll be a quiet night. Maybe all the trouble's played itself out."

"Could be," Cole grunted, but he didn't believe it for a second. The best they could hope for was a respite.

He walked back to the hotel and went upstairs to his room. After finding a visitor there the night before, he was a little more wary tonight, and as he approached the door he glanced down to see if there was any light coming from under it.

Sure enough, there was.

Cole stopped short and stood tensely in the hallway, wondering what the hell was going on. He hadn't really expected to see any light coming from his room, but the glow was unmistakable.

A grim cast stole over his face, and his hand went to the butt of the Colt. He lifted his left foot as he drew the gun, then sent the heel of his boot crashing against the door. It slammed open, smashing back against the wall behind it just in case anybody unfriendly was hiding there. Cole went through the opening in a hurry, the revolver leveled and ready to fire.

Simone McKay gasped and jerked to her feet from the chair where she had been sitting.

"What in blazes!" Cole exclaimed without thinking. "What are you doing here again, Mrs. McKay?"

Her face was a pale, blurred mask behind the veil. "Do you have to point that weapon at me, Marshal Tyler?" she asked, managing to sound a little dignified, which was quite an accomplishment under the circumstances.

Cole looked down stupidly at the gun in his fist, then said, "Oh. Sorry." He leathered the Colt, then went on, "No offense, ma'am, but I didn't expect to find you waiting in my room again tonight." He heard footsteps coming hurriedly up the stairs, drawn by the noise of the door being kicked open. "Maybe for the sake of your reputation, Mrs. McKay, we'd better move our discussion down to the lobby."

"I'm not overly concerned with my reputation, Marshal, but I thank you for your consideration." Her chin lifted defiantly. "I've been a widow for less than thirty-six hours, and besides, I own a great deal of this town now. I don't think the citizens will gossip too much about me. Furthermore, what I have to say to you tonight requires privacy."

Intrigued in spite of himself, Cole nodded. "If that's the way you want it." He swung around to the door as the clerk from downstairs appeared in the opening. Cole didn't even let him get the obvious question out. "There's no trouble here, mister. Everything's under control, so you can go on about your business."

The man looked at Cole, glanced at Simone, then nodded. Cole thought Mrs. McKay might be underestimating the power of gossip, but that was her business. Without saying anything, the clerk headed back down the stairs.

Cole shut the door. The lock was broken from his kick, but it caught enough to stay closed. He turned to face Simone and said, "What can I do for you, Mrs. McKay?"

"It's very simple, Marshal," she said. "You can prove that my husband's death was no accident. He was murdered, and I want you to find his killer."

CHAPTER 5

For several moments that seemed to stretch out even longer, Cole stared at Simone McKay and wondered if he had heard her right. There was no doubt about it, he finally decided. Frowning darkly, he repeated, "Murdered?"

Simone lifted her veil and draped it back over the shawl she wore on her thick, dark hair. When she looked at Cole again, he saw that although her features were still quite pale, the lines of shock and sorrow that had been there the night before were gone now, replaced by an expression of determination.

"That's correct," she said. "I believe that during that brawl on the station platform, someone took advantage of the confusion to shoot Andrew. It was a deliberate killing, Marshal, not an accident."

"You have any proof of that?" Cole asked, wishing he knew more about what a real lawman would do in a situation like this.

"I'm relying on you to discover the proof. That's part of your job."

Cole rubbed his jaw and shook his head slowly. "That may be, ma'am, but it doesn't tell me how to go about it. Do you at least have any idea who might have done such a thing?"

"As a matter of fact, I do." Again the defiant lift of the chin, the firming of the shoulders. "I think William Durand killed my husband."

Cole knew he was staring again, but he couldn't help it. "Durand?" he said. "But Durand and your husband were partners, and from what I've heard, your husband's holdings didn't go to Durand but to you."

"Not entirely. As a matter of fact, under the terms of the partnership agreement between Andrew and Durand, I received only the hotel and the newspaper. Everything else goes to Durand." She smiled faintly. "William Durand thinks of me as a sweet but helpless woman, Marshal Tyler. I'm sure he regards me as an easy target for his schemes and intends to swindle me out of *those* assets as well."

Cole wanted to let out a low whistle of admiration, but he suppressed the impulse. If that was really what Durand thought, then the man was in for one hell of a big surprise. Now that her initial grief had passed, Cole could see the iron in Simone McKay.

"You intend to look after your late husband's business interests?" he asked.

"Of course. And I'm going to keep an eye on Durand's activities, too. If it's proven that he killed Andrew, not only would my husband's share of their joint holdings revert to me, but so would Durand's, since he has no living relatives. To tell you the truth, Marshal, I'm not sure that William Durand is even his real name. I believe he may be wanted by the law back east."

"Then if you're right about him — and I can't say as I believe you are, just yet — but if you're right, you could be in danger, too."

Simone inclined her head in acknowledgment of his point. The movement had an innate grace to it, like the swaying of a pine in a mountain wind. "That's one reason I came to you tonight, Marshal, and told you of my suspicions. I want Andrew's death cleared up so that he can rest easily, wherever he is, and not have to worry about me."

Cole shook his head again. "Seems hard to believe. Durand was one of the men pushing so hard for me to take the job as marshal."

"Because he is being pushed in turn by

the other leaders of the community to bring some law and order to Wind River. Besides, it would look rather strange, wouldn't it, if he didn't have any reaction to his partner's death? He has to keep up appearances."

Cole thought about it some more and then said, "Reckon there could be something to it, all right. With all the confusion on that station platform, Durand could've slipped out a gun, shot your husband, and put it away before anybody noticed. Nobody searched him after the shooting. It seemed so obvious the shot was just a stray bullet. . . ."

"Which was exactly what he wished everyone to think."

Cole grunted. He didn't want to offend the widow, but he wanted things clear in his head before he let her rope him in on this notion of murder. "Well, for somebody who figures Durand killed her husband, you've been mighty friendly to him."

Simone arched her eyebrows. "Durand isn't the only one who has to keep up appearances. If he thinks I don't suspect him at all, I'll be better able to counter his schemes when he puts them into effect."

"And in the meantime you want me to prove somehow that he killed Mr. McKay."

"Yes. As I said before, Marshal, it's your —"

"My job. Yeah, I know," Cole finished for her. "I signed on to keep the peace, not to get to the bottom of a killing, but I reckon that comes with the territory." He nodded. "All right, Mrs. McKay, I'll look into it. But I can't promise anything. This is all pretty much new to me. In the meantime, keep your own eyes open. I don't want any more accidents."

Simone lowered the veil over her face again. "I assure you, Marshal, neither do I."

Cole didn't sleep well after Simone left his room in the hotel. He kept staring up at the darkened ceiling as he lay in the bed, thinking about what she had told him and what she had asked him to do. There was obviously going to be more to the job of marshal than he had bargained for. Finally, he dozed off.

And woke up what seemed like mere moments later to gunshots and shouting and the assorted sounds of all hell breaking loose.

Instantly, Cole rolled out of bed, his hand going instinctively to the butt of the holstered revolver he had hung on the bedpost. He hurried to the window and jerked on the shade, making it roll up with a loud rattle. Sunlight struck him in the face and he winced. Sleeping inside, on a real bed, was making him soft, he thought fleetingly. Most days he was up well before the sun, but today the morning was well advanced.

There was still all sorts of commotion going on outside. Cole stuck his head out the window, aware that he was wearing nothing but long underwear bottoms. He looked down Grenville Avenue toward the east and saw a huge cloud of dust hanging in the air outside of town. A loud rumble reached his ears. One of the townies was scurrying past on the street, just below the window of Cole's hotel room, and Cole shouted to him, "Hey! What's going on?"

The man paused long enough to throw a fearful glance up at Cole and wave frantically toward the dust and the ominous rumbling sound. "Cattle!" the man called. "Thousands of cattle! And they're stampeding this way!"

Stampede! Cole thought, his belly going cold with apprehension. He had never seen a herd of cattle running wild like that, but he had witnessed more than one buffalo stampede — and they could be awesome in their destructiveness. The herd of cattle coming toward Wind River couldn't be as big as the buffalo herds Cole had seen, some of which had probably numbered in the millions, but from the looks of the dust cloud, it was plenty big enough to do some damage.

He whirled away from the window and grabbed up his pants, pulling them on quickly and then reaching for his boots. He stomped into them, yanked the soft buckskin shirt over his head. After breaking the lock on the door the night before, he had wedged the room's single chair under the knob. He kicked it aside now and ran out, tucking the Colt in his pants and not taking the time to strap on the shell belt.

The rumbling from thousands of hooves was even louder as he ran out of the hotel lobby a few seconds later. The herd had not reached town yet, but it was drawing closer. Most of the people on the streets were terrified and running for cover, but a few men had managed to mount up and were riding east along Grenville Avenue, toward the stampede. Maybe they hoped to intercept the cattle and turn them before they reached Wind River. It was only a faint hope, Cole knew, but still the best chance for the town to avoid wholesale destruction.

A few of the stronger buildings might survive if the stampede swept through the settlement, but the tents would be trampled into the ground and most of the structures that had not yet been completed would probably collapse.

Cole turned toward the livery stable and broke into a run. He wasn't wearing his badge, but he was still the marshal of Wind River, and it was his job to do what he could to save the town.

He found Billy Casebolt in the barn, leading out the big golden sorrel and a sturdy-looking bay mare. "Figured you'd be wantin' your hoss when you heard what was goin' on," the deputy greeted Cole. "The hostler knew this big feller was yours and got him saddled up."

"That was quick thinking, Billy," Cole said as he grabbed Ulysses's reins from the older man and swung up into the saddle. "Come on. We've got to try to turn that herd."

Casebolt mounted up and rode out of the barn beside Cole. "You ever worked with cattle before?" he asked, raising his voice over the rapidly approaching thunder of hooves.

"A little," replied Cole. "Enough to know we've got our work cut out for us."

He heeled the sorrel into a run and headed down the street, which had pretty well emptied out. Most folks had found themselves a hidey-hole by now, Cole figured, but that wouldn't do them much good if the full force of the stampede hit the town.

As he reached the end of the avenue he saw the dark, roiling mass at the base of the dust cloud. The leading edge of the herd was less than half a mile away now. The cattle were galloping along parallel to the railroad tracks, and their path would take them through the main section of Wind River.

Cole spotted a few riders galloping along between the herd and the steel rails, firing six-guns into the air and shouting stridently as they tried to reach the leaders and urge them back to the south. That was the only way to stop a stampede, Cole knew — turning it in on itself until the cattle had run out their fright.

He leaned forward in the saddle, urging the sorrel on to greater speed. The riders he could see, probably the cowboys who had accompanied the herd on its journey from wherever it had come from, weren't going to be able to reach the leaders in time.

The townsmen who had ridden out here to see if they could help had all veered off, retreating to safety on the north side of the railroad tracks when they had seen the juggernaut bearing down on them. Cole and

Casebolt were the only ones who were still in position to have a chance to turn the herd.

And if they miscalculated . . . if their horses made one misstep . . . they would go down and the runaway herd would sweep over them — and likely there wouldn't even be enough left to bury.

With the crazed herd bearing down on them, Cole and Casebolt swung their horses to the south, the deputy following the younger man's lead. Cole jerked his revolver from the waistband of his pants and eared back the hammer. He and Casebolt were riding directly toward the flow of the stampede now, with less than a hundred yards separating them from the leaders of the herd. Cole started firing, and as he did so he yelled at the top of his lungs. Casebolt followed suit, trailing a few yards behind him.

For an awful moment he thought the noise and the distraction wasn't doing any good. The stampede didn't seem to be slowing or turning. But then a few of the leaders began to veer to the south in an attempt to avoid the two crazy men galloping in front of them. More of the cattle followed, and as the seconds dragged out it became more and more obvious that the herd was gradually swinging to the south.

Now the question was whether or not it would turn in time, Cole thought as he triggered off the last of his shots and then concentrated on getting all the speed possible out of the sorrel. He and Casebolt had to get clear, or they might still be trampled by the runaway cattle.

Cole waved Casebolt away and angled away from the herd himself. As the cattle continued to turn, the two lawmen eventually wound up galloping alongside the still-frantic animals. The cowboys who had accompanied the herd drew up even with them, still shouting and shooting to make sure the cattle didn't turn back toward Wind River.

Cole and Casebolt drew farther and farther away from the herd until they were finally well clear of it and could rein their exhausted mounts to a halt.

Blood was pounding inside Cole's skull, and he couldn't seem to get quite enough air into his lungs for a few minutes. When he looked over at Casebolt, he saw that the older man's face was gray and drawn, and Casebolt's gnarled fingers were clutched tightly around his saddlehorn. Casebolt was having trouble catching his breath, too.

"You all right, Billy?" Cole managed to ask.

Casebolt nodded jerkily. "That was close, Marshal, mighty close," he said.

"Too damned close," Cole bit off. He looked around. The herd of cattle was still streaming by, and the first tents on the outskirts of Wind River were less than fifty yards behind Cole and Casebolt. If they had taken another thirty seconds to turn the herd, it would have been too late to save some of the town.

Casebolt let go of the saddlehorn, took off his hat, and sleeved sweat from his forehead. As he replaced the battered hat he said, "Wonder who all them beeves belong to?"

"I was just asking myself the same thing," replied Cole. "Let's go see if we can find out." He lifted the reins and turned Ulysses toward the railroad tracks again. A few cowboys passed him as he rode toward the rear of the herd, but Cole didn't bother trying to get their attention. He was looking for a chuck wagon.

He located it a few moments later, parked on the north side of the tracks where the cook had driven it to get out of the path of the stampede. A young man was sitting on the driver's seat looking relieved as the herd milled on past the town without causing any

105

damage.

"You the cook for this outfit?" Cole called to the young man as he and Casebolt reined up on the south side of the tracks.

"That's right." The youngster nodded. His voice was excited as he went on, "You're the gents who turned the herd! I thought you were goners for sure."

Cole replied dryly, "The thought crossed our minds, too. Where's your trail boss?"

"Over yonder somewhere," the young cook answered as he waved a hand toward the cattle. "Mr. Sawyer took off after the leaders as soon as the herd spooked. Reckon you must've passed him."

Cole grunted. This Sawyer, whoever he was, would return to the chuck wagon sooner or later, unless some accident had befallen him in the effort to stop the stampede. Cole hoped that wasn't the case; he didn't want Sawyer getting off that easily.

"What the hell happened?" Cole demanded. "Did you see what started the stampede?"

The cook shook his head. "No, sir, I didn't. We bedded down the herd a couple of miles south of here last night, didn't know we were so close to the railroad or a town. This morning I came on ahead of the herd, just like usual, but I hadn't gone a mile when I heard 'em start running behind me. I took off in this direction as fast as I could, hoping I'd find some place the herd wouldn't go. I figured these railroad tracks would stop em."

"They didn't stop, they just turned and headed straight for town," Cole pointed out. "That accent tells me you're from Texas."

"Yes, sir. We brought the herd from Mr. Sawyer's ranch on the upper Colorado River. A mighty long drive, it was."

"Come to sell those cows to the railroad for fresh meat?" asked Cole. "If you did, you're liable to be disappointed. There's still plenty of buffalo in these parts to provide all the meat the track layers need."

"No, sir," the young man said. "We came to start a new ranch."

Cole frowned. He knew that a few cattlemen had been moving into the Wyoming Territory from Nebraska, but they hadn't yet come this far west. And why would anybody drive a herd all the way from Texas?

Before he voiced those questions, the cook pointed and said, "You can ask Mr. Sawyer about it, mister. Here he comes now."

Cole and Casebolt looked around and saw a man riding toward them. The newcomer was older, with white hair and a deeply lined face about the same color as the leather of his saddle. He wore a dark suit and hat that looked gray now from the thick coating of dust that had settled on them. As he drew rein wary eyes looked intently at Cole and Casebolt.

"Who're you?" he asked without preamble.

The cook spoke up, calling across the tracks, "They're the gents who rode out from that town and turned the herd, Mr. Sawyer. They ain't told me their names."

"*Helped* turn the herd, you mean, Lon," Sawyer said. He regarded Cole and Casebolt with a cold stare and went on, "My boys would've got that stampede under control sooner or later."

"After it had torn up the town and likely killed some innocent folks," Cole snapped. "What the hell's going on here, mister?"

The Texas cattleman shrugged. "A stampede's just one of the risks of driving a herd thousands of miles. If you'd ever worked much with cattle, you'd know that. And just who in blazes are you to be talking to me like that?" His voice crackled with indignation.

Cole was pretty upset himself after the close call. He said, "My name's Cole Tyler. I'm the marshal of Wind River, that town over there your herd nearly destroyed. This other fella's my deputy, Billy Casebolt."

The Texan grunted in acknowledgment of the introductions. "Kermit Sawyer, from West Texas. I thank you for your help turning the herd, Marshal, but you'd best back off a mite. We didn't stampede that stock on purpose, and we didn't even know your town was here."

Cole felt an immediate dislike for Sawyer. The man had an arrogance about him that he had seen in other cattle barons. Sawyer thought he was the cock of the walk, that everybody else had been put on earth to follow his orders and help him establish his own private little empire. It was an attitude especially common to Texans, Cole had found, but Sawyer was going to discover that it wouldn't wash here in Wyoming.

Still, it wouldn't help matters for him to lose his temper, Cole realized. Holding his irritation in check, he asked, "What started them running?"

"Who the hell knows?" Sawyer shot back. "We were getting the herd moving this morning like we have every morning since we left Texas. Maybe one of 'em stepped on a snake, or one of those damned prairie dogs popped his head up from his hole at the wrong time. *Something* spooked 'em, and that was all it took. They'd likely still

109

be running north if they hadn't come upon these railroad tracks."

Sawyer was right, Cole knew. It had been pure bad luck that the herd had gone wild, and more bad luck that the settlement had been in the way. But now that the animals were beginning to come under control again, it was important to know Sawyer's plans.

"What are you going to do now?" Cole asked.

The cattleman shrugged. "We'll bunch 'em up again and drive 'em north of the rails. They'll cross all right when they're calm. Then I intend to look for a place to start my new ranch."

"You're settling around here?"

"Damn right I am. From what I've seen, there's good grass, even if it is a mite sparse in places. And with the railroad right here, it'll be easy to ship the cattle back east to market."

That was another point in Sawyer's favor, Cole thought. In fact, Andrew McKay and William Durand had planned from the first for Wind River to serve as a shipping point for the herds of cattle that would be coming to this part of the territory. That much was clear from the loading pens that had already been built north of the depot.

"All right, blast it," Cole said impatiently. "But make sure you bed down those cattle well away from the town while you're looking around. I don't want any more stampedes threatening Wind River."

"You just do your job, Marshal, and let us do ours," Sawyer replied coldly. "And one more word of advice . . . don't cross me too often, Tyler. I'm not used to it, and I don't intend to get used to it."

With that, Sawyer jerked his horse around and headed back to the herd, which had slowed considerably and was now just milling around aimlessly while Sawyer's cowboys gathered up the strays and prodded them back with the other stock.

As Cole glared after Sawyer, Casebolt cleared his throat and commented, "That old boy ain't too friendly."

"No, he's not," Cole agreed. "But I'll be damned if I let him run roughshod over me or the town. Come on, let's see if things are settling down."

Cole urged Ulysses into a trot and headed for Wind River, not looking back to see if Casebolt was following him.

CHAPTER 6

Not surprisingly, a delegation of relieved citizens was waiting in the street when Cole and Casebolt rode back into town. William Durand and Dr. Judson Kent were in the forefront of the group as they came out to meet the lawmen.

"That was magnificent," Kent said with enthusiasm. "I've never seen anything like it. You gentlemen risked your lives to stop those beasts from rampaging through town."

Cole and Casebolt reined in and dismounted in front of the land development company with the marshal's office in the front room. Turning to face the townspeople, Cole raised his voice and said, "You don't have to worry now, folks. The fella who owns those cattle is going to drive 'em on north of town and keep them there. I reckon you can go on about your business." He wasn't sure, but it seemed like reassuring the townspeople in times of trouble ought to be part of the marshal's job.

"But what in God's name are all those cattle doing here in the first place?" demanded Durand.

"You were hoping that some ranches would be established in the area so you'd have something to ship out from those pens north of the tracks, weren't you?"

"Yes, of course. You mean —"

Cole nodded. "The fella who owns that herd, a man named Sawyer, brought them up from Texas to start a ranch here in Wyoming. He'll be looking for a spot that suits his fancy while he's camped to the north."

Cole didn't mention the hostility that had sprung up immediately between himself and Sawyer, that was none of Durand's business. As long as Sawyer kept his herd — and his cowboys — under control, Cole didn't expect to have any more dealings with the man.

Having a bunch of proddy cowhands nearby was worrisome, though. The atmosphere in Wind River was already strained enough due to the continuing conflicts between the railroad workers and drifters like Deke Strawhorn. Throwing some wild Texans into the volatile mixture was almost asking for trouble.

Maybe it wouldn't come to that, Cole told himself. He could always hope so, at least.

Michael Hatfield was also in the crowd. He spoke up. "Did this man Sawyer know what caused his cattle to stampede?"

Cole shook his head. "Claimed he didn't. And it doesn't really matter. All that's important is that they didn't run wild here in town. Now, if you folks will excuse me, I haven't had any breakfast yet."

The crowd broke up quickly. As it did, Michael came over to Cole and asked, "Do you think I should go out and interview Mr. Sawyer for the newspaper?"

"You're the editor," Cole said with a shrug. "I don't know much about the newspaper business, remember?"

Michael flushed a little. "I thought you and I had declared a truce, Marshal Tyler."

"We have," Cole told him. "Do what you want about talking to Sawyer. I warn you, though — he's a Texan, and that means he's pretty damned sure of himself. If he doesn't want to talk to you, he won't hesitate to run you off. And he might not be too gentle about it."

"I'm not afraid of him," Michael insisted. "But it might be wise to let him get his herd settled down completely before anyone bothers him."

114

"Yeah, that'd be a good idea," Cole agreed, a hint of a smile on his face.

Leaving Billy Casebolt at the office to handle any problems that came up, Cole returned to the hotel, put on his socks, hat, and gunbelt, and went looking for some breakfast. He had eaten at the hash house several times since arriving in Wind River, so he decided to try to find someplace different. As he looked down the street he spotted the strawberry blonde he and Casebolt had seen the day before. She was watching as several men unloaded a large iron stove from a wagon bed and wrestled it into the building. Cole started in that direction.

She noticed him coming, and he saw that she had a carefully neutral expression on her face, as if she was deliberately covering up her feelings. He nodded to her as he stepped onto the boardwalk. "Good morning, ma'am."

"Good morning," she returned, her voice as cautious as her face.

"I'm Cole Tyler, the marshal here in Wind River — as of yesterday morning. From the looks of things, we're both newcomers around here."

The woman nodded. "Yes. I'm new in town, too." She didn't offer her name.

Cole didn't let that bother him. Now that the harrowing encounter with the stampeding herd of cattle was fading into the background, he was getting back to normal, and that included being stubborn when there was something he wanted to know. He looked steadily at the woman and said, "And you would be . . . ?"

"Rose Foster," she replied as the men who had unloaded the stove reappeared from the building. Rose turned away from Cole and said to the leader of the other men, "Thank you for delivering my stove, Mr. Dunleavy. And thank you for keeping it in your freight warehouse until I got here."

"Glad to do it, Miss Foster," the boss of the freighters replied. "To tell you the truth, I'm glad for all the business I can get these days. We were really hoppin' when my wagons were haulin' all the stuff out here to set up this town, but now that the railroad's got here at last . . ." Dunleavy shook his head. "Well, there won't be as much wagon traffic in these parts, that's for sure."

"Thank you again," Rose Foster said, then she didn't add anything until Dunleavy and his men had climbed back onto the wagon and driven off. She turned to Cole once more and asked, "Was there something you wanted of me, Marshal? If not, I really have a great deal of work to do here."

"Moving in?" Cole asked. It seemed unlikely when all he had seen unloaded was a stove. If Rose was going to live here, she would need furniture, too, and dishes and rugs and all sorts of household goods.

She was moving in, but not to live here, he found a moment later as she said, "I'm going to open a restaurant in this building, Marshal. I'm leasing the place from Mr. Durand."

Cole nodded. "I see. When do you expect to be open for business?"

"Oh, not for another week or so. There's still a great deal to do."

He lifted a finger to the brim of his hat. "Well, good luck to you, ma'am. From what I've seen, Wind River can use a good eating place. I'll probably be taking some of my meals with you."

Rose put a perfunctory smile on her face. "That would be fine," she said.

She didn't sound very enthusiastic, though, Cole thought as he strolled on past the building and resumed his search for somewhere to eat breakfast. The way his stomach was growling, he wasn't going to be able to wait a week until Rose Foster opened her eatery. But then again, the food might not be any good.

But he would have been willing to bet that it would be, Cole mused with a slight grin.

That afternoon a finely appointed buggy rolled out of Wind River with William Durand at the reins, guiding a big, sleek black horse. Durand crossed the railroad tracks and drove north, quickly picking up the broad band of tracks left by the herd of cattle.

It had taken nearly an hour for the two thousand head to pass by the town once the herd was under control again. The cattle were out of sight now, and as Durand studied the gently rolling landscape to the north, he didn't see any dust cloud hanging in the sky. That meant the cattle had already come to a stop again.

A slight feeling of nervousness went through Durand as he left the settlement behind and passed out of sight of it. He had been raised in Baltimore and then spent time in New York, Boston, and Philadelphia before coming west, and he was still somewhat unaccustomed to all these wide-open spaces. He would always be a city lad at heart, he supposed.

But there was a fortune to be made here in the West, and besides, not all of those cities back east would welcome him if he returned to them. In fact, there were places where the only ones waiting for him with open arms would have been the authorities. . . .

Durand shook his head and scowled. He needn't worry about such things, he told himself, not as long as he remained here in Wyoming.

The tracks of the herd were easy to follow, even for a civilized man such as himself. The buggy rolled along briskly, and several miles north of town, at the top of a rise, Durand saw the cattle spread out over the broad valley in front of him. A tiny creek ran through the valley, providing enough water for a few scrubby trees along its banks and a thin coating of grass on the hillsides. Durand was not a cattleman by any stretch of the imagination, but even he could tell that there wasn't sufficient graze here for the herd to make a permanent home. This would be a temporary stop at best.

And since that fit right in with his plans, he allowed a momentary smile to touch his broad, bearded face.

He drove down the hill into the valley, and as he approached, several of the cowboys tending the now docile herd saw him coming and rode over to the chuck wagon to alert their employer. The wagon was parked at the eastern end of the valley, where the creek ran through a small saddle in the hills. Durand drove toward it, handling the reins skillfully.

A man wearing what appeared to be all black mounted up and rode out to meet him. As Durand pulled back on the reins and brought the buggy to a stop, he saw that the man had white hair and a weathered face. "Hello," he called when the rider was in earshot. "Would you be Mr. Sawyer, from Texas?"

The white-haired man reined in next to the buggy and nodded. "I'm Kermit Sawyer," he said. "And I'd appreciate it if you wouldn't bring that buggy any closer, mister. Those cattle are nice and calm again, and I'd like to keep 'em that way."

"I agree completely," said Durand, smiling. He leaned over on the seat of the vehicle and held out his hand. "William Durand is my name. I'm from that town you passed earlier, Wind River."

Sawyer grunted, hesitated for an instant, then took Durand's hand and shook it. "What can I do for you, Mr. Durand?"

"I'm told by our marshal that you've come to the Wyoming Territory to establish a ranch, Mr. Sawyer. Is that correct?"

"Yep. Pardon me for being blunt, Mr. Durand, but what business is that of yours?"

Durand's smile widened. "Business is exactly what it is, sir. I've come to make you a proposition that could prove profitable for both of us." He saw the skepticism creeping into the Texan's eyes, so he hurried on, "You see, my late partner and I are the ones who established Wind River, and we had high hopes for its future as a center of the growing cattle industry here in the territory. I still have those hopes, despite Andrew's recent untimely demise. Andrew McKay, that is, my late partner. At any rate, perhaps you saw the loading pens north of the railroad station in town . . . ?"

Kermit Sawyer nodded. "I saw 'em. Looked like you were ready for us, all right. That's pretty forward thinking, Durand."

"Exactly," Durand said, warming to his subject. "Right now there are no regularly scheduled trains passing through Wind River, since the railhead arrived only a few days ago, but soon there will be. You'll be able to ship your beef back to the markets in Kansas City with a minimum of trouble. That is, if you have plenty of beef to ship."

Sawyer jerked a thumb over his shoulder at the cattle behind him. "Two thousand head, give or take a few. And the herd'll grow."

"I don't claim to be a cattleman, Mr. Sawyer, far from it, in fact. But even I know that there's not enough grass in this valley to support your herd at its present size, let alone a larger one."

"Maybe not," Sawyer allowed curtly. "What's your point?"

"I know where you can find plenty of grass for your stock, plus good water and protection from the weather during the winter. The land would make a fine ranch."

Sawyer rested his hands on the saddle-horn and leaned forward. "I'm figuring on looking around until I find a place like that myself."

"Why waste time doing that when I can take you directly to the most suitable spot in the entire territory?"

The cattleman's bushy white eyebrows came down in a frown. "Now, just why is it that you're so anxious to help me out, Mr. Durand?" he asked, his tone shrewd.

Durand saw no point in being coy. He said bluntly, "I happen to have put in a claim on the land in question. I'm proposing a partnership between us. Your cattle on my land should provide sufficient profits for both of us."

Sawyer shook his head and said harshly, "I didn't come all the way up here to go in partners with anybody. No offense, mister, but I've always been my own man, and I aim to stay that way."

Durand held up his hands, palms out. "You misunderstand, sir. As I told you, I'm no cattleman, and I've no interest in becoming one. You would be, in effect, leasing the land from me, and the payment would be a percentage — a small percentage, mind you — of the money you make from your ranch."

"I thought this was open range up here."

"Some of it is," Durand said with a shrug. "But much of it was granted to the Union Pacific by the government, more than was necessary for the actual building of the railroad, since it was not determined at the beginning what the route of the line would be. The Union Pacific has, in turn, disposed of some of its holdings that are no longer needed."

"Disposed of 'em to gents like you," said Sawyer. "I reckon I'm starting to see how it works now. A little deal under the table here and there never hurt nobody."

Durand flushed, but he kept a tight rein on his temper. "I didn't come out here to debate the ethics of the business world with you, Mr. Sawyer. I merely want to present you with an opportunity that, frankly, I think you would be a fool to pass up."

For a moment Sawyer looked as if he was about to tell his visitor to go to hell. But then his expression became more speculative, and he asked, "Where is this property of yours?"

"In the foothills to the northwest, about ten miles from Wind River. Would you like to see it?"

"Reckon it wouldn't hurt to take a look," grunted Sawyer. "Come on."

"Right now?" Durand asked, surprised.

"Why not? If it's as good as you claim it is, I want to see it for myself."

"Oh, it's good range, I assure you," Durand said. "Very well, I'll show you." He flicked the reins and got the horse moving again, turning the buggy toward the northwest.

They followed ridges and valleys, the ride a fairly easy one. The terrain grew considerably more rugged to the north, where several ranges of mountains, including the Wind River range itself, were visible on the horizon. The country around here was still quite amenable to ranching, however, Durand thought. At least he had been told that it was.

The creek on which Sawyer's temporary camp was located veered off to the north, but after a mile or so Durand and Sawyer rode up to another small stream and began following it. "This creek leads into the valley I told you about," Durand said. "We'll be there shortly."

"I still say I can find some open range that'll be just as good," Sawyer replied. "But I'm willing to take a look at this place of yours."

The ground began to rise in a gentle slope that gradually grew steeper. The creek still bubbled and chuckled beside them. There were more trees along the banks now, and the grass under the hooves of the horses was thicker. The creek twisted to the north, away from the path Durand was following, and several hundred yards away it was visible tumbling down a steep bluff in a short waterfall.

Durand pointed and said, "The stream curves back to the west at the top of that bluff and runs through the valley. You'll see it in a few minutes."

They followed a winding path up to the top of the bluff, then Durand hauled the buggy to a stop and waved a hand at the scene spread out before them. "Did you ever see a more beautiful spot, Mr. Sawyer?" he asked the cattleman.

Sawyer had reined in beside the buggy.

The Texan's keen eyes swept over the valley, taking in the thickly wooded hills rising to each side and the broad, level plain in between. The creek meandered through the approximate center of the valley, its banks lined with cottonwood and aspen. Thick green grass carpeted its floor, which was perhaps five miles wide and twenty miles long.

Durand could tell from the way Sawyer caught his breath that the man was impressed by the sight. He waited for a few moments, letting Sawyer drink it all in, then said quietly, "Well, was I correct?"

"It's a mighty pretty place, all right," Sawyer admitted. His stubbornness reasserted itself, however. "But I still figure I can find some open range just as good."

"You won't," Durand said bluntly. "Not this close to a settlement and the railroad. Just think of the advantages, Mr. Sawyer. A short ride into town for all the supplies you might ever need, an easy drive to reach the railroad and ship your cattle to market. Plenty of water and grass, and those taller hills at the other end of the valley will block the worst of the storms in winter. It's ideal for a ranch such as the one you want to establish."

"Could be," mused Sawyer. "How big a

percentage would you want?"

Durand tried not to smile in triumph. Just like an experienced fisherman, he knew when the hook was set firmly. "One fourth of your profits is all I ask, and at the end of five years, I deed the land over to you free and clear."

"I run things, and you keep your nose out of it?"

Durand spread his hands. "As I told you, I've no wish to become a cattleman. Besides, I'll continue to make money from the fees you pay to use my loading pens in town once the ranch is completely yours." He made his voice as sincere as possible as he went on, "No, I can promise you that you'll have a free hand. I'm a businessman, not a rancher."

For a long moment Sawyer made no reply. Then he said, "I'll think about it. I want to take a look around for myself before I decide on anything, though."

"Of course. But I can tell you right now, you won't find anyplace as suitable as this one."

"We'll see," Sawyer said. "I'd better be heading back to my herd."

"I'll go with you part of the way, then there's a shorter route to town. Take all the time you like, Mr. Sawyer. My office is on

Grenville Avenue, across from the hotel in Wind River. Feel free to drop in anytime."

Sawyer nodded and turned his horse, but before he heeled it into a trot, he looked back at the valley. He was trying not to show how impressed he was with the location, Durand could tell. It was only a matter of time now, and it wouldn't be very long. The grass in that lower valley where Sawyer's herd was camped would only last a short while, then the cattle would have to be moved. Durand was confident that Sawyer would accept his proposal.

Then Durand would draw up an agreement they would both sign, and the real work would begin. By the time the five years were up — perhaps even before that — Sawyer would have been smoothly edged out of the arrangement, and William Durand would own the largest and best ranch in this part of the territory, in addition to controlling the town that was the hub of the whole thing.

Yes, indeed, Durand thought as he drove the buggy along beside the unsuspecting cattleman, everything was working out just fine.

That pudgy little townie figured he was really putting something over on the dumb ol' cowboy from Texas, Kermit Sawyer thought, keeping his gaze straight ahead so he wouldn't have to look at Durand's smirk. Thing was, he wasn't as dumb as Durand obviously believed him to be. The businessman probably planned to put some highfalutin legal language in the contract between them so that he could steal the ranch right out from under his "partner" after Sawyer got it established.

Sawyer wasn't going to have any of that. In fact, if he played his cards right, that valley would wind up belonging to him free and clear, just like Durand had said, only Sawyer wouldn't have to turn over any twenty-five percent of his profits for five years in order to claim it. And if Durand didn't like it . . .

Well, Sawyer had dealt with plenty of trouble in the past from redskins and wideloopers and all sorts of scalawags. He figured he could handle one overconfident city slicker, even if it came down to showing Durand the barrel of his gun and letting him know who was really boss. Sawyer wasn't worried overmuch about the law. He could handle that two-bit marshal in Wind River.

As soon as he had seen that high valley, he knew he'd found what he had come all this way to find. This was going to be his new home.

And anybody who got in his way could just watch out, including William Durand and Marshal Cole Tyler. *Especially* that high-and-mighty lawman . . .

CHAPTER 7

Cole was standing on the boardwalk in front of the hotel when he saw William Durand drive out of town in the fancy buggy. He had his saddlebags slung over his shoulder and the Winchester '66 tucked under his arm along with the big, oilcloth-wrapped Sharps.

The rest of his gear, consisting mainly of his saddle, was stored at the livery where Ulysses was stabled. Cole had never been one to burden himself with too many possessions; he liked to travel light, since it made moving a lot easier. He was on his way to Wind River's only boardinghouse to claim the room Durand had promised him as one of the benefits of the marshal's job.

The sight of Durand reminded Cole of the visit Simone McKay had paid him the night before. With all the uproar caused by the stampede that morning, the matter of Andrew McKay's death had receded to the back of Cole's mind. He hadn't forgotten entirely about it, however, and as he walked toward the boardinghouse he thought about the widow's claim that Durand had murdered her husband.

A frown creased Cole's forehead. He didn't know how the hell to go about proving a thing like that. Maybe a place to start would be to ask a few questions of folks.

The clerk at the hotel had told him where to find the boardinghouse. It was on one of the side streets, just around the corner from Grenville Avenue east of the hotel and the marshal's office. Construction was still going on, even though the house's owner was already accepting boarders. It would be a substantial three-story structure when it was finished, Cole saw. Several men were on the roof, hammering wooden shingles into place, while a couple of others were whitewashing the walls. Nearby, a man stood leaning on a cane, watching the work. Cole walked over to him and nodded.

"Howdy," Cole greeted the man. "Would you be Lawton Paine?"

"That's right." The man turned to face Cole. His features were those of a young man, but his hair was mostly white. He leaned heavily on the cane, using it to support the weight that his twisted right leg wouldn't. He went on, "What can I do for you?"

"I was told you rent out rooms. I'm the new marshal, and Mr. Durand said the town would pay for me to stay here."

Lawton Paine's lips tightened and he grudgingly admitted, "Yes, Durand came by and made the arrangements with me. My wife's got your room ready, Marshal."

Cole sensed that Paine had taken an almost instant dislike to him, and it had started with his mention of William Durand. Shifting his saddlebags slightly on his shoulder, he asked, "Don't you and Durand get along, Mr. Paine?"

The boardinghouse owner looked sharply at him. "What business is that of yours?"

Cole shrugged. "None, really, but I was curious. I got the feeling Durand's not one of your favorite people."

Paine looked away. As he stared up at the men working on the roof, he said, "I've got to get along with Durand. I'm still paying off what I owe him on this place."

"You bought the boardinghouse from Durand? I thought —"

"I bought the land," Paine cut in. "Or rather, I'm buying it. If I miss a payment, Durand'll take it over in a second. But at that, I'm lucky. Durand and McKay at least

133

let me buy the land. A lot of the businesses in town are having to lease their locations from the development company."

This wasn't the first time Cole had heard such a comment. He said, "Durand and McKay bought up a lot of land before the railroad ever got here, didn't they?"

"Damn right. While I was still in a hospital in Washington City, they were bribing somebody connected with the Union Pacific to find out where the route was going to go so that they could buy up all the good land through here. Then they advertised for settlers to come out and populate their new town. Made it sound like people could be independent and work toward bettering their own future." Paine laughed bitterly. "Too bad it didn't work out that way."

Cole shook his head. "I don't understand. The town's here, and it looks to be thriving. Folks are doing business —"

"And most of the money they make goes to either pay the rent that Durand and McKay charge them, or else to make payments on their notes. It'll be years before folks are out from under Durand's thumb, if then."

"So you didn't like McKay, and you don't care for Durand. Why don't you go back east?" Cole thought he already knew the answer to that question, but he wanted to hear it from Paine.

"I don't have enough money to go back," the man replied. "It took all I had, and all I got from the government after the war, to pay for coming out here and building this boardinghouse." Paine shook his head. "Did you ever hear of an indentured servant, Marshal? That's what I feel like."

Cole didn't say anything for a moment, then he asked, "What happened to your leg? Hurt in the war?"

"A Reb musketball broke the thighbone at Pea Ridge. They took me prisoner and shipped me off to a camp in Georgia called Copperhead Mountain. Ever hear of it?"

Cole grimaced. He had heard of the prison camp at Copperhead Mountain, all right. Most folks considered the hellhole at Andersonville to have been the worst of the Confederate prison camps, but Copperhead Mountain had been almost as bad. "Sorry," he muttered.

"So was I. Didn't get much medical care there, nor much to eat, and the leg didn't heal right. Never will be the same. But I didn't lose it, and I suppose I should be grateful for that. I'm told that one of the men who brought those tent saloons to town had his arm sawed off by some butcher

135

in a field hospital at Shiloh."

Paine was talking about Hank Parker, and Cole knew he was right. That was one of the causes of the hostility Parker had always felt toward him; Cole had ridden for the South, and Parker blamed everyone who ever wore butternut gray for the loss of his arm. Paine likely felt the same way.

"Might as well get this straight since I'm going to be staying here," Cole said, his voice hardening. "I was a Confederate, Paine. I've tried to put all those old hard feelings behind me, but if you can't abide a Reb under your roof, just say so and I'll find someplace else to live."

Without hesitation, Paine shook his head. "Hell, no. Your money spends as good as anybody's, Marshal. Or in this case, the town's money. Which means Durand's money, and I've got to admit, I sort of like taking it from him." He fixed Cole with a stony stare. "No, I'd be obliged if you'd stay. The room's clean and comfortable, and my wife's a good cook."

"That's all I ask." Cole put out his hand.

Paine hesitated, then took it briefly. The handshake was short and without much feeling, but at least it was a start, Cole thought.

He pressed on by asking, "What do you

think about Andrew McKay getting shot?"

Paine shrugged. "I feel sorry for his wife. Mrs. McKay seems like a fine lady. But I didn't shed any tears for McKay. Not after he and Durand gobbled up the whole town like they did."

Cole thought Paine was letting his bitterness color his thinking a little too much. True, from everything he had seen and heard so far, Durand and McKay were smooth customers, maybe even a little on the shady side in their dealings with the railroad. That didn't make them any different from hundreds, maybe thousands, of other entrepreneurs who had come west to make their fortunes.

But it cast an interesting light on McKay's death. If some of the other citizens of Wind River felt about the land speculators the way Lawton Paine did, that broadened the list of people who might have wanted to see Andrew McKay dead. For that matter, Paine himself might have been bitter enough to have pulled a trigger, had the opportunity presented itself. . . .

Trying to sound idly curious, Cole asked, "Did you go down to the railroad station the other day for the arrival of that first train?"

"No, I was busy here. Besides, with my

leg like this —" Paine slapped his withered leg and grimaced. "I don't like to get in a big crowd. I'm not that steady on my feet, and if I fell, I might get trampled."

He had a point there, Cole decided — not to mention an alibi for the time of McKay's death. But there had been plenty of other people on that platform, and some of them could have resented Andrew McKay as much as Paine seemed to, maybe even hated him.

Cole hitched up the rifles under his arm. "Well, if you'll tell me where to find my room, I'll take my gear up there."

"Sure. We're going to put you in the second floor front, on the south corner, if that's all right with you. The room's ready."

Cole nodded. "That'll do fine, I reckon. Durand's already taken care of paying you?"

"Yeah. You've missed lunch already, but supper will be at six sharp." A slight smile tugged at Paine's mouth, and his grim demeanor lessened a little. "It's chicken and dumplings tonight, and you haven't eaten until you've tried Abigail's chicken and dumplings."

Cole grinned back at him. "I'll be here," he promised.

He went inside and encountered Abigail Paine on his way through the foyer to the staircase leading up to the second floor. She came out of a partially furnished parlor and introduced herself. Cole liked her right away. She was a blond, plump, friendly woman with none of her husband's dourness.

"You just go right on up to your room, Marshal, and if there's anything not to your liking, you just tell me and I'll take care of it right away. You can always find me or one of my young'uns in the kitchen back yonder."

"How many children do you have?" asked Cole.

"Six," Abigail replied, beaming. "And don't you go trying to flatter me by telling me I look too young to have that many children."

"You must've read my mind," Cole told her gallantly, even though he hadn't been about to say any such thing.

"Go on with you. The mister told you about supper?"

"Yes, ma'am. I'll be here if I can. I reckon a lawman never knows when he'll be called away, even though I haven't been one for very long."

"I heard about what you and Billy Casebolt did this morning, stopping that stampede and all. My, that must have been frightening."

"I've had easier mornings," Cole allowed.

"Well, go up and get settled in, and we'll see you later. And don't mind Lawton's sour disposition. He's just like that sometimes."

Cole would have been willing to bet that Lawton Paine was like that most of the time, but he didn't say anything.

He went upstairs and found the room Paine had told him about. Like the man had claimed, it was clean, although the smell of sawed wood lingering in the air told him this part of the house had been only recently completed. Despite that, there was no sawdust on the floor.

A narrow bed took up about half the room; there was a chair and a washstand on the other side, along with an empty wardrobe. Nothing fancy about it, just a place to sleep — but that was all Cole needed. He tossed his saddlebags on the bed, put the Winchester and the wrapped-up Sharps in the wardrobe, and went downstairs again.

He didn't see either of the Paines as he left, although he heard what sounded like children shouting happily behind the house. Moving to Wyoming Territory had to be quite an adventure for the Paine youngsters, and Cole hoped their father's dissatisfaction didn't rub off on them. Life was hard sometimes, sure, but kids still deserved a chance to be kids and enjoy themselves.

As he walked downtown he passed the blacksmith shop and stopped to say hello to Jeremiah Newton. The massive smith nodded and said, "Good afternoon to you, Marshal. The Lord's given us a beautiful day today, hasn't He?"

Cole glanced at the blue sky with white clouds floating in it, felt a breeze with a trace of coolness in it to blend with the warmth of the sun. "It's mighty nice, all right, Mr. Newton," he agreed.

"Brother Newton, or just plain Jeremiah," the blacksmith told him. "The Lord loves a simple man."

"I've heard it said the Lord loves a poor man, and that's why He made so many of them."

Jeremiah was working the bellows on his forge, but he stopped at Cole's comment. "God helps those who help themselves," he said.

"And it's easier for a camel to pass through the eye of a needle than for a rich man to enter the kingdom of heaven."

Jeremiah threw back his head and laughed, a rich, booming sound. "You know the Bible, my friend. That's good."

Cole shrugged. "I know some of it. My

father was a mountain man, trapped beaver all over this part of the country and on up north to the Canadian border. He couldn't read a lick, but he could recite whole books of the Bible and some of Shakespeare's plays. I used to listen to him talk about how he and his friends would sit around a campfire and recite for hours all the things they'd memorized. I reckon when you're off by yourself, or nearly by yourself, in the middle of nowhere for months at a time, even being able to quote Bible verses is pretty entertaining."

"Better than guzzling whiskey and indulging the lusts of the flesh with poor, innocent Indian women," Jeremiah grunted.

Cole didn't say anything, but he reckoned his old pa had done his share of *that*, too. He didn't want to irritate the big blacksmith, though, especially when he was about to ask him another question.

"Not to change the subject," Cole went on a moment later, "but I was wondering if you rent this shop from Durand and McKay's land development company?"

"Indeed I do. My arrangement was with both Brother Durand and Brother McKay. I assume that Brother Durand will continue to honor the agreement now that Brother McKay has unfortunately passed on."

"Did you plan to buy the land when you came out here, instead of renting it?"

Jeremiah shrugged shoulders that seemed almost as broad as he was tall. "I don't concern myself that much with earthly possessions, Brother Tyler. I just want to help people and lay up treasures for myself in heaven."

If Jeremiah was telling the truth — and the sincerity in his voice was plain to hear — he was a pretty unlikely candidate to have killed Andrew McKay, Cole thought. Besides, the gun that had fired the fatal bullet had been a fairly small caliber, and such a weapon would have been almost lost in Jeremiah's hamlike hands. Cole could see Jeremiah Newton crushing the life out of somebody if he was provoked enough, but to do something as underhanded as shooting McKay during the confusion of the brawl at the railroad station . . . that just didn't seem believable.

He said his farewells and started to move on, but Jeremiah called after him, "Day after tomorrow is Sunday. Will I see you at services, Brother Tyler?"

"I'll try to be there," Cole promised.

"Under the big cottonwood on the western edge of town," Jeremiah told him. "You can't miss it."

"Thanks," Cole said with a wave. He didn't know if he would actually take Jeremiah up on the invitation or not. Despite the time he had spent listening to his father quote the Scriptures, he had never been a particularly religious man. Although there had been moments — usually when he was alone, far from anyone else in the high country — when he had felt a peculiar closeness with whoever had created the magnificent landscapes around him. For Cole, that had been enough.

During the rest of the afternoon, Cole continued his probing, walking around Wind River and talking to the various merchants, accepting their thanks and congratulations for turning the stampede away from town before getting on with his real reason for visiting them. He kept his questions fairly innocuous, but he discovered that what he had assumed was true: Durand and McKay — now Durand alone — owned practically the entire settlement.

A few of the business owners had had enough money to buy their land outright, although Durand and McKay had sold only grudgingly and at a high price. And there was a definite feeling in the community — resentment might have been too strong a word — that Durand and McKay had come out better on the deals than anyone else.

But did anyone in town feel so strongly that they would have pulled the trigger if they had the chance? Cole couldn't answer that question with his head, but his gut told him no.

Which left William Durand as the leading suspect in his partner's murder. *If* Andrew McKay had been murdered, as his widow claimed.

He'd been the marshal of Wind River for less than two full days, Cole thought, and already his head hurt from worrying at this problem. Between that and the stampede, the job sure hadn't turned out the way he had expected when he agreed to take it.

Late in the afternoon Cole saw Durand drive back into town, and he wondered where the land speculator had been for the past several hours. Durand lifted a hand in greeting as he drove past, and Cole thought he looked pleased with himself. Must've been working on a business deal of some sort, Cole thought. There probably wasn't anything else that would make a man like Durand seem so satisfied.

Abigail Paine's chicken and dumplings were as good as her husband had claimed, Cole discovered that evening when he returned to the boardinghouse for supper.

So were her greens and potatoes and biscuits and pie. The long table in the dining room was full, and the laughter and talk as the platters and bowls were passed around reminded Cole of other boardinghouses he had lived in briefly.

Abigail and the Paine youngsters were kept busy fetching more food from the kitchen, and Lawton Paine himself seemed to be in a better mood as he sat at the head of the table and ate with the other men.

After supper Cole walked downtown again and went into the marshal's office. Billy Casebolt sat with his chair leaned back and his boots on top of the desk, but he sat up hurriedly as Cole came in.

"Don't worry, Billy," Cole said with a grin. "I don't mind a man taking it easy every now and then. Everything been quiet around here?"

"Sure has," the deputy replied. "I swear, Marshal, this town's gotten downright tame since you been here. 'Cept for that stampede this mornin', there ain't been a lick of trouble. When I was the constable, seems like there was one or two fights every hour, and there weren't near as many saloons then as there are now. I reckon folks must be mindin' their manners since they know there's a real live lawman in Wind River now, 'stead of a broke-down ol' codger like me."

"I wouldn't count on that," Cole said dryly. "You ever heard of the calm before the storm? I reckon that's what we've got now."

Casebolt shrugged. "Maybe. But that fella Strawhorn ain't been around much since you had that run-in with him yesterday. If him and his pards lit out, that could be why things have gotten so peaceable."

"Well, we can hope," Cole said. "You had supper?"

"Yep. Hope that's all right."

Cole nodded. "Sure. I think I'll take a turn around town." He grinned. "Put your feet up and relax again. And don't jump up when I come in. You're liable to fall over in that chair and hurt yourself."

Casebolt gave the marshal a sheepish grin but nodded in agreement. Cole left him there in the office and strolled down the south side of Grenville Avenue.

Darkness had settled down over Wind River. The big emporium was still open for business, light spilling through its windows and doors, but most of the other shops had closed for the night.

All the saloons were still open, of course, and so was the hash house. A wagon rolled by in the street every so often, and men on horseback rode past Cole as he ambled along the boardwalk.

Women were outnumbered by men by ten to one in Wind River, and decent women were even scarcer. All of them were at home now, behind the walls of tents or new houses. The only females in evidence were in the saloons, and Cole heard their shrill laughter from time to time as he walked past the places.

He firmly believed what he had told Casebolt. Just because things had been fairly peaceful around town for a couple of days, there was no guarantee they would stay that way. In fact, it was likely there would be more trouble, and sooner rather than later.

That was what Cole was thinking when orange flame geysered from the shadows between a couple of half-finished buildings and a slug whipped past his head. Instinct drove him forward and down and sent his right hand streaking toward the butt of his Colt. He twisted as he fell, palming out the revolver and lifting it toward the darkness.

Another gunshot hammered against his ears, the muzzle flash almost blinding in the gloom. Cole fired twice toward the spot, the heavy pistol bucking against his hand. He didn't wait to see if his shots had done any good, rolling over quickly a couple of times instead and lunging to his feet again.

There was another shot from the opening between the half-completed buildings, but this time the bullet didn't come close enough for Cole to hear it. He leveled his own gun and squeezed off a couple of shots, then threw himself behind a wagon parked in front of one of the buildings. Since he kept the hammer of the Colt resting on an empty chamber, he only had one shot left without reloading.

Suddenly the sound of running footsteps came to Cole's ears. There was more than one set, and he frowned as he tried to sort them out. Several people were hurrying down the street toward him, coming to see what all the shooting was about, but he was convinced that one pair of feet was running down the alleyway between the buildings. And those steps were fading as the bushwhacker fled.

Cole didn't take the time to reload. He darted out from behind the wagon and ran toward the opening between the buildings. He might be running right into more trouble, he thought, but he didn't want the ambusher to get away if he could help it.

In the moonlight that was the only illumination in the alley, he spotted a running figure. "Hold it, you son of a bitch!" Cole shouted. The figure slowed and twisted toward him but didn't stop.

Cole went to one knee as the gunman fired again. The bullets went over his head. Cole steadied his aim and squeezed off his final shot, the explosion of black powder deafeningly loud in the close confines of the passage.

The bushwhacker kept running, never slowed down.

Cole bit back a curse and leaped to his feet, intending to give chase and try to reload as he ran. But then the fleeing footsteps halted abruptly, and a second later Cole heard the thud of a horse's hooves. The animal was galloping rapidly away from the settlement.

Cole grimaced in disgust, then heaved a frustrated sigh. The bushwhacker, whoever he had been, would be long gone before Cole could saddle up Ulysses and take off after him. There wasn't really any point to chasing him now. Out of habit, Cole reached for some fresh cartridges from his shell belt as he turned back to the main street.

"Marshal!" a voice shouted from nearby. "Marshal Tyler! You in there?"

"Down here, Billy," Cole called to his deputy.

Casebolt hurried down the alley to meet him, carrying a shotgun. "You all right, Marshal?" the older man asked anxiously.

"I'm not hurt," Cole told him. "Mad as hell, though. Somebody tried to bushwhack me from back here in the dark. I threw a few slugs at him as he ran off, but I don't think I hit him."

"Damn!" Casebolt said. "Who'd do a low-down thing like that?"

"I can think of somebody. Deke Strawhorn told me to watch my back."

"That's right!" Casebolt cursed. "If that no-good skunk shows his face in town again, I'll —"

Cole interrupted, "You won't do a thing unless he's breaking the law. I never got a good look at whoever shot at me. Can't accuse Strawhorn of it without any proof."

"No, I reckon not," Casebolt said reluctantly. He and Cole reached the mouth of the alley, where a curious crowd had gathered. The deputy raised his voice and told them, "You folks go on about your business! Ain't nothin' to see here."

The two lawmen walked back toward the office as the crowd broke up, muttering among themselves. Casebolt was doing some muttering, too, mostly about Deke Strawhorn and what he'd like to do to the drifting hardcase.

Cole wasn't paying much attention. He was thinking about the ambush attempt. A vengeful Strawhorn was the most likely one to be behind it, but the hardcase wasn't the only possibility. Cole had spent the day poking around in William Durand's business, and if somebody had told Durand about all the questions Cole was asking, the land speculator might have gotten nervous. If Durand was responsible for Andrew Mc-Kay's death . . . and if he thought that Simone suspected him and had enlisted Cole's help in an effort to prove his guilt . . . it was possible Durand might have decided getting rid of Cole would be better than waiting to be found out — even if it meant that Wind River would be without a lawman again. It was something to ponder, anyway.

"— figure it to happen so soon."

Cole looked up, aware that Casebolt was still talking to him. "What was that, Billy?" he asked. "Reckon my mind was wandering."

Casebolt snorted. "Hell, I wouldn't wonder, what with havin' to stop a stampede in the mornin' and then gettin' shot at this evenin'. I just said that when you said there'd be more trouble comin' along sooner or later, I didn't figure it'd be so soon."

"Neither did I," Cole admitted. "Well, it's been a pretty full day. We'll just have to wait and see what tomorrow brings."

More trouble? Cole wouldn't have bet against it, not with what he'd seen of Wind River so far.

CHAPTER 8

To Cole's surprise, and Billy Casebolt's as well, the next week passed peacefully in the railhead settlement. Of course, "peace" was a relative term, because Cole had to break up at least four fist-fights during that time. No one was hurt badly, though, and the damage to the various saloons was minor, so Cole was pretty well satisfied with the way his duties had settled down. Nobody tried to ambush him again, either, and Deke Strawhorn seemed to have left town.

Less satisfying was Cole's investigation into Andrew McKay's death. His conversations with the citizens told him that both McKay and Durand had been respected by the townspeople, although not particularly well liked. Nobody seemed to have hated McKay enough to have killed him, and nobody Cole talked to who had been there on the station platform that day had seen who fired the fatal shot. Everyone had been too concerned with their own part in the brawl.

Unless, of course, somebody was lying to him. Cole thought that was pretty likely, but he had no idea how to prove it or even to identify the liar.

On Sunday, Cole and Billy both attended Jeremiah Newton's religious service under the huge cottonwood on the western edge of town. Quite a few people were there, and Jeremiah led them in the singing of several hymns before stepping up onto an empty nail keg and beginning his sermon. The Bible he waved around in his right hand as he spoke was dwarfed by the long, thick fingers wrapped around it.

Jeremiah was fairly soft-spoken when he was working in the blacksmith shop, but not during the service. He preached hellfire-and-brimstone in a loud, ringing voice, and his descriptions of the fate awaiting sinners were so vivid that Cole winced a time or two. Billy Casebolt had a fine sheen of sweat on his forehead, as if he could feel the very flames of the pit itself.

Jeremiah got down to business at the end of the service, telling the congregation his idea of building a church in Wind River. A hat was passed and a collection taken up to buy lumber for the church, and several men volunteered their skills as carpenters. Watching Jeremiah work the crowd, Cole had no doubt that the church would indeed get built, and probably pretty soon. He even tossed a silver dollar into the hat when it came by.

Early on Wednesday morning, as Cole was walking from Paine's boardinghouse toward downtown, he saw that Rose Foster's cafe was open for business. The afternoon before he had seen workers putting up the sign on the awning over the boardwalk. It read WIND RIVER CAFE, not a very original name, to be sure, but one that summed up the nature of the establishment. Cole had already had breakfast — bacon and flapjacks and small mountains of scrambled eggs and fried potatoes dished up by Abigail Paine — but he crossed the street and stepped into the new business anyway. He could always use another cup of coffee.

Billy Casebolt greeted him with a grin. The deputy was sitting on a high stool at the counter along the back wall. Several other men were seated at the counter as well, and three of the eight tables in the room were occupied.

Cole hadn't been here since the first day Rose had begun moving in, and he was surprised by the change in the place. The walls were light and cheery with whitewash, and red-and-white curtains that matched the cloths on the tables hung in the windows. A menu with the day's specials chalked on it was on the wall behind the counter. Below the menu was a shelf containing several pies.

The air was full of delicious aromas from coffee brewing, bacon sizzling, and biscuits baking. Cole returned Casebolt's grin.

The door at the end of the counter opened and Rose Foster swung through it, a platter containing several plates in her arms. It was obvious that she had opened the door by bumping it with a hip. She paused for a second as she saw Cole standing there, then moved past him with a murmured, "Excuse me, Marshal."

Cole watched her deliver the food to one of the tables. Rose was wearing a blue dress with short, puffy sleeves and a white apron tied around her waist. Her thick reddish-blond hair was caught in a loose bun at the back of her head, but a few strands had escaped to dangle enticingly over her forehead. Cole thought she looked as pretty as the sunrise.

"Have a seat and try some of this grub, Marshal," invited Casebolt. "It's mighty good."

"I've eaten," Cole told him as he settled down on the vacant stool next to the deputy. "I reckon I could do with a cup of coffee, though."

"You sure?" Casebolt waved his fork at the plate full of food in front of him. "I ain't had flapjacks this light in I don't know when."

"Maybe tomorrow." Cole watched Rose hurry back to the door after delivering the order to the table, and as she went through to the kitchen he caught a glimpse of a wizened, middle-aged man at the stove. With a frown, Cole asked, "Is that Monty Riordan in there cooking?"

"I wouldn't know. The way that gal's been runnin' back and forth, though, she ain't had time to actually cook anything. Somebody else must be doin' it."

A couple of minutes passed, then Rose emerged from the kitchen again and seemed to notice Cole for the first time, even though she had obviously seen him earlier. She came over to him behind the counter and asked, "Is there anything I can get you, Marshal?"

"Just a cup of coffee will do me fine," Cole told her. "Was that Monty Riordan I saw out in the kitchen?"

"I hired Mr. Riordan to be my cook, yes,"

Rose said as she poured coffee from a pot she handled with a thick piece of leather, then placed the cup in front of Cole. "Do you know him?"

Cole nodded, picked up the cup and sipped the coffee, and then nodded again, this time in appreciation of the strong, rich brew. "He's been working for the Union Pacific. Ate many a buffalo steak Monty fried up from the meat I brought in."

"He's decided to make his home here in Wind River rather than moving on with the railroad. When he asked me for a job, I thought he'd be perfect. I can't do all the cooking and wait tables, too." Rose glanced at the shelf behind her and said with a hint of pride, "I made those pies last night."

"Well, I don't reckon it's too early in the morning for a piece of pie," Cole said with a smile. "I'll take one. What kind do you have?"

Rose's attitude, which had been almost friendly, changed abruptly. "It most certainly is too early for pie," she said. "Those are for lunch and supper."

"Anyway, I thought you said you already et," Billy Casebolt put in.

Cole tried not to glare at his deputy. "Are you saying you won't sell me a piece of pie?" he demanded of Rose.

"That's exactly what I'm saying. Come back at lunchtime."

"I reckon I'll probably be busy." If she wanted to be like that. Cole thought, then he figured he could be, too.

"That's a shame," Rose said without sounding like she really meant it. She moved on down the counter to inquire of one of the other customers if he needed a refill on his coffee.

Casebolt leaned over to Cole and asked quietly, "How come that gal acted so put out with you?"

Cole shrugged. "You're asking the wrong man."

"For that matter, you was a mite snippy with her. What's the matter, Marshal? Don't you like Miss Foster?"

"I don't even know her," Cole said with a shake of his head. "But if she made this coffee, she did a good job of it."

Casebolt mopped up the last of his bacon grease with a final bite of biscuit, then paid Rose for the meal. Cole left a coin on the counter to pay for his coffee, then joined his deputy on the boardwalk outside.

With a contented sigh, Casebolt loosened his belt a little, then asked, "You reckon there's somethin' wrong with that red-headed gal? She strikes me as a mite standoffish, and not just with you."

"A woman trying to make her way alone out here on the frontier, that's not an easy job," Cole replied after a moment's thought. "I reckon she's just being careful that nobody gets the wrong idea about her."

"Yeah, you could be right." Casebolt stretched. "Well, the day's off to a good start, anyway. That was the best breakfast I've had in a coon's age. Imagine, a gal that pretty, and she runs a cafe, too."

"Sounds perfect, Billy," Cole said. "Why don't you marry her?"

"Me?" exclaimed Casebolt. "Why, I never even thought . . . hell, I'm twice her age! And I never said nothin' about wantin' to get married. Of all the dang-fool ideas!"

Grinning, Cole left Casebolt there sputtering to himself. That ought to have taken care of any ideas the deputy might have had about playing matchmaker, Cole thought with satisfaction.

He couldn't have said what motivated him for sure — maybe the desire not to let Rose Foster think she had gotten the best of him — but Cole didn't eat lunch at the Wind River Cafe, returning to the boardinghouse and sitting down at Mrs. Paine's table instead. He couldn't argue about the quality of the food; Abigail was just about as good a cook as old Monty Riordan.

That was how Cole came to be on the boardwalk in front of Dr. Judson Kent's office, heading back toward his own office in the early afternoon. Just after passing the door of the doctor's office, Cole heard the man's unmistakable English accent as Kent called his name.

Cole swung around and saw the tall, bearded physician standing in the doorway in shirt sleeves and vest, wiping his hands on a cloth. "Do you have half a moment, Marshal?" Kent asked. "I'd like to speak with you, if I might."

"Sure." Cole nodded. "What can I do for you, Doctor?"

"Come inside. I was about to have a spot of tea. Care to join me?"

Cole looked dubious. "I'm afraid I'm not much of a tea drinker, Doc."

Kent grimaced. "Please, Marshal, I hear that dreadful appellation from so many of your compatriots here in Wind River. I'd prefer that you not use it, too."

"You mean you don't want to be called Doc?"

"Oh, I'll answer to it. What is it you Yanks say? Call me anything you like, just don't call me late for supper — or some such colorful phrase. But I prefer Dr. Kent, or even Judson."

"Judson's all right with me. I'm Cole."

"Very well." Kent ushered him into the building. "You're certain you won't have some tea?"

"I'll pass, thanks," Cole said dryly.

He looked around. The doctor's office was housed in a squarish frame building much like many of the others in Wind River. Cole suspected Kent's living quarters were in the rear of the building; the front room contained an examining table and several glass-fronted cases full of medical instruments and bottles of dark brown glass that no doubt held a variety of medicines, tonics, and nostrums. Kent's desk took up one corner of the room, and a small stove sat in the opposite corner. But the most eye-catching feature of the room was a complete human skeleton hanging from a stand between the desk and the stove. Cole looked at it and grinned.

"Who's your friend?" he asked Kent as the doctor was taking a pot of tea from the stove and pouring a cup for himself.

"Oh, you mean Reginald?"

"That thing's got a name?" Cole asked, surprised.

"Well, of course he has a name. What did you expect? He may be nothing but bones, but let's accord the poor devil a little dignity, shall we? Reginald, this is Marshal Tyler. Marshal, meet Reginald."

Cole frowned. Surely Kent didn't expect him to say hello to a damned skeleton! But the doctor stood there calmly, waiting for some sort of response, so after a moment Cole muttered, "Howdy, Reginald." He hoped Billy Casebolt never got wind of this.

"I'm afraid he can't answer you, but I'm certain if he could that he would be very pleased to meet you, Cole." Kent waved toward a chair in front of the desk. "Have a seat."

Cole reversed the chair and straddled it, more comfortable that way. Kent sat down behind the desk to sip his tea, and Cole asked, "You said you wanted to talk to me, Doc — I mean Judson?"

Kent nodded, his expression becoming more solemn. "I've observed you around town the past week, talking to the citizens and asking them all sorts of questions about William Durand and the late Mr. Andrew McKay. I was wondering about your purpose in this."

"Maybe I was just curious," Cole replied, frowning a little. "And any other reasons I might have would be law business, not medical ones."

"I see. I thought you might be trying to find out whether or not William Durand is responsible for the death of his late partner."

The calm statement uttered by Judson Kent was even more surprising to Cole than the skeleton had been. "What in blazes makes you say that?" he demanded.

"You don't have to worry, Cole," Kent assured him. "Mrs. McKay has taken me into her confidence concerning her suspicions. She and I are friends, as well as doctor and patient."

"Son of a —" Cole caught himself. "Do you know if she's told anybody else?" He was a novice at this sort of thing to start with, and Simone McKay was just going to make it harder on him if she was going around town telling people that Durand had killed her husband.

Kent put down his cup of tea and said, "No, she hasn't told anyone else. As I said, she confided in me, and she swore me to secrecy as well. But from your behavior since you accepted the position of marshal, I assumed that you were looking into the matter on her behalf."

There was no point in denying it, Cole decided. Kent had already figured out most of it. "She came to see me, all right. I don't know if there's anything to her suspicions or not, but I promised I'd poke around a little and see what I could find out. So far, not a damned thing."

"I see. Have you considered, Marshal . . . Cole . . . that Mrs. McKay may be wrong about Durand and her husband?"

"Sure. I was there that day, remember? I know it could've been a wild shot that killed McKay, just as easy as it could've been deliberate. But it *could* have been deliberate, that's the point."

Kent's high forehead furrowed. "Mrs. McKay is a grief-stricken lady. Such a woman might say things that had no basis in reality, that were in fact ill-advised."

"You're saying she shouldn't have accused Durand?"

"I'm saying I want only the best for Simone, and I'm not sure that indulging her suspicions is a good idea."

"What if she's right?" Cole asked bluntly.

Kent's shoulders rose and fell in a slight shrug. "Ah, yes, there is that possibility. But you've already admitted that you have found nothing to indicate that either William Durand or some person unknown murdered Andrew McKay. Do you intend to continue investigating indefinitely?"

Cole rubbed his jaw and admitted, "I don't know yet. Seems like sooner or later even the most determined cat's going to get tired of chasing his own tail around and around."

"Quite so," Kent said dryly. "Please understand, Marshal. I have no real opinion either way concerning Durand's guilt — or lack of same. I just don't want to see Simone hurt, and if Durand gets wind of this . . ."

"You think he wouldn't take it kindly?"

"I'm not sure how he would react, but it couldn't be good in the long run for Simone's relationship with him. I don't fully trust the man to start with to look after her best interests."

"But that's *what* you're *doing,* isn't it, Judson?"

Kent flushed slightly, and Cole knew his guess had hit home. The doctor had admitted to a fondness for Simone McKay, but Cole had to wonder if it was even more than that. Kent, of course, being the proper sort that he obviously was, wouldn't approach her until a suitable time had passed after her husband's death.

But the Widow McKay was quite an attractive woman, Cole mused, and she was damned well-off, too. . . .

"That's neither here nor there," Kent said curtly, as if he was reading Cole's mind. "I just want you to be careful, Marshal. If one goes poking and prodding around a nest of hornets, one has to expect them to come swarming out sooner or later."

"Don't worry, Doctor, I've smoked a few hives in my time —"

Before Cole could go on, a sudden clatter of hoofbeats in the street outside drew his attention. He looked up through Kent's front window in time to see a rider pull a horse to an urgent, skidding halt in front of the building. The young man, who wore the range clothes of a cowboy, practically threw himself out of the saddle and came bounding into the doctor's office. Wide-eyed and panting, he demanded, "You . . . you the doc?"

Kent stood up and nodded. "I am. What's wrong, lad?"

"I . . . I'm Lon Rogers . . . from the Diamond S."

"What's that?" Cole asked sharply.

Rogers huffed and puffed for a few seconds, then said, "Mr. Sawyer's ranch. We got trouble up there."

Cole wasn't surprised by the answer. He had recognized the young cowboy as one of Sawyer's hands. The information that Sawyer already had a name and a brand for his new spread came as news to him, however, although the brand part made sense. Sawyer would have put at least a road brand on his stock before starting up the trail from Texas.

"What's happened?" Kent asked as he came out from behind the desk.

"One of our punchers got himself stepped on by a longhorn. He's hurt real bad, Doc. You got to come out and take a look at him."

Without hesitation, Kent reached for his coat and shrugged into it. As he picked up his hat and his black medical bag from the desk, he said, "Of course I'll come. Let me get my horse."

Acting on impulse, Cole said, "I'll come with you, Doctor. You might need a hand."

Kent glanced at him. "I assure you, I won't need anyone arrested."

"That's not what I meant," Cole said. He hadn't been out to where Sawyer had the herd of longhorns camped, hadn't seen the rancher since the morning of the stampede, in fact. Even though Cole's jurisdiction ended at the edge of town, he thought it would be a good idea to keep up with what was going on in this part of the country, and that included Sawyer's activities. He didn't waste time explaining that to Judson Kent, however.

The medico shrugged. "You're welcome to come along, of course, Marshal."

Lon Rogers burst out, "As long as you

stop jawin' and come *on*!"

Cole and Kent hurried out of the office after the cowboy and headed for the stable to fetch their mounts. At Cole's suggestion, Rogers swapped his winded horse for another animal, promising the stable owner to bring the fresh horse back later. A couple of minutes later the three men rode out of Wind River and headed northwest toward the foothills, and Cole and Dr. Kent put their horses into a gallop to keep up with the frantic young cowhand.

Cole noticed right away that Rogers was leading them in a different direction than the herd had taken leaving Wind River. The cattle had moved almost due north from town, and now the three of them were riding northwest. He called to Lon, "Has Sawyer moved his herd?"

The young man nodded but didn't slow down. "Him and that Durand fella made a deal for Mr. Sawyer to start his ranch on some land up in the hills. Prettiest valley you ever saw."

Cole and Kent glanced at each other. Durand again. The man certainly had his fingers in a lot of pies.

The terrain quickly grew rougher than the area right around the settlement, but not so rugged that it kept the riders from making

good time. They reached a creek and followed it for a couple of miles, then took a
winding path that led them up a bluff to a
valley where they picked up the creek again.

Cole thought the place looked vaguely
familiar, and he figured he must have ridden through it a couple of years earlier
when he was scouting for the army here in
Wyoming Territory. As Lon Rogers had said,
it was a pretty place and a fine location for
cattle. Cole spotted a thread of smoke
climbing into the sky ahead of them and
thought that was probably where Sawyer
had established his camp.

That proved to be the case. As Cole, Kent,
and Lon Rogers rode up, Cole saw that a
couple of log cabins had already been built,
along with several large pole corrals filled
with bawling cattle. The smoke he had seen
came from a branding fire, and Cole figured
Sawyer's men had been slapping the Diamond S brand on calves that had been born
on the long trek up from Texas. The fire was
untended at the moment, though, because
all of the men on hand were clustered
around a spot near one of the corrals.

Kermit Sawyer heard them coming and
detached himself from the group, turning
and stalking out to meet them. He barely
spared a cold glance for Cole, then turned

171

his attention to Judson Kent. "You the doc?" he asked, echoing the question Lon Rogers had asked when he burst into the office in Wind River.

"That's right," Kent replied briskly as he swung down from the saddle of his roan gelding. Cole had already dismounted, too, and he took the reins of the doctor's horse without being asked. Kent went on, "Where's the injured man?"

"Right over here," snapped Sawyer. The cattleman was wearing the same dark clothes, or ones just like them. As he led Kent over toward the corral he barked, "Step aside, damn it! Give us some room."

Cole followed, moving up close enough to watch through a gap in the circle of cowboys as Kent knelt on one knee beside a young man stretched out on the ground. Someone had put a bedroll under the hurt cowboy's head and covered him with a blanket. Kent pulled the blanket back carefully.

Cole's jaw tightened as he saw the way the injured man's midsection was caved in, almost flattened. The cowboy was breathing loudly and harshly, seeming to struggle to draw each breath into his body.

Kent glanced up at Sawyer. "What happened to him?" he asked.

"We cut out a calf for branding and took

it out of the corral," Sawyer explained. "It was Sammy's job to swing the gate closed before the calf's mama could come after it. He was a little too slow. The cow hit the gate, knocked him down, and trampled right over him trying to get to her baby."

"I . . . I'm sorry, boss," Sammy whispered as his eyes flickered open. "I tried to . . . get it closed. . . ."

"Don't you worry about it, Sammy," Sawyer assured him. "It wasn't your fault."

"The hell it . . . wasn't . . ."

"Please lie quietly," Kent told the young man as he examined the injury. Sammy closed his eyes again and subsided. Cole couldn't see the doctor's face from where he stood, but he could tell by the stiff set of Kent's back that what he saw wasn't good. Cole wasn't sure how Sammy had managed to live even this long, stove in like that.

One of the cowboys standing around the injured man spoke up suddenly. "You got to save him, Doc, you just got to. Sammy's a good fella. He don't deserve to die."

"Few people do," Kent snapped. "Now stand back, please."

Several of the other Diamond S hands echoed the sentiments, calling out to Sammy to hang on and exhorting Kent to do something for him. Finally, after several minutes of carefully probing Sammy's mid-section, Kent looked up grimly at Kermit Sawyer.

"There's nothing I can do," the doctor said.

Sawyer's lips thinned and his brows drew down. "Sure there is," he insisted. "Sammy's busted up, sure, but I've seen men hurt worse —"

"Not that lived," Kent said bluntly. "The lad's back is broken, and there are massive injuries to his internal organs, not to mention internal bleeding. I'm afraid I simply can't save him."

Without warning, Sawyer's revolver was in his hand, the barrel staring at Kent's face. "You funny-talking son of a bitch," the cattleman grated. "You do something for him, and you shut your mouth about him dying. You want him to hear you?"

Kent's eyes widened slightly as he looked at the gun, but he sounded calm enough as he said, "The young man *can't* hear me, Mr. Sawyer. He's lost consciousness. I daresay that within a few moments it will all be over."

Several of the cowboys shouted angrily at Kent. This had gone on long enough, Cole decided — too long, as a matter of fact. He said loudly, "Holster that gun, Sawyer, or —"

"Or what?" Sawyer demanded curtly as he lifted his glower to meet Cole's angry stare. "Or you'll arrest me? You got no authority out here, Marshal. This is Diamond S land. I'm the law here, not you."

"Maybe so, but you know damned well that threatening the doctor's not going to do you any good. What are you going to do, shoot him if he doesn't work a miracle?" Cole snorted in disgust. "Hell, man, you need that Scripture-spouting blacksmith out here to say a prayer over the boy. There's nothing else Dr. Kent or anybody else can do."

"I'm afraid Marshal Tyler is correct, Mr. Sawyer," Kent said quietly. He reached down and rested a couple of fingers on Sammy's neck. "In fact, the poor lad has passed on, I'm sorry to say."

"He's dead?" The gun shook a little in Sawyer's hand as he asked the harsh question.

Kent nodded.

Some of the Diamond S hands started to shout angrily again, but Sawyer silenced them with a curt gesture. He shoved the revolver back in its holster and said, "All right, that's enough. I'm as sorry about

Sammy as the rest of you boys, but he was right — it was his own damned fault for not watching that cow closer and getting that gate shut in time. Now let's get on about our business." He squared his shoulders. "Somebody put out that branding fire. We've got burying to do." Sawyer looked at Cole with hate-filled eyes and added, "And we can do our own praying over him, by God!"

Kent stood up, and Cole said to him, "Come on, Judson. We're not needed here anymore."

Sawyer said, "You weren't needed here to start with, Tyler. You'd best stay in town and leave the range to those who belong on it. I don't want to see you on my land again."

"Fine by me," Cole told him. It was obvious that he and Sawyer rubbed each other the wrong way, and he didn't foresee that situation changing.

He kept an eye on the cattleman as he and Kent mounted up for the ride back to Wind River. Sawyer had called off his dogs, but the Texans were still proddy and muttering among themselves. One word from their boss, and there could still be trouble. Cole backed Ulysses away from the corrals while Kent turned the roan and rode back the way he had come. Not until the circle of cowboys closed in around their fallen comrade did Cole turn his own horse and gallop after the doctor.

"For a moment there, I thought those young men were going to avenge their friend on us, as if we had something to do with his death," Kent commented as Cole drew alongside him and eased his horse back to a walk.

"They might have if Sawyer hadn't stopped them," Cole said. "Texans fly off the handle pretty easy, especially cowboys. I'd think twice about coming out here again to doctor them."

Kent stared at him. "I can't do that," he said. "If they need my services, I'll come, regardless of the danger. You should understand a man's devotion to his duty, Marshal, being a lawman and all."

"I'm starting to learn," Cole muttered. "I just hope our duties don't get us killed one of these days."

CHAPTER 9

Michael Hatfield leaned back in his chair and lifted the pencil he was holding to his mouth. His teeth clamped down on the wood without him even being aware of what he was doing. He stared at the sheet of paper on the desk in front of him, chewing on the end of the pencil as he read the words he had written.

Michael had always been his own harshest critic, and from time to time he crossed out a word and scribbled another in its place, then returned the pencil to his mouth and resumed gnawing on it. Only when he reached the end of the story he had just written did he stare in surprise at the wet, chewed end of the pencil and begin spitting flecks of wood from his mouth.

It was a good story, Michael thought, full of color and pathos. He had gotten the basics of the young cowboy's death from Dr. Judson Kent, then filled in a few more details by talking to Lon Rogers.

Michael had been a little hesitant about approaching the Texan when he spotted Lon in the Wind River Cafe the previous evening, but Lon was about the same age as Michael and seemed friendly enough. He had told Michael that the dead cowboy's name was Sammy Vaught and that like everybody else connected with the Diamond S, he had come from West Texas.

The story of the young man's tragic death was finished and ready to go in the next edition of the *Sentinel,* Michael judged. It wouldn't go to press for a couple of days, since the paper came out only twice a week and the previous edition had appeared the day before. Michael tossed the story into a wire basket with the other stories he had already written for the next edition.

This was one of his favorite days in the routine of newspaper publishing, the day when things began to pick up again and enthusiasm began to grow for the next edition. Of course, he had other favorites as well — the hustle and bustle of determining the layout and setting the type; the clatter of the press working as the paper was actually printed; the satisfaction of taking stacks of the finished paper around to the various stores in town where it was sold. . . . In fact, he loved virtually everything about the newspaper business, from the potent smell of the ink to the crisp sound of a freshly printed paper being unfolded. As the old saying went, printer's ink was in his blood.

The front door of the office slammed open, and a familial-voice said angrily, "Michael!"

He sat up sharply in his chair and looked up to see his pretty, pregnant, redheaded wife advancing toward him. As was becoming more and more common these days, Delia did not look happy. In fact, her green eyes were blazing and she was practically spitting fire.

Michael came to his feet and tried to grin. "Hello, darling," he ventured uneasily. "What brings you here?"

"You know perfectly well what brings me here!" she accused.

All Michael could do was shake his head in bewilderment. "I promise you, sweetheart, I don't."

"No, you probably don't." Delia crossed her arms over her chest and glared at him. "You spend so much time here at this newspaper office that you have no idea what really goes on in your home. Have you even noticed that I've been unhappy recently?"

Only every time he stepped through the

door of the little house he and his wife rented from Mr. Durand, Michael thought, but wisely he kept that reply to himself. He put his hands on Delia's shoulders and said, "Of course I've noticed. But why don't you tell me what's got you so upset today?"

She started to jerk away from him, then relented and sighed. "A horse — I don't know who it belonged to, probably some awful cowboy — but a horse was in our garden! It ate all my tomatoes and destroyed the bean plants, and when I ran out to shoo it off, I thought it was going to trample right over me! Nothing of this sort could ever happen back in Cincinnati!"

It seemed to Michael that a stray horse could cause some mischief just as easily in Cincinnati as in Wind River, but he knew Delia was in no mood to listen to logic. "I'm sorry, dear," he said sincerely. "I'll try to put up a better fence around the garden so that it won't happen again."

"You don't have to worry about that," Delia muttered. "The garden's already ruined."

"There, there. I'm sure the horse didn't eat *everything*."

"What he didn't eat, he stepped on!"

It might be time to change the subject, Michael decided. He asked, "Where's Gretchen?" Usually Delia brought their daughter with her when she came down here to stage one of her tirades.

"I left her over at Abigail Paine's house. Abigail promised to have her daughters look after Gretchen."

Michael frowned. "Are you sure that was wise? After all, this *is* the frontier. . . ."

Delia's head jerked up so that she could glower at him, and he knew too late that he had played right into her hands — again. "So you admit that this wilderness is no place to raise a child?" she demanded.

"Now, I didn't say —"

"You most certainly did! You said it wasn't safe for our daughter to be left with the neighbors. Good heavens, Michael, back in Cincinnati when I was a child, I practically lived at our neighbors' house."

He tried again. "You misunderstand me, Delia —"

"On the contrary, I think I understand you all too well, Michael Hatfield!" She waved a hand at the newspaper office surrounding them. "You think more of this . . . this clutter than you do of your own family!"

"Now, that's just not true," insisted Michael. "You know I love you and Gretchen both."

"Enough to take us back to civilization?"

Ah, there it was, Michael thought. The ever persistent *question.* Did he love his family enough to take them back east?

What Delia really meant, although she would never understand it, was did he love them enough to give up the dream that was finally in his hands?

Michael took a deep breath. "You know how much this job means to me, Delia. I've wanted to edit a newspaper for years, ever since I've known what a paper is."

"It's a *job,* Michael. You can get another job." She let a pleading tone come into her voice. "It would mean so much to Gretchen and me."

"I thought Gretchen was happy here. She's always playing and laughing when I'm around."

"Of course! She feels safe when you're there. But you don't hear her asking me if the badmen or the Indians are going to get her if she steps out of the house."

"The Indians have signed a peace treaty, and now that we have a marshal, we don't have to worry about badmen."

"Try explaining that to your daughter!" Delia snapped. "You know perfectly well you could take us home, Michael — if you weren't so selfish." Her voice was cold now, and to Michael that sounded worse some-how than the heat of anger.

Feeling suddenly weary of this argument, he told her, "I won't go back to being a printer's devil. I'm doing an important job here, Delia. A territory needs newspapers, especially a new territory like Wyoming. We're . . . we're the banner of civilization!" He added, "Besides, I can't let Mrs. McKay down. She's counting on me to keep the paper running."

"Oh." Delia packed a world of meaning into the syllable. "You won't let down Mrs. McKay, but you're perfectly willing to disappoint your wife and daughter." A shudder went through her, and she whispered, "I don't know you anymore, Michael Hatfield, and I'll not live with a man I don't know."

He took hold of her shoulders again. "What do you mean by that?"

This time she jerked out of his grasp. "I mean that I'm taking Gretchen and leaving."

Michael's eyes widened in shock. "You're going back to Cincinnati?" he asked in a stunned voice.

Delia hesitated. "I . . . I don't know. I was raised to believe that a wife doesn't desert her husband. . . ." An idea seemed to occur to her. "I'll take a room at the hotel. Gretchen and I will live there until I've decided what to do."

Michael shook his head, almost overcome by anger, frustration, and sorrow. "Come on, Delia! You can't leave me just because a horse got into the garden!"

She stared at him for a moment and then said quietly, "You actually believe that's all there is to this, don't you?" She laughed humorlessly and turned away from him.

Michael wanted to reach out for her, to call after her and stop her somehow as she walked slowly out of the newspaper office. At the very least he ought to follow her and try to talk some sense into her, he thought. But he had been talking to her ever since he had answered Andrew McKay's advertisement seeking an editor for the newly founded *Sentinel* and made the decision to come to Wind River. Sometimes it seemed he had done nothing *but* talk to Delia during the past couple of months. It was too late now for talking to do any good.

She stalked out of the office and Michael slumped back in his chair. At least she hadn't committed herself to leaving town with Gretchen just yet. That would be easy enough for her to do. The Union Pacific crews were building a roundhouse just west of the depot, and soon trains would be running regularly to Rawlins, Laramie, and points east. The journey back to Cincinnati would be much faster and easier than the trip by wagon out here. If Delia wanted to go through with this, there was nothing Michael could do to stop her.

He sat there in the office as the sun set and the room grew dim, and he wondered just how everything in life could go so wrong, so fast.

Michael Hatfield was not the only one with a visitor this evening. As Dr. Judson Kent was straightening his office after his last patient of the day had left, he glanced up in slight annoyance when the front door opened. It had been a long day, and Kent was ready for his supper and some reading in the medical journals he had brought west with him. However, he was nothing if not a professional, as he had told Marshal Tyler, and he put a carefully solicitous expression on his bearded face as a young woman stepped nervously into the room. "Yes?" Kent said. "Can I help you, miss?"

"I . . . I sure hope so," she said as she clutched a small purse tightly in her hands. "You're the doctor, ain't you? Dr. Kent?"

"That is correct. And you are . . . ?"

She looked surprised at the question. "You

need to know my name?"

"It's customary for a doctor to know the names of his patients," Kent told her gently. "You've nothing to fear from me, young woman. Are you ill?"

She nodded. "Yeah, Doc. I'm sure sick. And my name . . . well, it's Becky Lewis."

Kent held out a hand toward her. "Come in, Miss Lewis. Or is it Mrs. Lewis?"

She laughed a little, but there was no humor in the sound. "It's miss, all right," she said.

Kent ignored that for the moment. "Have a seat, and tell me what seems to be troubling you."

She came over to the chair in front of the desk, still looking rather apprehensive. Kent studied her in the light of the lamp on the desk and saw a young woman — a girl, really — who was probably not yet out of her teens. Her long hair was a little darker than the color of straw and was pulled back from her face. She wore a red dress with a neckline cut daringly low, but her figure was so slender and her bosom so skimpy that the effect was one of incongruousness rather than sensuality. Her features were plain but heavily painted. Kent didn't recall having seen her before, but he recognized her type. She was one of the *nymphes des Prairies* who had inhabited certain sections of Wind River even before the arrival of the railroad. The soiled doves had become even more numerous since the first train had rolled in with its cargo of hell-on-wheels saloons and brothels.

Becky Lewis kept her eyes downcast as she sat in front of the desk. Kent lowered himself into his own chair and waited for her to explain the purpose of her visit. When she didn't, he prodded, "You were going to tell me the nature of your problem, Miss Lewis?"

"I . . . I been sick lately. Can't keep nothin' down. Don't matter what I eat, it comes right back up."

"Does this condition go on all the time?" Kent asked.

"Well . . . I reckon it seems worse in the mornin's."

Kent closed his eyes for a second and tried not to sigh. Young women in Becky Lewis's profession were exposed to certain occupational hazards, and from the sound of what Becky was saying, she was suffering from one of the most common ones. He said carefully, "I don't wish to be indelicate about this, my dear, but have your breasts been rather tender lately, perhaps even swollen slightly?"

She frowned. "Yeah, they have. How'd you know?"

"And your, ah, monthlies . . . ?"

Becky's eyes widened. "They've got to where I can't depend on 'em at all, Doc. I ain't even sure when the last one was. I think it's been a couple of months."

Kent rubbed his eyes wearily. It was so obvious to him, and he was surprised the answer hadn't occurred to her. He asked, "How long have you been in your current line of work?"

She flushed in embarrassment, and that partially answered Kent's question. She was so new at it that she was still ashamed of herself. "Only about a month and a half," she said. "I didn't really want to do it, but I ain't got no kin anymore, nor any schoolin'. And a gal's gotta eat, don't she?"

"Indeed," Kent said, trying not to sound judgmental. He stood up and gestured at the examining table. "Climb up there, please. I think a quick examination will determine what we need to know."

Becky looked scared, like a doe that wanted to bolt but didn't dare, but after a moment she did as Kent asked. As he had promised, the examination was a quick one, and when he was through, he helped her sit up on the end of the table. Wiping his hands, he said, "It's just as I thought. Miss Lewis, you're with child."

She gaped at him. "You mean I'm goin' to have a baby?"

Kent nodded. "That is correct. I would say that you are approximately six weeks pregnant, which means that conception coincided with your entry into your current profession." He wasn't sure she followed what he was saying; he had already decided that she perhaps wasn't completely competent mentally.

"You're sayin' the first fella who done me is likely the one who got me this way?" she asked, proving that she was somewhat quicker-witted than he had estimated.

"I'd say that's probably correct, yes. Before you came here, had you engaged in any, ah, intimate relations in the recent past?"

She shook her head. "No, I'd never even done it before. That's why it was so hard. If that first fella hadn't been so nice . . ." Her eyes widened even more. "If he's my baby's daddy, then he ought to do right by me, oughtn't he?"

"That seems a reasonable assumption." Kent nodded. "You may have trouble convincing him of his responsibilities, however. In your line of work, the, ah, potential for fatherhood is spread around among a great many likely candidates, I would imagine."

"If you mean a lot of fellas've had me, Doc, you're right about that. But I remember the first one, sure enough." Her expression fell. "But he can't do nothin' for me and the baby now. He's dead."

"That *is* a shame. If he was any sort of gentleman, he would have provided for you once the circumstances were explained to him."

"Oh, he was a gentleman, all right. A really swell gentleman." Becky looked up at the physician, a cunning gleam appearing in her eyes. "His name was Andrew McKay."

CHAPTER 10

Kent stared at her in shock for a moment after that astounding claim. When he was finally able to speak again, he said, "You must be mistaken. I knew Andrew McKay. He was not the sort of man to . . . to . . ."

"Bed down with a whore?" Becky smiled. "No offense, Doc, but I reckon you didn't know him as well as you thought you did."

"But his wife is a very attractive woman —"

"I may be new to the game, but I've already learned it don't matter what you got, if you ain't willin' to use it. Andrew told me his wife didn't want him in her bed 'cept every once in a blue moon."

Taut lines of dismay appeared on Kent's face. He didn't want to hear this sort of thing about a man he had considered a friend and a woman he greatly admired. A married couple's private lives were just that — private. Unless, of course, there was a legitimate medical reason for him to be involved.

In this case, there was indeed a medical reason — Becky's pregnancy — but still Kent felt awkward and uncomfortable hearing such intimate details about the McKays.

The look of cunning on the young prostitute's face had grown more intense. As she laced her fingers together over her stomach, she said, "Andrew and his wife didn't have any kids, so this one here is his only, what you call it, heir. Ain't that right?"

"Well, the legitimacy of such a claim would be very difficult to prove," Kent hedged. "At any rate, most of Mr. McKay's business holdings went to William Durand under the terms of their partnership agreement."

"Yeah, but she got something — the wife, I mean. I reckon she's pretty well-off, and some of that money ought to go to my baby, by all rights."

Beads of sweat popped out on Kent's forehead. If this young woman came forward with her claim of having been impregnated by Andrew McKay, it would cause a great deal of embarrassment for Simone. In fact, the widow would be devastated, Kent judged. He could not allow that to happen if he could prevent it.

"Perhaps you have a case," he said to Becky, "but as I told you, it would be virtually impossible to prove in court. And you would cause a great deal of trouble for some innocent people if you pressed your claim."

"Innocent people? You mean Andrew's wife, don't you?" She gave him a sly smile. "Are you sweet on that widow woman yourself, Doc?"

Kent's bearded features hardened. "I'll thank you not to speculate on things that are none of your concern, Miss Lewis. What we have to decide is what we're going to do about this situation."

"Ain't nothin' to decide. I'm goin' to have a baby."

"Yes, indeed you are." Kent sighed.

"And I'll bet that Mrs. McKay'd be happy to pay to keep her husband's name from bein' dragged through the mud. Long as I keep quiet about it, I don't have to prove nothin' in court."

Kent had been hoping that Becky wouldn't arrive at that conclusion, but it was a futile hope, he knew. She had the survival instincts of a wild animal.

It was even possible, he thought abruptly, that there was no truth to her story. She could have concocted the tale about Andrew McKay being her first lover solely to extort money from Simone. Her seeming ignorance about her pregnancy could have been nothing but a sham, her visit here this evening only a ruse to lay the groundwork for her financial claim.

Kent couldn't afford to take that chance, however, not and be sure that Simone's good name and that of her late husband were protected. Making his voice as stern as possible, he told Becky, "You will not approach Mrs. McKay."

"No? What's to stop me, Doc?"

"I will," Kent said. "If you insist on bringing this out into the open and exposing Mrs. McKay to all sorts of ridicule, I will have no choice but to also make public the medical knowledge that Andrew McKay was physically incapable of fathering a child."

"But that's not true!" she exclaimed.

"No, it's not," Kent admitted. "But the community will take my word over that of a young woman such as yourself. Your claim will be seen as nothing but a venal scheme to enrich yourself at the expense of one of the town's founders, and you'll wind up with nothing."

Becky's hands clenched into small fists, and for a second Kent thought she was going to attack him. "You wouldn't do that!" she said desperately.

"Not unless you force me to. As long as you keep your knowledge to yourself, so will I."

"But it ain't fair! McKay got me this way, and he ought to have to take care of me."

"Allow me to handle this," Kent said, thinking furiously. "It's a very delicate situation and will require caution in bringing it to a conclusion that is satisfactory for all concerned." He went behind the desk and opened one of the drawers, then took out a small metal box. "I have a bit of money. I'll give you some to help out with your expenses, in return for your silence until I can decide what to do."

"How much?" Becky asked sullenly.

Kent opened the box and took out a gold double eagle. "This to start," he said as he handed the coin across the desk to her.

She snatched the double eagle, bit it to make sure of its genuineness, then cached it in the bosom of her dress. "All right," she agreed. "But twenty dollars ain't goin' to keep me quiet forever. Not with all the money McKay had. You figure it out, Doc. You figure out some way to get me what I want and keep your lady friend in the dark at the same time. We're all countin' on you, although I reckon Miz McKay don't know it."

Kent sighed. This was perhaps the thorniest set of circumstances he had ever encountered, but there was a way out of the tangle. There had to be.

"I'll say good evening to you now, Miss Lewis."

"Sure, I'll leave. But I'll be back to see you, Doc. You can count on that."

Kent did not doubt for a moment that she was telling the truth. She would be back, and he would have to have an answer for this dilemma — or else things would never be the same for Simone McKay.

And he could not allow Simone to be hurt. At all costs, he could not allow that. . . .

Cole Tyler paused just outside the entrance flap to Hank Parker's tent saloon and listened to the loud talk and shrill laughter within. Parker was doing a booming business; all the saloons in Wind River were.

The settlement would serve as the railhead for another month or so until a lengthy section of track had been laid to the west. Cole had been told by acquaintances who worked for the Union Pacific that a place over on the Green River called Rock Springs would likely be the next railhead. Once the tracks reached that spot, Hell on Wheels would roll again.

That time couldn't come too soon for Cole. Strawhorn's bunch had moved on, but Wind River was still full of Irish work crews from the UP, as well as cowboys from Kermit Sawyer's Diamond S.

There were rumors that other trail herds were on their way, and once they arrived, the settlement would fill up even more with potential troublemakers. Added to that was the fact that a payroll train was scheduled to arrive any day now, meaning the railroad workers would have more money to spend on liquor and gambling.

Fights were still rare, but they were becoming more commonplace. Cole figured that within a few weeks he and Billy Casebolt would be kept busy breaking up a couple of fracases every night.

Cole pushed the flap aside and stepped into the saloon. A few heads turned in his direction, and the noise in the place might have subsided just a little. It didn't cease, however, and most of the people who had paused in what they were doing to look at him turned their attention back to their poker hand or bottle of rotgut or calico cat or whatever was occupying them. Lawman or no lawman, life went on in the saloons.

As Cole approached the bar Hank Parker

caught his eye and nodded a curt greeting.
Parker seemed a little nervous about something, his eyes darting from Cole to a spot
down the bar. Cole stepped up to the plank
and asked over the noise in the room,
"What's wrong, Parker?"

"I just don't want no shooting in here,
that's all," replied the burly saloonkeeper.
"Gunfights are bad for business."

Cole frowned. "I don't plan on shooting
anybody."

"Wasn't necessarily talking about you,
Marshal." Again Parker's eyes cut toward
the other end of the bar.

Cole leaned forward and looked along the
line of men who were bellied up drinking
Parker's whiskey. He stiffened as he saw the
man standing at the end of the bar. Immediately, he recognized the white hat with
the rolled brim, the long blond hair, and
the drooping mustache.

The drifter had a bottle of rotgut at his
elbow and a shot glass of the fiery stuff
cradled in his left hand. He was lifting the
glass to his mouth when he saw Cole. The
glass stopped midway to his lips, and for a
second Strawhorn looked as if he wanted to
toss it aside and reach for his gun.

But then he gave Cole a lazy, sardonic
smile and lifted the glass even higher before

he tossed back the drink. The mocking salute made Cole's jaw tighten. He hadn't forgotten the attempt on his life or the fact that Strawhorn might have been behind it.

"I told you, I don't want any trouble," Parker said nervously.

"Won't be any unless Strawhorn starts it," Cole snapped. He stepped away from the bar and sauntered along behind the line of drinkers, making sure that his right hand hung close to the butt of his .44.

"Howdy, Marshal," Strawhorn greeted him coolly as Cole reached the end of the bar. "Have a drink with me?"

"Nope. I'm particular about such things."

Anger flared in Strawhorn's pale eyes, but he kept the fires carefully banked. "Suit yourself." He shrugged.

"I intend to. What are you doing back in Wind River, Strawhorn?"

The drifter tipped up the bottle, splashed more whiskey into his glass. "Didn't know there was any law against visitin' this town," he said without looking around at Cole. "You intend to arrest me, Marshal?"

"Depends on what you've done."

Strawhorn sipped the rotgut this time, which took some control considering how raw the stuff was. "All I've done is sit here and have a few drinks, peaceable like."

"Deke's tellin' the truth. Marshal," said the man standing beside him. Cole recognized him now, along with a couple of other men at the bar, as cronies of Strawhorn who had been with the gunman during his earlier visit to Wind River.

"Stay out of it," Cole told him. "This is between me and your boss."

"I ain't nobody's boss but my own," Strawhorn protested. "Me and the boys are just pards who like to ride together."

Cole nodded. "Sure. You wouldn't happen to know anything about some shots that were fired at me from an alley a while back, would you, Strawhorn?"

"Why, Marshal, are you sayin' that somebody tried to bushwhack you?" Strawhorn shook his head and clucked his tongue. "I reckon this town is more lawless than I ever figured."

"You left town right around the same time," Cole pointed out. "Maybe you had a good reason for not showing your face around here for a while. Maybe you thought if you laid low, I'd forget about what happened." He shook his head. "You were wasting your time, Strawhorn. I don't forget about cowardly skunks who try to back-shoot me."

Again the hatred blazed up in Strawhorn's

eyes. Cole was deliberately baiting him, hoping to prod him into admitting that he was behind the ambush attempt. Of course, if that happened, Strawhorn might go for his gun in an attempt to finish things, and he had three of his cohorts backing any play he made. Cole was alone and without any friends in this place, at least real friends who would be willing to put their lives on the line for him.

Something thumped on the planks that formed the bar, and Hank Parker said in a loud voice, "I told you I didn't want no shooting in here." A few muttered, surprised curses from the other drinkers followed on the heels of his statement.

Cole glanced along the bar and saw that Parker had produced a sawed-off shotgun from somewhere. The saloonkeeper had his hand resting on the stock of the weapon, near the trigger. Parker glowered at both Cole and Strawhorn, his heavy brow creased in a menacing frown. Men began backing away from the bar.

"Put that greener away, damn it," Cole rasped. "You let it go off in here and innocent folks'll get hurt."

"That's right," Parker said. "And it's your job as marshal to see that don't happen. So back off and quit prodding Strawhorn, Tyler. You always were a hotheaded son of a bitch, and that star on your chest don't change anything."

Cole could hear the blood pounding in his head as he struggled to control his anger. As much as he hated to admit it, Parker was right in a sense. The way things had been going, Cole could have goaded Strawhorn into a gunfight, regardless of the odds against him. His own dislike of the hard-case had nearly betrayed him into foolishness.

He looked at Strawhorn again and warned, "Stay out of my way, mister, and don't even think about breaking the law. I won't bother trying to lock you up. I'll just kill you."

Strawhorn laughed coldly. "Some lawman you are, Tyler, threatenin' law-abidin' folks that way. Me and the boys just came to town for a little fun. We'll be gone soon enough."

"See that you are," Cole said, unwilling to give Strawhorn the last word. He turned on his heel and stalked out of the saloon, the skin between his shoulder blades prickling as he turned his back on Strawhorn. It was doubtful that the man would try to gun him down in cold blood in front of so many witnesses, though.

Cole pushed the flap aside and stepped

out into the night. There was a cool breeze that felt even cooler as it brushed against the sweat that suddenly popped out on his face. He had come damned close to losing control of himself in there. What was the line he'd heard his pa quote from one of those old plays? *Cry havoc, and let slip the dogs of war.* Maybe war was too strong a word for what had nearly happened, but he had sure enough almost let those dogs slip away from him.

He would have his chance to settle things with Strawhorn. Now that the hardcase was back in town, it was only a matter of time until he made a play of his own. Cole was sure of it.

And he would be waiting.

The trouble came even sooner than Cole had expected. He was still making his evening rounds less than an hour later when he walked past a wagon piled high with empty barrels. The wagon was parked beside the boardwalk, near the emporium. As Cole reached the end of the walk he stepped down into the street and started to cross behind the wagon.

With a rumble like sudden thunder, the barrels shifted and started to roll off the wagon.

Cole tried to dart out of the way, but one of the barrels struck his left shoulder and knocked him off his feet. Despite being empty, the barrels were heavy, and if enough of them landed on him, they could crush the life out of him. He rolled desperately in the only direction that promised any hope of safety — underneath the wagon.

He heard a man curse and then booted feet thudded against the dusty street next to the wagon. The man had been hiding there among the barrels, Cole figured, just waiting for him to go by so the barrels could be toppled over onto him. That might have been enough to kill him right there, but the ambusher would have been ready to finish him off if necessary.

Those thoughts flashed through Cole's mind as he scuttled toward the front of the wagon, his numb left arm dragging and making progress awkward. He knew he had to get out in the open again; as long as he was bottled up underneath the wagon, he was an easy target for the would-be killer.

His feet and legs drove him forward. The wagon team had been unhitched and led away, so he didn't have to worry about them spooking and pulling the wagon over him.

Some of the barrels were still rolling and falling, the noise from them even louder under here. Cole couldn't hear the man's gun being cocked, but he heard the blast of the shot and winced as the bullet sang past his head and hit the ground, kicking dust into his eyes. He had just cleared the front wheels, so he dropped and rolled again as he reached for his own gun.

Luckily, the Colt hadn't fallen out of its holster. Cole's fingers closed around the butt and jerked the weapon free. He fetched up to a stop against the low boardwalk and blinked rapidly until his vision cleared. He spotted the feet and legs of his assailant as the man hurried along the other side of the wagon toward the front of the vehicle.

Cole eared back the hammer and fired, rewarded instantly by a howl of pain that blended with the roar of the shot. The man's feet went out from under him and he rolled in the street, clapping a hand to the calf Cole's bullet had just ripped through. Cole fired again and then again, the attacker's torso giving him a bigger target now. He heard both slugs thud into flesh. The man shuddered under the impact, rolled onto his back, and lay still with his arms outflung.

Feeling was coming back into Cole's left arm, and he used it to balance himself as he scrambled to his feet. He kept the revolver trained on the dark bulk of the ambusher as he stepped over the wagon tongue and approached the fallen man. People were coming on the run to investigate the shooting. Cole called out to them, "Stay back! This is Marshal Tyler talking!"

The townspeople stopped in their tracks as Cole cautiously approached the man he had shot. He prodded the bushwhacker in the side and got no response, then knelt and used his left hand to check for a pulse. He wouldn't have risked coming this close if he hadn't spotted the man's gun lying a dozen feet away where it had fallen when Cole's first shot dropped him.

The bushwhacker was dead, all right, no doubt about that. He'd had two good chances at Cole, but failing both of them had been his death warrant. He just hadn't been lucky.

And, Cole saw in the moonlight, he wasn't Deke Strawhorn, either. In fact, Cole didn't recall ever seeing him before.

"Need some light over here," Cole called to the bystanders. "And somebody fetch Deputy Casebolt."

"Right here, Marshal," Billy replied as he pushed his way through the crowd and then hurried over to join Cole. Casebolt dug a block of lucifers out of his pocket, broke off one of the soft sulfur matches, and scraped it into life. The glare that came with the stink of brimstone illuminated the face of the dead bushwhacker.

"Who in blazes is that?" Casebolt asked.

"You don't know him, either?"

"Never seen him before, not that I recollect, anyway." Casebolt looked around. "What're all them barrels doin' layin' in the street?"

Cole straightened and gestured at the dead man. "He tried to dump them on my head, and when that didn't work, he tried to finish me off with a bullet." He rubbed his shoulder, which was starting to ache. There would probably be a pretty bad bruise on it tomorrow, Cole thought.

Casebolt glared down at the corpse. "What'd he want to go and do a thing like that for?" he asked.

"Don't know. I figured somebody would make another try for me, but I thought it would be Strawhorn."

"Strawhorn?" exclaimed Casebolt. "Is that sidewinder back in town?"

"I had a run-in with him in Parker's place less than an hour ago," Cole explained. "He and three of his partners were there."

"You should've sent for me then, Marshal. We'd've cleaned out that rat's nest in a hurry."

Cole shrugged. "I figured Strawhorn couldn't resist coming after me. Looks like I was wrong."

" 'Less'n he sent this hombre after you," Casebolt speculated as he rubbed the silvery bristles on his jaw.

"You might have something there, Billy." Cole looked up to see the livery-stable owner, who doubled as the town's undertaker, approaching. "Got a job for you," he told the man. "Reckon you can go through this gent's pockets and claim whatever he's got on him as the price of planting him."

"Sure, Marshal." The liveryman nodded. "Are you all right?"

"I'm fine," Cole said.

To tell the truth, he was far from fine, even though the banged-up shoulder was his only physical injury. But he was mad as hell, both at the attempt on his life and the fact that the dead man had turned out to be somebody besides Deke Strawhorn.

It was possible, even likely, that the bushwhacker was a new member of Strawhorn's gang. Strawhorn could have sent the man after Cole, or he could have made the attempt on his own, hoping to impress Strawhorn by killing the marshal. Either way, the end results were the same. The man was dead, and Strawhorn was still alive to cause trouble.

In fact, Cole saw, Strawhorn was saunter-
ing down the boardwalk toward the scene
of the shooting, his men ambling along with
him. He paused on the boardwalk and
called over, "What happened, Marshal?
Have some trouble?"

Cole stiffened, his breath catching in his
throat. He took a step toward Strawhorn,
but Billy Casebolt put a hand on his arm
and stopped him. In a low voice, the deputy
said, "I ain't anxious to stick up for that
ranny, Marshal, but if you was thinkin'
straight, you'd see that he wants you to
come after him. He'd have plenty of witnesses that you started the fight."

Cole dragged a deep breath into his lungs
and then jerked his head in a nod. "You're
right, Billy," he said. Keeping a tight rein on
his temper, he indicated the dead man. "You
know this man, Strawhorn?"

"Now, why in the world would you figure
a thing like that, Marshal?" Strawhorn
asked, his cool arrogance grating on Cole.
"The only souls I know in this whole town
are my three friends here. I never saw that
gent before."

"Take a good look at him," Cole ordered.
"Billy, strike another match."

"That ain't necessary —" Strawhorn

began, but Casebolt had already struck another lucifer. The deputy knelt beside the body and held the flame so that its glow washed starkly over the contorted features of the dead man.

Cole thought he saw a muscle twitching in Strawhorn's jaw, but he couldn't be sure. The drifter's voice was flat and hard as he said, "I told you I don't know the man, Marshal. Now, if you're through with us, we got places to go and things to do."

"Sure." Cole waved them on, then called after them, "Just remember how bushwhackers wind up in this town."

Strawhorn might have broken his stride just for an instant; Cole couldn't tell. But then he strode on, accompanied by his friends, and turned a corner, going out of sight.

"That fella don't like you, not even a little bit," Casebolt said worriedly.

"The feeling's mutual," Cole snapped. He nodded to the liveryman to get on with the job of dragging away the corpse, then started toward the marshal's office. Casebolt fell in step beside him, and Cole went on, "I've got a special job for you, Billy."

"Sure, Marshal, anything you want."

"You said you did some scouting for the army. I reckon you're pretty good at keep-

ing an eye on somebody without him knowing that anybody's watching."

Casebolt nodded and said proudly, "I can
track a flea through a sandstorm without
him ever seein' me, Marshal, and that ain't
a brag."

"Think you can watch Strawhorn and find
out what he's up to?"

"Sure. But don't you figure he came back
to Wind River to have another go at you?"

"Could be," Cole said as his brow furrowed in thought. "Could be that's just part
of it, though, and he's really here for some
other reason. A man like that's usually looking for some sort of payoff."

"Yep, that's true," Casebolt mused. "Don't
you worry. If he's up to any mischief, I'll
find out about it."

"Be careful, Billy," Cole advised as they
reached the marshal's office. "I figure
Strawhorn would be glad to shoot any lawman he could get in his sights, and you're
the best deputy I've got."

" 'Course, I'm the *only* deputy you've got"
— Casebolt grinned — "but still the best
one you're ever likely to have."

CHAPTER 11

Billy Casebolt hummed silently through his teeth as he slouched against the wall of a newly built hardware store and watched the saloon across the street. Deke Strawhorn and his cronies had gone in there an hour earlier. From where he stood, the deputy could see both the batwinged main entrance of the saloon as well as the side door. Strawhorn hadn't come back out, and Casebolt intended to stay where he was until the hardcase emerged.

There had been no more trouble since the attempt on Cole Tyler's life the night before, but Billy shared Cole's opinion that it was only a matter of time. He also thought there might be something to the marshal's theory that Strawhorn had returned to Wind River for some other reason than revenge. Strawhorn wasn't likely to pass up the opportunity to settle the score with Cole, however.

Casebolt had picked up Strawhorn's trail the night before, locating the hardcase and his friends in one of Wind River's many saloons. Strawhorn and the other three drifters had made the rounds of several barrooms before settling down for the night at a so-called hotel that was little better than a flophouse frequented by out-of-work railroad men, down-on-their-luck gamblers, and assorted shady characters.

Casebolt would have figured Strawhorn was the type to seek out better accommodations, but maybe he was low on cash right now. That could be why he had returned to Wind River to start with.

So far this morning, Strawhorn and his friends had eaten breakfast at the hash house, then immediately started hitting the saloons again, despite the early hour. Most of the places never closed; a man could drink twenty-four hours a day in a railhead town if he wanted to.

Casebolt had gotten his own breakfast at the Wind River Cafe, although he hadn't eaten it there. Rose Foster had wrapped up some biscuits and sausage for him and he had taken the food with him so that he could keep an eye on Strawhorn. Cole had given him this responsibility, and Billy didn't want to let the marshal down.

The saloon across the street was the third one Strawhorn and his companions had visited today. The morning was well advanced, and Casebolt was beginning to get hungry again. He was considering going across the street and into the saloon to try out the free lunch. That would put him in the same room as Strawhorn and the others, but Casebolt didn't think that would alarm the hardcases.

He had stayed out of sight so far during his surveillance of them, so they oughtn't to think anything of him stopping into a saloon for a drink and some hard-boiled eggs and ham and stale crackers.

"Good day to you, Deputy."

The unexpected greeting made Casebolt jump a little. He looked around and saw William Durand standing there on the boardwalk. "Oh . . . Howdy, Mr. Durand. Didn't see you comin'."

"I certainly didn't mean to startle you, Deputy." Durand had an amused expression in his eyes.

Casebolt swallowed the anger that welled up inside him. He knew that Durand thought he was barely competent as a lawman; the businessman had made that clear enough when he relieved him of his duties as constable, before Cole Tyler's arrival in town. But to give Durand credit, he was the one who had suggested that Billy might make a good deputy for the new marshal. Still, Casebolt didn't particularly like the man.

"What are you doing?" Durand went on, gesturing at the wall where Casebolt was leaning. "Is the building in some danger of collapsing?"

"Not that I know of," Casebolt answered. "I'm just standin' here keepin' an eye on the town, Mr. Durand. That's what you folks pay me for, ain't it?"

"Yes, indeed. And I'm sure we all sleep better at night knowing that you're watching out for us." Durand lifted a finger to the brim of his bowler hat. "Good day."

Billy watched the land developer move on down the boardwalk, then step off at the end of the walk and cross to the livery stable. The deputy wondered where Durand was going, and his curiosity grew even more when Durand drove out of the stable in a finely appointed buggy a few minutes later. Durand turned the big black horse toward the western edge of town and drove briskly along Grenville Avenue.

His house was in the other direction, Casebolt knew, and anyway, Durand wouldn't have bothered getting his buggy out of the livery stable just to go home.

Durand followed the trail to the west out of town and dwindled out of sight as Casebolt watched. Maybe he was going out to have a talk with the railroad construction foreman about something, the deputy decided. He knew the work crews had already laid several miles of track to the west.

It was none of his business what Durand did, Casebolt reminded himself. His job was to watch Deke Strawhorn.

And by letting himself get distracted, he realized a second later, he had almost made a big mistake and allowed Strawhorn to get away from him. The drifter and his friends had left the saloon and were walking along the opposite side of the street.

Casebolt was about to turn and trail them from across the street when Strawhorn suddenly stepped off the boardwalk and started toward the livery stable, trailed by his friends. Stepping back quickly, Casebolt put himself in the recessed doorway of the hardware store, where he wouldn't be so visible.

Through the front window of the store, he watched Strawhorn and the other three men angle across toward the stable and disappear. When Billy leaned out from the doorway, he spotted the last of the men entering the barn.

They were probably getting their horses, he thought. There was no other reason for them to be going to the stable in the middle of the day. And there was no reason to get their horses unless they were planning on leaving town.

Which meant he had to be ready to ride, too, or he was going to lose them.

Casebolt moved out of the doorway and went quickly to an alley that led him to the area behind the buildings along Grenville Avenue. He hurried toward the rear of the livery stable. There was a back door to the place, but it was closed. Casebolt came to a stop beside the door and leaned his ear against it. A few moments later he heard the thud of hoofbeats as several men rode out of the barn.

As soon as those hoofbeats had faded, he jerked open the back door and went into the stable. The young hostler looked around at him in surprise as Casebolt asked, "Did four men just leave here, boy?"

"Yeah, that fella Strawhorn and his friends," the youngster replied. "What's the matter, Mr. Casebolt? You after 'em for something?"

"That's law business," muttered Casebolt.

"You just get my horse ready to ride, quick like."

The boy nodded his head. "Sure, Mr. Casebolt."

Casebolt watched approvingly as the hostler saddled up his horse. At least some people in this town still knew how to treat their elders with respect, he thought. It took only a couple of minutes for the hostler, who was experienced despite his youth, to get Billy's horse ready to ride.

The deputy nodded his thanks, took the reins, and swung up into the saddle. As he rode toward the front entrance he asked the hostler, "Did you see which way Strawhorn and the rest of 'em went?"

"They headed west," the boy said. "Seemed like they were in a little bit of a hurry, too."

Casebolt nodded again, waved a hand, and then turned his mount to the west and heeled it into a trot. A few people on the street gave him curious glances as he rode purposefully out of town. They probably weren't used to seeing him moving so fast. At his age, Casebolt liked to maintain a deliberate pace whenever he could.

No time for that now, though. As he left Wind River eyes that were still keen in spite of his age scanned the horizon, and it didn't take him long to notice the thin plume of dust rising to the west of town. Casebolt rode toward the dust, knowing it probably came from the hooves of the horses ridden by Strawhorn and the other drifters.

The country here was fairly flat, so Casebolt hung back a good distance and didn't push his horse for fear of raising a dust cloud of his own. Men like Strawhorn were in the habit of watching their back trails, and Casebolt didn't want to alert him that he was being followed. Once Strawhorn and the others stopped, then there would be time to catch up to them and see what they were doing.

The telltale plume of dust gradually veered a little south of west, away from the route of the Union Pacific. They were already past the last point where the tracks extended, although the roadbed had been graded beyond that for a considerable distance.

As he rode, Casebolt's stomach reminded him that he hadn't eaten since breakfast. He had followed Strawhorn out of town before he could implement his plan to sample the free lunch at that saloon where Strawhorn had been drinking. With a sigh, Casebolt told himself he would just have to put up with the hunger pangs. He wasn't going to turn back until he had tracked Strawhorn to wherever the hardcase was going.

And the way Strawhorn and the others were riding, they had some definite destination. They weren't just ambling across the prairie. For another thing, most folks wouldn't come so far from town in this direction without a good reason, because even though peace treaties had been signed with the Sioux and the Shoshone, there was always a chance the Indians would momentarily forget about those treaties if they saw a small group of whites traveling alone.

Casebolt kept an eye on the dust he was following, but he was watchful of his surroundings, too. Hills rose to the north and south, with mountains looming in the distance to the north. Somebody in the hills could be watching him, just as he was watching Strawhorn.

The rolling plains seemed deserted, and gradually Casebolt relaxed. Once he knew what Strawhorn was up to, he decided, he would head back to Wind River as fast as he could and tell Cole all about it. That thought reminded him that he hadn't told the marshal where he was going. Cole might worry about him dropping out of sight this way. But Cole would also know that Billy had been shadowing Strawhorn, and he might assume that the deputy's disappearance was related to that chore. Besides, if Cole got to worrying too much, he would likely go to the livery stable to see if Casebolt's horse was still there, and the hostler would tell him about Casebolt riding out right after Strawhorn and the others had left.

As he topped a small rise Casebolt reined in abruptly. The dust he was following had stopped rising, but a faint haze of it hung in the air about half a mile ahead of him, indicating that was where Strawhorn's bunch had come to a stop. Casebolt thought about it for a minute, then heeled his horse into a walk. He would take it slow and easy now as he approached the spot where Strawhorn had halted.

He saw a line of brush along the banks of a creek as he drew closer. There were even a few scrubby trees sucking life-giving water out of the rocky ground along the stream. Casebolt thought he caught a glimpse of some riders under the trees, but he couldn't be sure. When he estimated that he was only a few hundred yards away from the spot, he dismounted and led his horse forward on foot.

This was just like the old days, Casebolt

thought, slipping around like some sort of redskin himself. Of course, when he was scouting for the army, he had been hunting hostile Indians, and now he was trailing white renegades. But the game was sort of the same, still mighty exciting — and mighty dangerous.

He started up a last shallow slope and knew that on the other side of the little hill was the creek he had seen earlier where Strawhorn had stopped. At least he hoped the dust had been coming from Strawhorn's bunch. He was going to feel like seventeen different kinds of fool if he had been following the wrong trail all the way from Wind River.

That wasn't the case, he saw when he reached the top of the rise and bellied down to study the scene spread out before him. The creek was there, about seventy-five yards away, and four riders were sitting their horses in the sparse shade of the little trees. Casebolt recognized Strawhorn's hat and knew the other three men had to be the hardcase's friends.

But Strawhorn's presence wasn't the most interesting thing; Casebolt had been expecting that.

What he hadn't expected was that William Durand would be sitting there beside the creek in his fancy buggy, talking loudly and gesturing emphatically as he spoke to Strawhorn.

Casebolt frowned. What in blazes did Durand have to do with an owlhoot like Strawhorn? The drifters weren't holding up the businessman, that much was certain. Strawhorn and the others all had their guns holstered, and they seemed to be listening intently as Durand spoke. Billy wished he was close enough to hear what Durand was saying.

Twisting his head, Casebolt looked back down the slope to where he had tied his horse well out of sight of the other men. The animal was contentedly cropping on a little patch of cheat grass.

What little breeze there was blew out of the west, toward Casebolt, which meant that the horses down there wouldn't be able to smell his mount and start whinnying. The slope leading down to the creek was dotted with brush, enough so that Casebolt thought he would have plenty of cover if he tried to sneak closer on foot.

It would mean running a risk, but hell, he had run plenty of risks in his life. And he wanted to know what the connection was between Strawhorn and Durand. He sensed that it was mighty important, whatever it was.

He moved back to his horse and took off his hat, hanging it on the saddlehorn. "You just stay right here for a spell," he told the horse quietly as he patted its flank. "I'll be back for you."

Then he returned to the crest of the hill, took a deep breath, and catfooted his way over the top, crouching so that he was behind a greasewood bush.

Carefully, Casebolt worked his way down the slope toward the creek. He could see that Strawhorn and Durand were still talking. The other men seemed to be concentrating on the discussion, and none of them was looking in his direction. Excitement grew in Casebolt. Pretty soon he was going to be close enough to hear what they were saying. . . .

". . . sure of the schedule." The words came faintly to Casebolt's ears. Durand had spoken them, and the deputy heard part of Strawhorn's reply.

"Damn well better . . . riding on this . . ."

". . . need to worry . . . be rich men soon enough."

Casebolt's eyes narrowed. Sounded like Strawhorn and Durand were planning some sort of business deal. Billy knew about Durand's business, but he was damned if he could see where Strawhorn had any profession except being a gunman and probable outlaw. If he and Durand were mixed up together in something, it had to be a crooked deal.

That was news Cole Tyler had to hear, and as soon as possible. Casebolt started backing up. He had seen and heard enough.

He never knew where the snake came from. Slithered out from under one of the bushes he had passed, more than likely. But suddenly it was there, under his boot as he took a careful step backward, and as it whipped and coiled around his booted ankle, Casebolt's instincts took over and sent him jumping backward with an involuntary yelp.

He landed hard on his rump as the offended snake slid off under another bush. He got a good enough look at it to recognize it as a harmless bull snake. But the real danger had never been from the snake. It came from the men involved in the clandestine meeting nearby. At the sound of Casebolt's outcry, the heads of Strawhorn and Durand had jerked around, and Durand leveled a pointing finger and said harshly and angrily, "There!"

"I see him!" Strawhorn yelled. Casebolt

scrambled to his feet and turned to run. He didn't know if Strawhorn and the others had seen him well enough to recognize him, but that didn't matter. If they were up to no good, they wouldn't want anybody spying on them. Casebolt knew he had to reach his horse.

He threw a glance over his shoulder, just in time to see Strawhorn leveling the Winchester he had pulled from his saddleboot. Billy saw smoke spurt from the barrel of the rifle and a split second later heard the sharp crack of its report. At the same instant something slapped him hard in the right side.

Casebolt spun half around, staggered, and almost lost his balance. He stayed upright somehow and kept running toward the spot where his horse was tied. His whole right side was numb, and he couldn't lift his arm. He reached across his body with his left hand and felt the sticky wetness soaking his shirt. There was no way of knowing if the slug from the Winchester had torn all the way through him or was still lodged in his body. Either way, he was hurt bad.

As he stumbled over the top of the rise, he looked back again and saw Strawhorn and the other men riding after him. Durand's buggy was rolling east, bouncing over the rough spots on the ground as Durand whipped the black to greater speed. Durand was heading back to Wind River, Billy figured, leaving Strawhorn and the others to take care of this minor distraction.

Casebolt struggled to reach across his body again and snag the butt of the pistol on his right hip. He lifted it, the gun feeling awkward in his left hand, and triggered off a couple of shots at Strawhorn and the other riders.

He didn't expect to hit any of them, but he wanted them to know he still had fangs. He turned and staggered downhill to his horse, which shied away from him at the smell of blood. Jerking loose the reins from the small bush where he had tied them, Billy grasped the saddlehorn with his good hand and tried to get a foot in the stirrup.

It seemed to take forever, but finally he had his foot in place and used it to lift him. He swung his other leg over the horse's back and settled down in the saddle. Pain doubled him over as the horse leaped into motion, but he managed not to fall off. He turned the horse and headed east as his eyesight began to blur crazily.

At least he thought it was east, but when his vision cleared somewhat a few minutes later, the country in front of him didn't look familiar. Maybe he was headed in some other direction. Maybe he had gotten turned around and was riding right into the guns of Strawhorn's bunch. He peered up, trying to find the sun, but a gray haze seemed to have been drawn across his eyes.

Casebolt let out a groan as he realized that somewhere along the way he had dropped his gun. Now he couldn't even defend himself if he ran into Strawhorn.

Luckily, the horse underneath him was running well. It took the dips and rises of the ground in stride. The terrain around here might look flat, but it was surprisingly rugged. Gradually, Casebolt became aware that his surroundings were growing even rougher.

He didn't remember crossing the roadbed of the Union Pacific, which meant he was probably heading south. Unless of course he simply hadn't noticed the route of the railroad, and given his condition, that was all too possible. His head was spinning and it was all he could do to hang on to the saddlehorn and stay on top of the horse.

He looked around from time to time, whenever his head cleared a little, and saw no sign of Strawhorn. Had he managed to give the slip to his pursuers? If so, it was either a miracle or a pure-dee accident, because he hadn't been coherent enough to know what he was doing.

Pain washed through him with every jolting step of the horse. His right side felt like liquid fire was flooding over it. He felt himself slipping and knew that regardless of how much of a lead he had on Strawhorn, he had to slow down or be bounced out of the saddle. Pulling back weakly on the reins, he called out to his mount, "Whoa there . . . steady . . . steady . . ."

The horse eased back to a walk, and Casebolt tried to heave a sigh of relief. It hurt too much to do so, however, so he settled for slumping over the saddlehorn and drawing in short, gasping breaths. His sight seemed to be going again. Everything was darker than it had been only moments earlier, even though he knew it was still a long time until sunset.

He was dying, Casebolt thought. He had failed in the job Cole had given him, and now the marshal wouldn't find out until it was maybe too late that Durand and Strawhorn were working together.

More than anything else in the world, he wanted to hang on and make it back to Wind River so that he could warn Cole. But it was no use. Billy felt himself slipping again, and this time he was too weak to hold himself in the saddle. He fell, and it seemed to take forever for him to hit the ground.

In fact, he never did feel it when he landed. . . .

Time passed, and the bloody, huddled figure still lay on the Wyoming prairie, unmoving. The horse wandered away, looking for some grass on which to graze, and a few prairie dogs stuck their heads up from their burrows to study the strange shape on the ground nearby. Once they had decided that it did not represent any sort of threat, they emerged from their holes to scurry around looking for food.

Suddenly one of the prairie dogs jerked its head up and emitted a loud, startled squeal. All of them bolted for safety, diving back into the burrows they had come from. The warning had done its job. Someone was coming.

The sun beat down on Billy Casebolt's face, and he never stirred as several pairs of moccasin-clad feet slowly surrounded him.

CHAPTER 12

"Damn it, Billy, where the hell are you?" Cole muttered to himself as he stood in front of the livery stable and frowned toward the prairie west of Wind River.

It had been nearly twenty-four hours since Casebolt had ridden out of town on the trail of Deke Strawhorn, and there had been no sign of the deputy since then.

The evening before, when Cole realized that he hadn't seen Billy since that morning, he had gone to the livery stable to see if the deputy's horse was gone. The hostler had told him about Casebolt's questions and the fact that the deputy had ridden out right after Strawhorn, and Cole had leaped to the reasonable conclusion. Billy was keeping an eye on the hardcase, just as Cole had asked him to.

But he hadn't returned, and Cole was getting downright worried. He had just checked at the livery stable to make sure

Casebolt's horse was still gone, and it was, along with the mounts of Strawhorn and his friends.

Had something happened to Casebolt out there on the plains? Cole didn't want to think so, but it was becoming more likely with each passing moment.

Grim lines around his mouth, Cole stalked down the street toward Hank Parker's tent saloon. When he reached the place, he pushed aside the flap and stepped inside. At this time of day there were fewer customers, but still more than half a dozen men stood at the bar and an equal number were seated at the tables scattered around the room. The burly, bullet-headed Parker was behind the bar, and Cole had to wonder if the man ever slept.

Parker looked up as Cole came over to the bar, and the saloonkeeper grunted. "I suppose it'd be too much to hope that you just came in here for a drink."

"Have you seen Strawhorn last night or today?" Cole asked, ignoring Parker's comment.

"Why?"

"Just answer the question," the marshal said coldly.

Parker shrugged his broad shoulders. "I've had other things on my mind. Look around,

233

Tyler. Folks are getting edgy because that payroll train still hasn't gotten here."

"That's the Union Pacific's worry, not mine."

"It'll be yours if those Irishmen start to thinking they're not going to get paid," Parker said. "They're liable to tear this town up."

"I'll deal with that if it happens," Cole snapped. "What about Strawhorn?"

"Haven't seen him," Parker said with another shrug. "Like I said, I've got other things to worry about."

"Thanks," Cole said grudgingly. "If he happens to come in, will you send somebody to let me know?"

"So you can come over and start some more trouble?" Parker held up his hands at the blaze of anger in Cole's eyes. "All right, all right," he said. "I'll let you know."

Cole nodded and left the saloon. Parker's place seemed to be Strawhorn's favorite watering hole, but there were plenty of other saloons in Wind River where the hardcase and his friends could have gone. Cole moved on down the street, stopping in at each saloon to ask if Strawhorn had been seen in the past day.

By the time he had gone halfway down the street, it was obvious a pattern was developing. No one had seen Strawhorn or any of the drifter's friends since the previous morning. It could be they had simply left Wind River, but if that was the case, Billy Casebolt should have turned back by now and returned to town. He wouldn't still be trailing them.

Cole decided that he would finish his questioning of the bartenders and saloonkeepers, then, if no one had seen Strawhorn, he would have to think about organizing a search party. Casebolt could have run into some hostile Indians, or his horse could have thrown him. There were several possible explanations for his disappearance.

And Strawhorn could have discovered him and taken exception to being spied upon, too. If that was the case, Cole thought grimly, then he was partially to blame for whatever had happened to his deputy. He had given Casebolt the job of watching Strawhorn.

Before Cole could continue down the street, he heard a sound that made him lift his head and frown in surprise. It was a high, distant keening, almost like the wail of a lost soul. A few seconds passed before he realized the noise was the steam whistle of a locomotive. The whistle grew louder and didn't tail off, and Cole knew the engineer must be hanging on to the cord for all he was worth.

That meant trouble. Cole broke into a run toward the train station.

He wasn't the only one. The shrill sound of the whistle had alerted other citizens, who hurried toward the depot out of concern or simple curiosity. Cole saw Michael Hatfield emerge from the newspaper office and look around in confusion until he located the source of the commotion. Then the young editor joined the flow of people toward the station.

Quite a few people were on the platform by the time Cole got there, gesturing along the tracks to the east and talking excitedly. Cole made his way to the edge of the platform and looked along the tracks, spotting the billowing clouds of steam from the big Baldwin locomotive as it rolled toward Wind River. The stationmaster and telegrapher, a man named Barkley, stood nearby with a worried frown on his face. Cole caught his eye and asked, "What's going on?"

"I don't know," Barkley replied with a shake of his head. "My key went dead a little while ago, so the lines must be down somewhere east of here."

Cole scanned the horizon. Sometimes

prairie fires burned the telegraph poles, making them fall and snapping the wires. There was no pall of smoke to be seen in the sky, though. In the past, the Sioux had sometimes pulled down the lines after learning that the so-called singing wires were important to the white men. There hadn't been any reports of trouble like that for a while, and Cole hoped it wasn't about to begin again.

Obviously, there was a connection between the downing of the telegraph lines and the train that was rolling in with its whistle screaming. The train would be there soon enough — it was less than half a mile away now — and Cole was anxious to question its engineer.

Cole and Barkley moved people back from the edge of the platform as the locomotive approached. Anybody who was bumped from behind and fell under those wheels would be killed instantly. Cole turned to watch grimly as the train slowed to a stop. The whistle was still blowing, and it was almost deafening now at this close range. The locomotive rolled past the platform. Cole peered into the cab and saw the arm hanging limply through the window. There was a dark stain on the upper part of the man's sleeve.

"Son of a bitch!" Cole exclaimed.

He broke into a run again, this time alongside the cab. The train was moving slowly enough now for him to risk vaulting up into the cab. He latched onto the grab bar and pulled himself up with his left hand while his right palmed out the Colt on his hip, just in case.

The danger was over, he saw immediately. There were two men in the cab, the engineer and the fireman, but neither of them was in any shape to threaten anybody. The fireman was the one with an arm dangling out the window of the cab. His coat was sodden with blood, and his eyes were glazed over in death. Somehow the fingers of his right hand were still wrapped around the whistle cord, locked tightly there, and the weight of his arm held it down.

The engineer was still alive, but he was hunched over against the pain in his midsection. He was probably gut-shot, Cole realized from the way he seemed to be trying to hold himself together with an arm pressed over his belly. With his other hand, the engineer had managed to work the throttle and brake well enough to bring the train into Wind River.

Now that he had done his job, the man's stamina played out. He let go of the brake lever and slumped heavily to the iron floor of the cab. Cole holstered his gun and pried the fireman's dead fingers off the whistle cord, silencing it abruptly and making an eerie silence fall. Quickly, Cole knelt beside the wounded engineer.

"What happened?" he asked urgently, hoping the engineer could still hear and understand him. The man's eyes were closed now. "Who did this to you?"

The engineer's eyes fluttered open weakly. "Eight of 'em . . ." he gasped. "Stopped the train . . . five miles east . . . burning logs on the track . . . damn near derailed us . . . Had to stop . . . and then they come up with guns."

"Why did they want to stop the train?"

"Carrying . . . payroll . . ."

Icy fingers touched the back of Cole's neck. He had heard of trains being held up and robbed back east, but not this far out on the frontier. Still, the outlaws couldn't have picked a better target. The payroll for the work crews added up to a hefty sum.

Cole forced his mind off that and gently eased the wounded man's arm aside. He winced at the sight of the injury. The engineer had been shot in the stomach, just as Cole had thought, maybe more than once. It was a hell of a way to die, and death was a long time coming. Cole was surprised the engineer had managed to hang on this long without passing out from the pain.

He heard an angry voice demanding, "Let me through, you bloody fools!" Dr. Judson Kent stepped up into the locomotive's cab a moment later, took a look around, and said, "Oh, my Lord."

"This fella's still alive," Cole said, "although I don't reckon there's much you can do for him. If you'll tend to him, I need to check the rest of the train."

Kent went to one knee beside the wounded engineer. "Of course. I'll take over here, Marshal."

Cole left Kent bending over the injured man and leaped down from the cab, again motioning the curious bystanders back from the edge of the platform. He drew his gun again and started past the coal tender. The train was a short one, only one boxcar and the caboose behind the locomotive and tender. Cole stopped beside the boxcar and reached up to slide open the door.

The car was loaded with railroad ties and sections of track bound for the area several miles to the west where new tracks were being laid. Cole glanced around inside, satisfied himself that no one was hiding there, then hurried on to the caboose. He noticed as he reached it that Michael Hatfield was trailing him closely.

"Better stay back," he warned the editor. "I don't think there's going to be any trouble back here, but I can't be sure."

"I heard what the engineer said to you," Michael replied. "This was the payroll train, and someone stopped it and held it up, didn't they?"

Cole glanced sharply at the young man, intending to warn him to keep quiet about that for the time being, but the damage was already done. Shouts of alarm went up from those citizens standing closest, and soon the news had spread all over the platform. Men began running down the street, carrying the word even farther. Soon the whole town would know that the Union Pacific payroll had been stolen.

There was nothing that could be done about that now, Cole realized. He went up the steps leading to the platform on the rear of the caboose and stepped carefully inside.

The first thing that caught his eye was the sprawled body of the conductor, lying facedown in a pool of his own blood. Two more men were inside the car, also dead, lying on their backs where they had been gunned down by the robbers. Cole recognized both of them and knew they had served a dual role as guards and paymasters for the Union Pacific. They would have given out the wages to the work crews if the train had arrived here safely.

Too late for that now, Cole thought. The money was long gone, hauled off in the canvas pouches in which it was usually carried. A quick look around the caboose told Cole the pouches were gone.

He stepped out wearily, holstering his gun, and questions from the crowd bombarded him. He held up his hands for silence, and when it came after a few moments, he said, "The men inside are dead, and it looks like the payroll's gone, all right."

Howls of dismay rose. A few of the railroad workers were here in town for one reason or another, primarily for putting the finishing touches on the nearby roundhouse, but most of them were west of town laying track. They would be coming back to Wind River tonight on the work train, however, and when they found out their pay had been stolen . . . Well, there was no way of knowing what would happen, Cole thought.

But one thing was certain. It wouldn't be good.

Cole recognized one of the men in the crowd as the supervisor of the roundhouse construction. He motioned for the man to join him, then said, "You'd better take a handcar and go on up the line to find your boss. Let him know what's happened."

"I don't know if that's a good idea, Marshal," the railroad man said dubiously. "If those section gangs find out their pay's been stolen, they're liable to cause trouble."

"Maybe not if you tell them a posse has already gone after the outlaws and intends to get the money back."

"A posse?"

Cole nodded. His worries about Billy Casebolt would just have to wait. This holdup could affect the whole town. If the track layers rioted, they might burn Wind River to the ground.

Raising his voice to be heard over the uproar on the platform, Cole shouted, "I want volunteers for a posse! We're going after those thieves!"

"I'll ride with you, Marshal," Michael Hatfield said immediately, "but doesn't your authority end at the edge of town?"

"Maybe so, but I know the country around here and I can read sign," snapped Cole. "Besides, recovering that payroll money is the only way I know of to make sure there's no trouble here in Wind River. I reckon that gives me the right to head up a posse."

"Nobody's going to argue with you about that, Brother Tyler!" called Jeremiah Newton. The massive blacksmith stood on the platform wearing his apron and carrying a sledgehammer. "The Lord said, 'Thou shalt not kill,' so I reckon it's our Christian duty to go after those murdering heathens."

"Thanks, Jeremiah," Cole said. He had two volunteers now, Michael and Jeremiah, and most of the other men didn't waste any time in speaking up. They were all eager to start tracking the desperadoes responsible for this outrage.

Dr. Kent stepped down from the cab as the platform was emptying. The volunteers were hurrying back to their houses or businesses to fetch their rifles and horses. With a weary shake of his head, Kent told Cole, "The engineer is dead. He bled to death, both internally and externally, as victims of that sort of wound usually do."

"I figured he was a goner as soon as I saw him," Cole said. "At least he lived long enough to bring the train in and tell us what happened."

"Did I hear you say that you're going after the highwaymen who committed this atrocity?"

"That's right. A posse is, anyway, and I'm leading it."

"I wish you the best of luck. Would you like for me to accompany you?"

Cole considered the offer for a moment, then shook his head. "I'm a pretty fair hand at patching up bullet wounds when I have to be," he said, "and that's likely all we might run into. I'd rather have you here in town to sort of look after the place."

"I appreciate the faith you have in me, Cole, but I'm not a lawman. Far from it, in fact."

"I know that, but you've got enough common sense to keep people from flying off the handle. And if there's any trouble from the railroad workers, your medical skills will be needed for sure."

Kent sighed. "I fear that you are correct, my friend. Very well, I shall do what I can to keep the town from being overrun by barbarians. I suggest, though, that you bring back that payroll money as soon as possible."

"That's just what I intend to do," Cole said firmly.

Less than thirty minutes later a posse of twenty men rode out of Wind River, following the railroad tracks to the east so that they could pick up the trail of the robbers where the holdup had taken place. Cole rode at their head, surprised that the group

245

also included Hank Parker. He supposed the saloonkeeper had a stake in this matter; if the railroad crews were all broke, they couldn't spend their money on Parker's watered-down rotgut and brightly painted women.

Try as he might, Cole couldn't completely forget about Billy Casebolt's disappearance, just as he hadn't stopped worrying about Andrew McKay's death and the possibility that William Durand might have killed his partner. But he hadn't been able to unearth any new facts concerning the case for over a week, and circumstances now prevented him from looking for Casebolt, who had been headed in the other direction when he vanished. Cole grimaced as he urged the golden sorrel on at a brisk trot.

This business of carrying a badge was damned frustrating.

Cole found out just how frustrating over the next day and a half.

He found the spot where the holdup had taken place; it was easy enough to locate because the remains of the flaming barrier the locomotive had smashed through before coming to a stop were still scattered along and on top of the tracks. And the tracks of the robbers were equally easy to find. The hoof prints of eight horses led almost due north, toward the mountains. Cole hoped they could catch up to the outlaws before they reached those distant peaks. Once they were in the mountains, it would be easier for the thieves to cover their trail and slip away from the posse.

But the outlaws had a lead of several hours, and it was always slower following someone. Losing the trail meant backtracking until the sign could be cut again. That happened a couple of times and threw the posse even farther behind. The delays grated on Cole, but there was nothing he could do about them.

Nightfall found the men from Wind River miles north of the railroad, but the mountains didn't seem much closer in the fading light. Distances were deceptive out here, Cole knew, and he hoped the mountains were still far enough away so that he and his companions would have time to catch up to the thieves.

There was a lot of grumbling in camp that night. Cole had insisted that everyone bring enough provisions for a chase that might last several days, but he figured the townspeople had been hoping to find the robbers, recover the money, and be back in Wind River by dark. He knew how unrealistic that expectation was, but most of the settlers had spent relatively little time on the frontier. They still had a lot to learn about the hardships out here.

Including a cold camp. Cole ordered that no one light a fire. "If those outlaws see a campfire, they'll know we're back here on their trail and they'll push on that much faster," he explained when several men complained. "We want 'em overconfident and thinking nobody's after them."

The night passed uncomfortably for most of the men as they tried to sleep in bedrolls on the hard, rocky ground. A chilly wind sprang up toward morning, making them even more miserable. As for Cole, he had slept in much worse conditions. He kept that thought to himself, though, knowing it wouldn't make the others feel any better.

As they were mounting up after a breakfast as cold and unsatisfying as supper the night before, Michael Hatfield groaned. "Every muscle and bone in my body aches," he said as he tried futilely to stretch into a more comfortable position. He was riding a borrowed horse and carrying a rifle from the general store that had been provided by Durand. The businessman had armed several members of the posse, loaning them the weapons free of charge. It was in his best interests, too, if the railroad payroll was recovered quickly.

"I reckon you're pretty sore, all right," Cole said, offering what little sympathy he could muster. "Wish I could say it was going to get better before it gets worse."

"Thanks." Michael laughed humorlessly. "I'm not surprised. The way my life has been going, I ought to expect one problem after another."

Whatever the youngster was talking about, Cole didn't want to hear it. He had more on his mind than Michael's troubles, whatever they might be. He twisted around in the saddle, saw that the other men were mounted, and called, "Let's ride."

The trail still led north, but during the day it began to curve toward the west. That lifted Cole's spirits even more, and he began pushing the posse harder. They had left the dusty, rolling prairie behind and were riding now over grassy meadows flanked by wooded hills.

At midmorning, they passed the remains of a small campfire, and Cole figured that was where the gang had spent the night before. The outlaws were only a couple of hours ahead of them.

Noon came and went, and the posse took only ten minutes for lunch, more to rest the horses than anything else. Cole ignored the complaints as he ordered the men back into their saddles. The next time he needed a posse, he thought wryly, most of these men wouldn't be so quick to volunteer.

He stopped a couple of times during the afternoon to check the tracks they were following. The edges of the hoof prints were sharper now, not as crumbled. That meant the marks were fresher. The posse was closing the gap, drawing nearer and nearer their quarry.

The trail led down a canyon toward a bluff of red stone that rose at the far end. From a distance Cole couldn't tell if there was a path to the top or not, but as they drew nearer he thought he could pick out a narrow ledge angling back and forth across the face of the bluff. The ledge probably wasn't wide enough for more than one horse, so they would have to climb it single file.

A feeling of unease prickled along his backbone. That narrow path would make a good place for an ambush, he realized. Once the posse was strung out along the ledge, gunmen at the top of the bluff would be able to fire down and pick off the pursuers almost at will. But an ambush would assume that the outlaws knew they were being followed, and Cole had taken pains to avoid that.

Still, it was damned hard to conceal a group of riders this big from someone who really knew how to look, and he was certain the outlaws were the type to watch their backtrail. As the posse approached the base of the bluff, Cole held up his hand to signal a halt.

The tracks of the outlaws led up the ledge, just as he had expected. Cole studied them for a few seconds, then said to the other men, "You fellas wait here. I want to ride up there and scout around a little before the rest of you come up."

Jeremiah Newton reined his horse up alongside Cole's. "If you're afraid those sinners might be waiting up there for us, Marshal, you shouldn't be riding into the lions' den alone. I'll go with you."

"So will I," Hank Parker said, surprising Cole. The saloonkeeper moved forward to join Cole and Jeremiah.

"I'm going, too," Michael spoke up. "If something's going to happen, I have to be able to write about it for the paper."

Cole's features hardened in exasperation. Riding into an outlaw trap might get them all killed, and then Michael wouldn't be able to write about anything. He wasn't sure Michael would understand that line of reasoning, though. Besides, the other three were grown men and had the right to make up their own minds.

"All right," he said curtly. "Let's go. But keep your eyes open and follow my lead in case of trouble."

He sent Ulysses onto the path. Jeremiah came next, followed by Parker and then Michael bringing up the rear. The other members of the posse waited at the bottom of the bluff, rifles held ready.

Cole felt sweat popping out on his forehead as he led the way along the ledge. He had experienced moments like this before, during the War Between the States and since. Moments that seemed to stretch out into hours as a man waited for the crash of guns, waited to see whether he was going to live or die. Despite the coolness of the morning, the air was hot and dry now, and there was no sound except the ringing of horseshoes on the stony path.

Cole saw the pebble come bouncing down in front of him, rebounding off the ledge and flying off into the air. Before the little rock could fall the rest of the way to the ground, Cole's .44 was in his hand and he was calling to his companions, "Watch out!"

He twisted his head to look up at the top of the bluff as gunfire rolled down from above like thunder. Powder smoke puffed out from the rimrock. Cole triggered a couple of shots, hoping to drive the bush-whackers back as he jabbed his spurs into Ulysses's flanks and sent the golden sorrel lunging up the path. There was no time to look behind him and see if the others were following.

Cries from below made him aware that at least some of the ambushers were concentrating their fire on the posse members who had stayed at the foot of the bluff. "Get back!" Cole shouted at them, hoping they would have enough sense to move along the face of the bluff and put themselves at a bad angle as targets. Of course, that would also mean they were in an awkward position to return the fire. The four men climbing the winding path were on their own.

That was why Cole was attacking. There was no place to hide, no place to run. Charging into the face of the ambush and maybe taking the bushwhackers by surprise was really their only chance.

Bullets kicked up dust and slivers of rock as they impacted on the path around him. Cole caught a glimpse of a man's shoulder and part of his head as he fired from behind a boulder at the top of the bluff. Instantly, he fired twice and was rewarded with the sight of the bushwhacker spinning back away from the rimrock. A shotgun boomed somewhere behind Cole on the path, and he knew Jeremiah Newton was getting into the fight. The big blacksmith had brought a greener with him.

As Ulysses reached a bend in the trail Cole hauled on the reins and guided the horse around the steep hairpin turn. He and the others were taking the path too fast for safety, but there was no safety in sitting there and letting the ambushers cut them down, either.

Once around the turn, Cole could look back the way he had come and see that Jeremiah, Michael, and Parker were all still mounted. Parker was firing his rifle toward the top to the bluff as he rode, but Michael had his hands full just controlling his mount.

Cole jammed his revolver back in its holster and pulled the Winchester '66 from the saddle boot. There was only one shot left in the Colt, and Cole wanted to save it in case he needed it badly later. In the meantime the fifteen-shot magazine of the rifle known by the Indians as the Yellow Boy was full. Cole worked the lever, jacking a shell into the chamber.

Guiding Ulysses with the pressure of his

knees, Cole brought the rifle to his shoulder and began firing, throwing lead toward the rimrock as fast as he could work the lever and press the trigger. Fewer slugs were whipping around him now, and he hoped the bushwhackers were pulling back.

He stopped firing long enough to take the sorrel around another bend in the trail, and then he was galloping along the final section before it reached the top of the bluff. Cole lifted the rifle again, his eyes scanning the rimrock for targets.

Obviously, the ambush had been less successful than the gunmen had intended, because as he reached the top of the path Cole spotted several of them racing toward horses tied nearby. He dropped the reins and brought the Winchester to his shoulder again, slamming shots toward the running men.

One of them spun around a couple of times before falling limply, while another simply pitched forward on his face as Cole's bullets drilled into him. The shotgun boomed again behind Cole, and he twisted his head long enough to see Jeremiah firing the scattergun one-handed. Anyone else might have wound up with a broken wrist from trying such a stunt, but the blacksmith's massive hand and arm were strong enough to withstand the recoil.

Michael Hatfield appeared next at the top of the path. He was still struggling to control his mount. Hank Parker was right behind him, the rifle in his hands spitting smoke and fire as he sent bullets among the rocks where the bushwhackers had hidden.

Cole was drawing a bead on one of the outlaws when a man suddenly appeared on top of a large rock and launched himself at the marshal in a desperate dive. The man crashed into Cole, wrapping long arms around him, and drove him off the sorrel's back. Cole slammed into the ground with the outlaw on top of him, knocking the breath out of his lungs. The Winchester skittered away on the rocky ground as Cole lost his grip on it.

Gasping for air, Cole saw the man slashing at his head with the barrel of a pistol. He jerked his head aside as the gun barrel thudded against the hard-packed earth. The blow would have crushed his skull if it had landed. Twisting his body, Cole brought up a leg, hooked it around the man's neck, and thrust savagely, throwing the outlaw off to the side.

As he rolled over, Cole's left hand found the leather-wrapped hilt of the Green River knife sheathed on his left hip. With a whisper of cold steel, he brought the knife out and up as the outlaw leaped at him again. The razor-sharp point of the blade caught the man just below the sternum and slid smoothly into him, angling up to pierce his heart. His eyes opened wide with pain and surprise as he died.

The body sagged limply against Cole, who shoved it aside, ripped the knife free, and came to his feet, looking for another enemy. That familiar red haze had slid down over Cole's vision again. He was panting with the need to strike out, his lips drawn back from his teeth in a grimace. He spun around sharply as he sensed as much as heard movement behind him.

"Brother Tyler!" Jeremiah exclaimed as he saw the killing rage in Cole's eyes. "It's just me, Brother Tyler!"

"Take it easy, Marshal," Michael put in as he finally brought his horse under control enough for him to dismount. "It's all over."

Cole drew in a deep, ragged breath. "The bushwhackers?"

"All dead," replied Hank Parker. "You did for three of 'em yourself, and Newton and me finished off the other three."

Cole shook his head, forcing the last of the cobwebs out of his brain. "Six of them?" he asked. "We've been following eight men."

"Well, there's only six here, and none of 'em got away that I saw," Parker said. "There's only six horses, too."

Cole rubbed a weary hand over his face and then looked around. Like the others had said, there were six bodies scattered around here at the top of the bluff. Cole checked them to make sure they were all dead. He recognized several of them.

"These men rode with Deke Strawhorn," he said grimly.

Parker nodded. "I recall seeing them with him, too."

"But Strawhorn's not here, Marshal," Michael said.

"I can see that." Cole peered toward the west. "I reckon if we look, we'll find the tracks of two horses heading that way. But we won't find that railroad payroll. Strawhorn and the other man will have taken it with them. They left these men here to deal with anybody who was following them. Probably planned to meet later and split up the money. It damned near worked. We were lucky to survive that ambush, even luckier to have downed all these owlhoots."

"The Lord was on our side," Jeremiah said simply.

"You may be right," Cole said, "but He hasn't delivered that payroll into our hands yet. We've still got work to do." At that moment a voice called out from below, asking what was going on up there, and Cole swung toward the edge of the bluff. "Come on. We'd better see how much damage those bushwhackers did."

CHAPTER 13

Delia Hatfield paced anxiously back and forth over the rug on the hotel-room floor. Her arms were crossed and her forehead was creased in a frown of worry. This was the third night since Michael had impulsively ridden out of Wind River along with the posse pursuing the train robbers, and none of the men had come back to town.

She wondered if her husband was still alive, or if Michael was lying out there on the prairie somewhere, his lifeless body torn by outlaw bullets. A sob tried to well up her throat, but she swallowed it, determined not to let Gretchen see just how upset and frightened she was.

Gretchen was sitting on the floor beside the bed talking nonsense to a rag doll. Ever since the little girl had begun talking, Delia hadn't had to watch her to keep track of her. Gretchen usually stopped talking only when she was eating or sleeping, and not always then. One time at the supper table, Delia remembered, Gretchen had pointed to the food on her plate after jabbering for several minutes and asked, "Hot?" And Michael, with that grin of his, had answered, "It shouldn't be. The wind from your flapping tongue should have cooled it off by now, Gretchen."

The child hadn't understood the joke and had just sat there glaring at her father, but Delia had laughed and laughed. . . .

And now she sobbed, despite all her best intentions, as the memory of that moment pierced her like a dagger. She and Michael had argued more and more since she became pregnant, culminating in her moving out and renting this room in Simone McKay's hotel, but she still loved Michael, loved him desperately. If anything happened to him, she didn't know how she would be able to go on.

Delia caught hold of one of the posts at the foot of the bed and hung on to it for a moment as she fought off the attack of tears that threatened to overwhelm her. She couldn't allow this to happen. If Gretchen saw her like this, the little girl would be scared, and Delia didn't want that. She wanted Gretchen to be safe and secure and happy —

The silence suddenly assaulted Delia's ears. There was no sound in the room except her harsh breathing.

She turned around quickly, expecting — hoping — that Gretchen had simply gone to sleep on the rug next to the bed. That wasn't what had happened, though, Delia saw to her shock.

The door into the hotel corridor was standing open about six inches, and Gretchen was nowhere to be seen.

William Durand and Dr. Judson Kent came to a stop on the boardwalk in front of the hotel entrance. They had run into each other at Rose Foster's cafe, eaten supper together, then strolled back down to the hotel. The two men had never been close friends, but as two of the civic leaders of Wind River, there was a surface politeness between them.

And tonight both of them shared a concern for the young town's continued well-being as well. An air of tense expectancy hung over the settlement. More than forty-eight hours had passed since the train bringing the Union Pacific payroll to Wind River had been stopped and held up.

The UP crews had not rioted, but work on the line had ground to a virtual standstill as the Irish laborers converged on the saloons to drink and wait to see if their wages were going to be recovered. Most of the saloon owners were letting them drink on the cuff, hoping to keep them happy for a little while longer. The saloonkeepers would recoup their losses quickly enough once the payroll money was brought back.

But if the posse led by Cole Tyler didn't recover the money . . . well, then, that would be a disaster, and Durand and Kent both knew it.

"Did Marshal Tyler give you any indication before he left of how long he expected to be gone?" Durand asked as he and Kent paused on the boardwalk to mull the situation over one last time before going their separate ways for the night.

"None," replied Kent. "He said something about taking enough provisions for several days, though." The physician sighed. "I hope he returns soon and brings that payroll with him. Those railroad men are liable to go on a rampage if they find out they won't be paid anytime in the near future."

"I appreciate what you've done to keep them calm, Doctor. I know you've been going around town and talking to them, steadying them."

Kent shrugged. "Cole asked me to try to keep a lid on things, I believe was how he phrased it. I've given the task my utmost effort."

"I would hate to see this town torn down around our ears after all the time and money Andrew and I spent on establishing it. Of course, we all have a stake in seeing that the peace is kept."

"Indeed," Kent agreed. He frowned slightly. "You haven't seen Deputy Casebolt the past few days, have you? He didn't ride out with the posse, I'm sure of that. It might help if he was here."

Durand shook his head and waved a hand in contempt. "Billy Casebolt is a worthless old man," he said harshly. "I haven't seen him, but I know I wouldn't feel any more secure if he were here."

"Still, he is one of our legally appointed guardians of the peace."

"He's probably drifted off somewhere and forgotten all about his responsibilities," snorted Durand. "I'm not going to hold my breath waiting for him to show up again."

"No, none of us can afford to do that." Kent nodded at the businessman and went on, "Well, I'll say good night, Mr. Durand. The town has survived this long. Perhaps it can muddle along a bit longer, eh?"

Durand just grunted and nodded his own good night. He turned and went into the hotel as Kent proceeded down the street toward his combination office and living quarters. Durand nodded to the clerk behind the desk and then went up the stairs to the second floor. He could have gone down the street to his own house, but he didn't want to be alone in the big house tonight. There was a hot, dry wind blowing outside, but somehow it made Durand feel cold.

When he and Andrew McKay had built this hotel, they had seen to it that each of them had a suite permanently reserved for their private use. The plan had been that important guests, such as politicians and officials of the railroad, could stay there when they visited Wind River. Since McKay's death, however, his widow had been staying in the hotel, probably because *she* didn't want to be alone in her house except for the servants. Durand had decided that he would stay in his suite tonight; if there was a riot, he might be safer here than in his house — as if anywhere in Wind River would be safe under those circumstances.

He reached the suite, which was at the far end of the second-floor corridor, and unlocked the door. As he stepped inside a match flared suddenly. Durand jerked to a stop, and his hand darted toward the small pistol underneath his coat.

"You won't need that, Durand," a familiar voice said. "It's just me and Benton."

Durand relaxed slightly as the match was brought over to the wick of a lamp on a side table. The lamp caught and flared up, the yellow glow revealing the dusty, stubbled face of Deke Strawhorn. The outlaw looked gaunt and tired, as did his companion, a dark-haired man in faded range clothes. Both men had their guns drawn, but Strawhorn holstered his and Benton followed suit.

"My God," Durand said hoarsely. "What are you two doing here?"

Strawhorn gestured lazily at the canvas pouches lying on the sofa in the suite's sitting room. "Reckon you know that," he said. "We brought the money, just like it was agreed."

"You were supposed to deliver it to my house," Durand hissed. "You weren't supposed to take a chance on coming *here*."

Strawhorn shrugged. "You weren't home. Figured we'd find you here. We rode mighty hard to get back here ahead of that posse, Durand. We took a lot of chances for that money. Weren't in much of a mood to wait for our share."

Durand sank down in a heavily padded

armchair and passed a hand over his face. "What about the other men?" he asked.

Strawhorn's features took on a grim cast. "Dead, all of em," he said bluntly. "There's nobody left but Benton and me."

"Dead?" echoed Durand. "But how —"

"That bastard Tyler," Strawhorn spat. "I set up an ambush for him, but he got out of it somehow. Not only that, but him and that posse killed all the boys I left behind. We watched the whole thing from a ridge about half a mile off, didn't we, Benton?"

"That marshal's a lucky son of a bitch," grated the other hardcase. "I don't reckon I want to go up against him again. I'm pullin' up stakes."

"You can't do that," Durand snapped. "We had an agreement."

"And it's a good thing for you that I'm an honorable man, Durand," Strawhorn said dryly. "Benton wanted to take all the money and light a shuck for the high lonesome, but I wouldn't let him. A deal's a deal, says I, and we had a deal, you and me and McKay. The two of you were to bring the money out here with the town and the railroad, and me and my boys'd help you steal all of it."

"Yes, yes, I know," Durand said impatiently. "Didn't I tip you off that that payroll was about to come in? It wasn't easy finding out exactly which train the money was going to be on, I can assure you. But my information was correct, wasn't it?"

Strawhorn inclined his head. "Can't argue with that."

Durand thumped a fist down on his leg. "What are we going to do now? With your gang destroyed —"

"I can get other men," Strawhorn cut in. "Benton here'll stay if there's enough good payoffs down the road, and there ought to be. I can find plenty of other boys who'll be downright eager to ride with us. This is going to be rich country, and we'll be the first ones to loot it proper like, Durand, just you and me and my boys now that McKay's gone. There's just one thing. . . ."

"And what might that be?" Durand asked coldly.

"We're going to have to have a bigger cut."

"It was agreed we would split three ways," Durand said without hesitation, "and with Andrew dead, his share goes to me." He shrugged his heavy shoulders. "It's not my fault those were the terms of the partnership agreement."

"Yeah, I'll bet you didn't have anything to do with settin' it up that way" — Strawhorn chuckled — "just like you didn't have anything to do with McKay gettin' hisself shot." He held up a hand as Durand flushed and opened his mouth to deny the accusation. "Don't waste your breath and my time. We split fifty-fifty from now on, or I'll just take all this payroll money and you'll never see me again, Durand."

"That . . . that's robbery!" sputtered Durand.

"Well, what the hell do you expect from a gent like me?" Strawhorn laughed, but there was nothing in the sound except menace. "You still come out ahead, Durand, because I'll take care of my boys out of my half. But it's an even split from now on or nothing."

Durand sighed, ran his hand wearily over his face once more, and then nodded. "All right. An even split. Just be careful slipping back out of town. We can't be connected in any way."

"Those Irish apes goin' to riot if they don't get paid?" Strawhorn asked idly.

"I don't think so. In the long run it won't really matter. The Union Pacific will bring in troops to put down any riot and see that the work resumes. The government wants this railroad built, no matter what the disturbances along the way."

Strawhorn nodded and turned toward the sofa. He picked up one of the pouches and opened it, ready to get started splitting up the stolen money.

A new voice suddenly came to Durand's ears as he sat in the chair. A high-pitched, childish voice that came from the direction of the doorway. Durand's head snapped around and his eyes widened slightly as he saw that in his surprise at finding Strawhorn and Benton in the suite, he had neglected to close the door completely. It was open a couple of inches, and it abruptly swung open even more as someone in the hall pushed on it.

Strawhorn whirled around, his gun appearing in his hand with a flicker of motion. Durand stared in horror at the young blond child standing in the doorway as the muzzle of Strawhorn's pistol lined up on her. A fraction more pressure on the trigger would blast a slug right into the child's startled face.

"No!" Durand cried in a choked voice.

Strawhorn held off on the trigger at the last possible instant, his face blanching as he realized that he had nearly gunned down a toddler. In the next instant a voice exclaimed in the hall, "Gretchen! There you are! Thank God, for a minute I didn't know where you had gotten off to."

Delia Hatfield stepped into view and

reached down to pick up her child. She glanced through the open doorway and went on, "I'm sorry if Gretchen bothered you folks —"

The words froze in her throat as her eyes took in the scene before her. There was William Durand, the town's leading businessman, sitting calmly in a chair while also in the room were the notorious Deke Strawhorn holding a pistol and another man who looked like a desperado, and there on the sofa were several pouches with UNION PACIFIC stenciled on them, one of which was open and had fallen over or been dropped, so that wads of money were spilling out of it. . . .

"Oh, my God," Delia whispered.

"Get them!" snapped Durand as he leaped to his feet.

Strawhorn was across the room in a flash, his free hand shooting through the open doorway to close over Delia's arm and jerk her roughly into the room. The man called Benton darted forward and grabbed Gretchen at the same time. Strawhorn holstered his gun and clapped his hand over Delia's mouth so that she couldn't scream. Benton did likewise with the child.

Durand cursed bitterly to himself. He did not know Delia Hatfield all that well and wasn't sure just how intelligent the woman was, but he had seen the realization dawning in her eyes. She had seen him together with Strawhorn, just as that damned Billy Casebolt had a few days earlier, and even worse, she had seen the stolen payroll.

Those facts had come together in Delia's mind like the pieces of a puzzle, and she hadn't been able to hide her surprise at the conclusions to which they led her, namely that Durand was involved in the payroll robbery right up to his eyebrows.

Of all the damned bad luck!

"I'm truly sorry about this, Mrs. Hatfield," Durand told her as he faced her. "I never intended for anyone to find out about the arrangement Mr. Strawhorn and I have, certainly not someone such as yourself." He sighed. "Now we'll have to do something about this, won't we?"

Delia's eyes were wide and terrified, and the little girl was sobbing and struggling in the grip of Benton, who had picked her up. Strawhorn still had his hand over Delia's mouth and his other arm locked tightly around her thick waist, pressing her up against him.

"You want us to get rid of 'em like we did that old man?" Strawhorn asked as Durand shut the door, firmly this time.

"I want you to handle this situation better than you did the one with Casebolt," Durand said. "Remember, you never found his body. You can't be certain that he's dead."

"Oh, he's cashed in his chips, all right," Strawhorn said confidently. "He was bleedin' like a stuck pig the last I saw of him." He grinned down at Delia. "But you won't have anything to worry about this time, Mr. Durand. Benton and me'll make sure of that."

Delia whimpered even more. All this casual talk of killing Billy Casebolt had to horrify her, and it was plain enough that her captors intended the same fate for her and her daughter. Again Durand felt the briefest flash of sympathy for them.

But then he thought about the money he had made so far, and the money he would make in the future, and suddenly the lives of a few innocent people didn't seem so important.

"Take your share of the money," he told Strawhorn, "and take the woman and the little girl. I'll trust you to take care of everything."

Strawhorn just grinned and leaned his head closer to Delia's. "Oh, yeah," he said. "We'll take care of everything, all right."

CHAPTER 14

Simone McKay lifted the tumbler of brandy and sipped from it, enjoying the smooth taste. She had always liked brandy, but she had not been able to indulge herself as much when Andrew was alive.

It was perfectly fine for gentlemen to adjourn to the library after dinner for brandy and cigars, but the women had to content themselves with sherry or perhaps port. Now Simone could drink whatever she wanted, whenever she wanted. She could even smoke a cigar if she wanted to.

She had to smile at the image of herself puffing away on a cheroot. It was ridiculous, of course.

Sighing, she carried the brandy over to an armchair and sat down. She had explained her move to the hotel by telling the servants that she didn't want to rattle around in the big house by herself, and there was some truth to that, of course. But nothing had really changed. She was alone here, too.

Alone . . . except for the brandy.

With a rueful smile, Simone shook her head and downed the rest of the drink. She stood up and replaced the tumbler on the sideboard.

It wouldn't do to sit here in solitude and get drunk. A man could do such a thing when the need hit him, but not a lady. Especially not a lady such as herself, who already had her hands full with all the changes that had come since her husband's death. She had to keep her wits about her at all times.

A faint noise caught her attention, and Simone turned toward the doorway with a frown. It had sounded like the cry of a baby or a young child, she thought, but as far as she knew, there were no infants in the hotel. And the only young child belonged to Delia Hatfield, Simone recalled. She had been surprised that Delia had taken little Gretchen and moved into the hotel, leaving Michael. To all appearances, the Hatfields' marriage was a happy one, and Simone couldn't help but wonder what had caused the rift between them. She wasn't going to interfere, though; the young couple's personal problems were none of her business, and besides, Michael was an employee of hers now that she owned the newspaper. It was never wise to mix in the private affairs of one's employees.

But still she was curious, and she went to the door and opened it, looking out to see if Gretchen Hatfield had slipped away from her mother and was wandering in the hallway.

A door closed sharply, all the way down at the other end of the corridor. Simone caught just a glimpse of it swinging shut. She frowned; that was the door to the suite used by William Durand, she recalled. There was no reason for a young child to be in that room, and Simone didn't know whether Durand himself was in the hotel tonight or not.

Curiosity deepened her frown. She had nothing to do tonight anyway — except drink, and she didn't want to do that — so she might as well see what was going on, she decided. After all, she had a right. This was *her* hotel now.

Quietly, she closed her own door after stepping out into the hall. The blue silk dressing gown she wore swished around her ankles as she walked down the corridor. Her slipper-clad feet made little or no noise. When she reached the door of Durand's suite, she raised a hand to knock, then paused as she faintly heard voices coming from inside. They were male voices, she decided. She must have been imagining that she had heard a child.

Leaning closer to the door, Simone put her ear against the panel. She felt more than a little ridiculous, eavesdropping like this, but she sensed somehow it might be important for her to know what Durand was up to. Durand and Andrew had been partners, but that was over. Simone viewed the man now as a rival, and quite a dangerous one at that. She held her breath and listened carefully.

She heard two, perhaps three, different voices coming from inside the room, but the door was too thick for her to make out the actual words the men were saying. From the tone of the exchange, though, the men were tense, even a little angry at times. Simone kept an eye on the corridor as she listened. It wouldn't do for one of the townspeople to see her here with her ear pressed against someone else's door. The story would get around quickly and make her appear foolish. Simone couldn't abide that.

But the hallway was deserted at the moment except for her, and she thought she would hear the footsteps if anyone started up the stairs from the lobby, even concentrating as she was on what was being said inside Durand's suite.

One of the voices — she thought it was Durand's — suddenly sounded louder as he approached the door. Simone drew back quickly, ready to move away down the hall. She certainly didn't want Durand to catch her snooping around. She backed off several steps and then turned, ready to go back to her own suite. Her curiosity wasn't really satisfied, but she couldn't risk any more eavesdropping.

That was when the woman screamed inside Durand's suite.

Dr. Judson Kent tried to hide the annoyance he was feeling. He knew full well, of course, that a doctor's calling was different from that of any other profession. He was expected to be on duty twenty-four hours a day, every day of the year. He had tended to patients at all hours of the day and night, delivered babies at every hour from midnight to high noon, worked for two and sometimes even three days with no sleep when he was serving as a field surgeon in the Crimea.

But now that he was growing older, he had hoped that this new settlement on the

American frontier would offer a somewhat more sedate existence, an opportunity to practice medicine during the day and relax at night.

It hadn't always worked out that way, needless to say. Tonight, for example, he had returned to his office after leaving William Durand at the hotel and found two young women waiting for him. He had realized right away that they were of the fallen variety, but his oath did not allow him to use his skills only on those who met with his moral approval. He smiled and said, "Good evening, ladies. What can I do for you?"

Their names, it developed, were Susie and Blaze — or so they claimed — and each of them had a medical complaint. Susie's was a simple case of the grippe, while Blaze had a minor infestation of a particularly nasty sort of vermin. Kent dealt with both of their problems as well as he could, giving Susie a bottle of tonic that would relieve at least some of her symptoms temporarily and prescribing a special soap and more frequent bathing for Blaze. That done, he faced the two young women across his desk and said, "Now, is there anything else I can do for you?"

Susie shook her head. "I don't think so, Doc. At least we ain't come down with the ailment plaguin' poor ol' Becky."

The two prostitutes looked at each other and giggled, and Blaze said, "Yeah, I hear the nine-month complaint is pretty bad."

Kent looked down at the desk and frowned. His late-evening patients might be women of the world, at least in their own minds, but they were also little more than girls. He doubted if either one of them was more than seventeen, and he felt uncomfortable with their giggling and smirking. "I'm sure I have no idea what you're talking about," he muttered.

"Oh, sure, you do, Doc," Susie said. "Becky told us she came to see you when she got sick."

"Oh?" Kent raised an eyebrow, interested in spite of himself. He hoped Becky Lewis hadn't been doing too much talking about her condition. He still had not decided how to approach Simone about the delicate matter of the Lewis girl's child, and he didn't want Becky ruining everything by spreading rumors about Andrew McKay. "What else might she have told you?"

"Well, she might've told us who the father was," Blaze said, "but she didn't. She can be a close-mouthed little bitch when she wants to."

Thank heavens for small favors, Kent

thought.

"I figure she told the fella about it, though," Susie took up the story. "She rents the crib next to mine, down the alley, you know —"

"No, I wouldn't know," Kent said, trying to maintain his dignity.

"Well, anyway, she has the place next to mine, and those walls ain't thick. A while back I heard her really lightin' into some poor gent, tellin' him how it was all his fault and how he had to do the right thing by her. Of course, I reckon he told her to go to hell, because I ain't noticed a ring on her finger lately and she's still entertainin' as many fellas as ever."

Kent's frown deepened as he thought about what he had just heard. He despised gossip, but in this case there might be something important to be gleaned from it. "You say Miss Lewis approached the gentleman who was most likely to, ah, be the father of her child?"

Both young women nodded. "That's right," Blaze said. "Susie told me about it. It was right after that she came to see you."

"Then she knew she was expecting *before* she came to see me?"

Susie snorted. "Well, hell, of course she knew. Gals in our line of work find out how to tell things like that mighty quick. Anyway, we all talked about it. It was Blaze and me who told her she ought to go see a doc 'fore she waited too long." An expression of genuine concern appeared on her face. "Tell us, Doc, is she goin' to be all right?"

"What? Oh, yes, physically she seems fine, quite sturdy. I'm sure she'll deliver a fine, healthy baby when the time comes."

Blaze said, "Well, that's good to know. Say, Doc, what's eatin' you? You look like you got a lot on your mind all of a sudden." She leaned forward, allowing the already drooping neckline of her dress to sag a little more. "If you got some worries, we can sure help you forget 'em. We're good at that sort o' thing, ain't we, Susie?"

Both girls giggled again.

"No, no, that's all," Kent replied abruptly, standing up to show them that their visit was concluded. When they had paid him — Susie commenting that it seemed strange giving money to a man, instead of the other way around — he ushered them out of the office and sent them on their way, not caring whether they were offended by his brusque refusal of Blaze's offer. He had a great deal to think about, and he didn't want to be distracted.

He sank slowly into his chair again, deep

lines creasing his forehead. If what Susie and Blaze had told him was true — and they'd had no reason to lie about it — then Becky Lewis had not only been aware that she was pregnant before coming to see him, she had even confronted the man she suspected was responsible for her condition. Only after he had refused to do the right thing by her had she come to Kent's office, pretending ignorance about the child growing inside her. Just as Kent had suspected, her attitude was a sham. She had merely been laying the groundwork for the claim that Andrew McKay was the father of her child.

Quite a convenient claim that was, Kent thought. McKay was dead and could no longer deny his involvement with Becky. She was a shrewd young woman and knew there was a good likelihood McKay's widow would pay to hush up even the slightest suspicion of anything that might blacken her beloved husband's memory. The real father of Becky's child was undoubtedly some railroad worker or cowhand, and she had made up the whole thing about McKay.

But, Kent suddenly thought, what if she hadn't made it up? What if Andrew McKay really was the baby's father? That made things entirely different.

283

Entirely different, indeed . . .

Delia Hatfield didn't think about what she was doing. As Strawhorn leaned against her, his breath hot in her ear, she let her instincts take over and sank her teeth as hard as she could into the palm of the hand he had pressed over her mouth.

He yelped in pain and jerked his hand away. Her teeth came loose with a tearing of flesh and her mouth was suddenly filled with the hot, brassy taste of blood. Strawhorn's other hand suddenly slammed into the back of her head and knocked her forward. "You bitch!" the gunman gasped.

Delia spat blood out of her mouth, pulled in a deep breath, and screamed as loud as she could.

Durand lunged at her, exclaiming, "Stop her! Shut her up!" He grabbed her shoulder and jerked her toward him.

The hardcase called Benton had his arms full with Gretchen, whose struggles grew even more frantic as the little girl saw her mother in trouble. Strawhorn shook his injured hand back and forth, slinging drops of blood onto the rug. His lips drew back in a snarl as he reached for Delia and got his hands around her neck.

"I'll take care of her," he growled.

"Lemme have her, Durand!"

Suddenly the door to the corridor was thrust open, and Simone McKay stood there in a silk dressing gown that was belted tightly around her slender waist. Her lovely face was full of anger. "Let go of her!" she shouted at Strawhorn.

"Simone!" Durand cried as the woman surged into the room like some sort of avenging angel. His bearded features were etched with stark dismay. Obviously, everything around him was suddenly going wrong.

Delia didn't have time to notice any of that. She was too busy striking out at Strawhorn with her fists and trying futilely to drag some air into her lungs past his brutal grip on her throat.

One of Gretchen's flailing legs connected by accident with Benton's groin. The outlaw groaned and doubled over, losing his grip on the child. As she started to slip away he snagged her arm and flung her savagely backward. She landed on the soft cushions of the sofa, but the impact was still enough to make her lie there, stunned.

That left Benton free to get between Durand and Simone McKay, who was advancing on the businessman with her fingers hooked into claws, the long fingernails threatening to gouge out Durand's eyes if they found their targets. Benton grabbed her around the waist and swung her away from Durand. She turned her fury on the hardcase instead, slapping his hat off with one of her wild blows.

Benton growled and let go with one arm so he could bring up a tightly clenched fist. The blow smacked into Simone's jaw and jolted her head back. Her eyes rolled up and she sagged against Benton, out cold.

Strawhorn had Delia down on the floor by now, with a knee driven against the unborn baby and into her midsection while he choked her. He had intended to have a little fun with the pregnant young woman once he got her out of Wind River, before killing her. But his rage was too strong to be blunted by lust now. His hand throbbed with pain where she had bitten him, and he was going to return that pain a hundredfold and enjoy choking the life out of her.

Durand grabbed him by the shoulder and shook him urgently. "Not here, man!" Durand said. "For God's sake, don't kill her *here*!"

Strawhorn tried to shrug off Durand's grip, but after lowering Simone's unconscious body to the floor, Benton took hold of him from the other side. "Take it easy,

Deke!" the outlaw warned. "Let's get 'em out of here and then take care of 'em!"

"Damn it, let go of her!" Durand ordered.

Their words finally got through to Strawhorn's fevered brain. He took a deep, ragged breath and pried his fingers loose from Delia's neck. Her head fell back against the floor with a thump and rolled limply to one side. Her neck was already showing bruises from Strawhorn's fingers, and one side of it was smeared with blood from the palm of the hardcase's hand.

For a harrowing moment Durand thought she was already dead, but then he saw her chest rising and falling and heard the harsh sound of air making its way down her tortured windpipe.

Strawhorn came to his feet and staggered back a step, glaring down at Delia's senseless form. "Damn bitch," he muttered as he looked at his wounded hand.

"We've got to move quickly," Durand said. He was breathing heavily, and sweat stood out on his face. "Take the sheets off the bed and wrap them up, then take them down the back stairs. You have to get them out of town as quickly as possible before they cause more trouble. Once you're safely away, kill them and dispose of the bodies."

"All three of them?" Strawhorn asked.

"Of course," Durand panted.

"Even Mrs. McKay?"

"Especially Mrs. McKay." Durand wiped some of the sweat off his forehead and went on, "I've never trusted her, and I think the feeling is mutual. Now that she's seen the two of us together, she'll be nothing but a threat as long as she's alive. I don't know if she had time to notice the payroll money or not, but at this point it doesn't really matter, does it?"

"I reckon not," Strawhorn said. He went over to the bed and tossed aside the expensive comforter, exposing the fine silk sheets underneath. He took out his knife and cut a strip off one of the sheets, then bound it tightly around his hand with Benton's help. Dryly, Strawhorn said, "Mighty fancy bandage, but I reckon that's all right. After all, we're all goin' to be rich men."

"Only if you get rid of these damned females," said Durand.

Strawhorn nodded, his face grim now. "Consider 'em dead," he said.

Just outside the western edge of Wind River, a group of about a dozen riders reined in. Only one of them rode a horse with a saddle and shod hooves. The others rode only with woven blankets thrown over the backs of their mounts. Each man wore buckskins and had eagle feathers adorning his long, dark hair. A couple of them carried rifles, but the others were armed only with bows, arrows, and knives.

"Thanks, Two Ponies," Billy Casebolt said as he turned and nodded solemnly to the leader of the Shoshones who had saved his life. "I don't reckon I'd be here if it wasn't for you and your people."

"You must go home, rest now, Billy," Two Ponies replied. He gestured at Casebolt's midsection, which was still tightly bandaged underneath the soft buckskin shirt the tribe's women had given him to replace the torn and bloody one he had been wearing when he was found. "Lose much blood, take many suns to be strong again. Should have stayed longer with Shoshone. Billy has many good stories."

"Glad somebody thinks so," Casebolt muttered, then went on, "Your offer was mighty temptin', Two Ponies, but I got things I got to do. I sure appreciate you bringin' me all the way here to town. Some folks might get a little spooked if they was to see you and your boys this close to the settlement."

"The Shoshone have promised peace. We have made a treaty with your chiefs in

289

Washington City saying so. The whites have no reason to fear the Shoshone."

"I can sure testify to that," Casebolt said. "If it wasn't for you gents findin' me out there on the prairie and takin' me back to your village, I'd've died for sure. Tell your wives and daughters I ain't never seen any better nurses."

"Come back and tell them yourself someday, Billy Casebolt," Two Ponies told him with a smile. "Farewell." He turned his horse and heeled it into an easy lope that carried it away into the darkness. The other warriors followed.

Casebolt waited until the Shoshones had disappeared, then put his horse into a walk along Grenville Avenue. Music and laughter came from the saloons he passed, but Casebolt didn't slow down. His side was aching where Strawhorn's bullet had struck him, tearing through flesh and glancing off a rib.

After Two Ponies and the other men had taken him back to the Shoshone village, the women had cleaned the wound, packed it with a poultice made of mud and moss and herbs, and bandaged it. Casebolt had been too stiff and sore to move for the first couple of days, and he suspected he had been running a fever, too, because he didn't remember much of that time. But then he had started growing stronger, and this afternoon he had persuaded Two Ponies to bring him back here to Wind River.

As he had told them, the Shoshones had saved his life, and Casebolt would always be grateful to them. But as much as he would have enjoyed taking advantage of their hospitality for a while longer, there was something he had to do.

He had to find Cole Tyler and tell the marshal about how he had seen Strawhorn and Durand plotting together, up to no good sure as shooting.

The office in the front room of the land development company was dark, though, and the building was locked, Casebolt discovered when he dismounted stiffly and went up onto the boardwalk. Could be Cole was making his rounds, Billy thought with a frown. He looked up and down the street. The saloons were just about the only places still open at this time of night, and he didn't see the familiar figure of the marshal going into or coming out of any of them. That meant he was going to have to check each one, he supposed.

Casebolt spotted a light on in Dr. Kent's office and decided to stop in there first. The doctor might happen to know where Cole was, and he could also take a look at the wound and see if it was healing as well as Billy hoped it was. Leaving his horse tied at the rack in front of the marshal's office, he started down the street to Dr. Kent's place.

The front door was unlocked, and as Casebolt came in Kent glanced up first in annoyance and then shocked surprise. "Good Lord, Deputy!" the doctor exclaimed. "Where have you been? What's happened to you?"

"Well, that's quite a yarn, Doc," Casebolt said with a tired grin. "I'd be glad to tell it to you, but right now I got to find Marshal Tyler. You know where he is?"

"He and the posse are still out chasing those train robbers, I daresay."

"Train robbers!"

Kent nodded. "A Union Pacific special train was stopped and held up east of town a few days ago. It was carrying the payroll for the work crews. Marshal Tyler led a posse after the bandits, and we haven't seen any of them since then." The physician looked shrewdly at Casebolt. "Are you injured, Deputy?"

"No time for that now," Casebolt muttered with a curt gesture. He swung toward the door. "I got to find out about this." As he reached the entrance he staggered a little and might have fallen if he hadn't reached out to grab the side of the door.

Kent hurried around the desk and went to his side. "Come over here and sit down immediately," he said in a brisk tone that didn't allow for any arguments. "You're hurt, and you're not going to do anyone any good by falling on your face."

"Just a mite weak still," Casebolt protested as Kent steered him over to a chair. "Took a bullet in the side from Deke Strawhorn the other day. Don't worry, though, it went on through. Just lost a little blood and got bunged up a mite."

"Strawhorn?" repeated Kent. "He seems to have dropped out of sight again, and I for one am quite thankful, since the town is already full of angry railroad workers who're wondering if they're ever going to get paid again."

"Strawhorn's been gone, huh?" Casebolt mused as Kent lifted the buckskin shirt and began examining the bandages around the deputy's midsection. "Ever since right before that train robbery, I'd reckon."

Kent glanced up sharply. "Now that you mention it, I believe you're correct. Do you think Strawhorn might be responsible for that holdup?"

"Durand said something about a schedule when he was talkin' to Strawhorn. Could've been a train schedule. Could've been the one that payroll was supposed to be on."

"What did you say?" Kent demanded incredulously. "Durand was talking to Strawhorn? William Durand?"

"They rode about ten miles southwest of here to have their meetin'," Casebolt told the doctor. "Reckon they must've had a good reason for bein' so careful — like they were plannin' to hold up that UP train and take the payroll. And they were sure spooked when they found out I saw 'em. So spooked Strawhorn started shootin' and come after me. Damn near got me, too."

"My God," muttered Kent. "Durand and Strawhorn working together . . . It makes sense of a sort. I wish Cole Tyler was here."

Casebolt tugged his shirt back down. "If you'll leave off pokin' me, I'll tend to it myself. Where's Durand?"

"I left him at the hotel. I believe he's using his suite there for the time being."

Casebolt stood up, his weathered features set in grim lines. "I'll just go pay a visit to Mr. Durand and see what he's got to say for himself."

"I'm coming with you," Kent declared as he reached for his coat. "You really should be in bed resting, but after what you've gone through, I doubt you'll agree to that until this matter is settled."

"Damn right," Casebolt said. "Durand's got some mighty tall explainin' to do."

CHAPTER 15

Durand acted as the lookout, despite the fact that he found the whole concept somewhat demeaning. He was a powerful man, after all, the lord and master of Wind River.

But if he wanted to stay that way, he knew he had to make sure that Strawhorn and Benton got the three unfortunate witnesses out of town.

Everything started out as smoothly as Durand could have hoped. The hotel corridors were deserted, and as he motioned urgently to Strawhorn and Benton, the two hardcases hurried out of the suite with the sheet-wrapped bundles. Strawhorn had Delia Hatfield draped over his left shoulder and was carrying Gretchen in his right arm. Over Strawhorn's right shoulder were a set of saddlebags containing half of the stolen payroll money. Benton followed, grunting under the burden of Simone McKay. Durand shut the door of the suite behind them, then hurried ahead to go down the rear stairs first.

His confidence grew as he saw that there was no one on the stairs or in the alley behind the hotel. Strawhorn and Benton's horses were there, along with a couple of other mounts Benton had stolen a few minutes earlier. He had slipped out of the hotel and untied a couple of horses from the hitch rack in front of one of the saloons, leading them back here to the alley so that Delia and Simone could be draped over their saddles.

Durand looked up and down the alley, then motioned for the two outlaws to come ahead with their prisoners. Strawhorn and Benton hurried into the narrow, shadowy lane. As they were arranging the bundles on the horses and tying them in place, Durand tugged a handkerchief from his breast pocket and mopped some of the sweat off his face. "Get out of town as quickly as you can without drawing attention to yourself," he told Strawhorn. "Lie low for a while, and I'll get in touch with you when the time is right for you to pull another job."

"Just make sure it ain't too long," Strawhorn said. "This loot won't last forever."

"I'll be in touch, I assure you —" Durand

began as he turned back toward the rear door of the hotel.

That was when he saw a sight that froze his blood and would haunt him for the rest of his life. Billy Casebolt stood there, a grim, determined expression on his face and a gun in his hand. "Don't move, Durand!" the deputy called out. "Strawhorn, you and that other fella, elevate — now!"

Durand stared, eyes wide with horror. He saw Judson Kent standing behind Casebolt, angry realization on his bearded face. Kent might not have believed what was going on in this alley if he hadn't seen it with his own eyes, but now it was too late, Durand thought. Here he was with a pair of outlaws, a couple of unconscious women, and a child, the latter three on their way to be killed on his orders. Too many witnesses, too much guilt . . . It was all over, he thought, all over.

"I thought I killed you, old man," Strawhorn said, his voice cool and mocking.

"Wasn't for lack of tryin', you son of a bitch. Step out from behind them horses and drop your guns, the both of you. What's that you got there in them bundles?"

Simone McKay picked that moment to regain consciousness and start squirming and trying to shout through the gag in her mouth. Or perhaps she had already come to and had been waiting for the proper moment. At any rate, Judson Kent exclaimed, "Good Lord! There's someone wrapped up in there!" He started past Casebolt, heading toward the horses.

"Damn it, Doc, stay back!" Casebolt ordered, but it was too late. Strawhorn stepped into the clear, his hand sweeping down to his pistol. The Colt flashed out of its holster and geysered flame from its barrel.

Casebolt ducked to the side as the outlaw's slug sang past him and thudded into the wall of the hotel. He lifted his gun but hesitated, obviously afraid of hitting one of the prisoners if he fired. Strawhorn and Benton didn't have to worry about that. Both owlhoots slammed shots at the deputy as Casebolt threw himself backward through the rear entrance of the hotel.

Kent had flung himself on the ground when the shooting started. He looked up to see Strawhorn and Benton swinging into their saddles. Durand was moving around agitatedly, taking a step one way and then the other, clearly at a loss as to what to do. Strawhorn looked at him and shouted, "Get on that horse if you want to come with us, Durand!" He motioned with his gun hand to the mount carrying Delia Hatfield.

Strawhorn was right, Durand knew. His burgeoning empire had collapsed around him in a matter of moments. His only chance now was to get out of Wind River and start over somewhere else.

It wouldn't be the first time, he thought fleetingly.

Grabbing the bundle containing Delia Hatfield, Durand started to sling her off the horse, but Strawhorn yelled, "Put her in front of you! We'll need the women if anybody comes after us!"

Durand understood. Delia and Simone would make excellent hostages. But there was no need for the child to be endangered, now that it was too late to preserve any secrets. "Let the little girl go," Durand ordered as he shifted Delia and climbed up behind her.

For a second Strawhorn looked like he wanted to argue, but then he nodded and let the bundle containing Gretchen tumble to the ground. Durand hoped she was all right.

Then it was too late to worry about such things, because Strawhorn and Benton were spurring their horses into a gallop and throwing a few final shots at Casebolt as they fled the alley.

Casebolt returned the fire, but his bullets went wide. Durand smacked his heels against the flanks of his own mount and felt the horse leap into motion. He hung on for dear life, one hand clinging to the saddlehorn while the other grasped the reins.

He hoped Delia Hatfield wasn't bounced off by the rough ride and tried to hold her in place with his legs. Awkwardly, he galloped after the two outlaws. Only there were *three* outlaws now, he thought, because he was every bit as much a fugitive as Strawhorn and Benton. William Durand, businessman, financier, entrepreneur, was hitting the owlhoot trail.

Judson Kent picked himself up from the dust of the alley and hurried over to Casebolt. "Are you all right, Deputy?" he asked anxiously.

Casebolt was wincing as he came out into the alley. "Jumpin' around like that wasn't much good for that wound in my side, I reckon," he said. "But I'm good enough to go after those low-down skunks!" He waved the pistol he had borrowed from the desk clerk in the hotel, then suddenly sagged forward. Kent grabbed him and held him up.

"There's blood on your shirt," Kent said.

"You've torn the wound open again and you're bleeding badly. I'll get you back to my office —"

"The hell you will! I got to go after Durand and Strawhorn. They had some folks hog-tied in them bundles."

"I know," Kent said. "I saw and heard them, too, and they left one of them behind. You're on the verge of collapse, Deputy, and if we don't get that bleeding stopped, the situation could become serious."

"Dad-blast it! The marshal's dependin' on me —" Casebolt's protest came to an abrupt end as his eyes rolled up in his head and he sagged even more in Kent's grip. He was only semiconscious as the doctor dragged him back into the hotel, shouting for help.

Curious townspeople were already hurrying toward the spot, drawn by the gunfire, and Kent quickly had enough volunteers to carry Casebolt back to his office.

Some of the saloon women took charge of Gretchen Hatfield, who was sobbing as she was unwrapped from the tangle of sheets. One of the soiled doves picked her up and cuddled her, calming her and displaying an unexpected maternal instinct. Kent told her to bring the girl along to his office. As they went down the street Kent told the townspeople about the probable arrangement between Durand and Strawhorn to steal the railroad payroll. Howls of outrage went up from the listeners.

"We're goin' after 'em!" one man shouted. "We'll string up them thievin' bastards!" There were angry yells of agreement from the other men as, in the distance, lightning flickered and thunder rumbled faintly. A storm was rolling down from the mountains, Kent realized.

He was far from an experienced Westerner, but it only made sense that a storm would wipe out any tracks the fugitives left. And he doubted that any of the townspeople had the skills necessary to track someone at night. If the posse waited until morning to leave, chances were the trail would be gone, destroyed by the storm.

Kent wished he knew where in blazes Cole Tyler was at this moment.

William Durand watched the lightning as he and his companions rode northwest, leaving Wind River far behind them in the night. It was quite appropriate, he thought, that on the same night he lost everything he had worked so hard to establish, he would also be soaked by a rainstorm.

So far, though, the rain had held off.

There was a light breeze from the south, a hot, dry wind. Maybe the distant storm wouldn't break, Durand thought. At this point, he would be thankful for any small favor.

Almost an hour had passed since he had left Wind River with Strawhorn, Benton, and the two women. Simone and Delia were both conscious now, and although their hands were tied in front of them, the sheets that had been wrapped around them and the gags in their mouths had been discarded when Strawhorn first called a halt to rest the horses. The women were riding astride now, in front of Strawhorn and Benton. Strawhorn was leading the extra horse.

"Reckon we'll get rained on?" Strawhorn asked Simone. He had put her in front of him and kept an arm looped around her waist as they rode.

"I don't care about the rain," she replied. "But it would be all right with me if God would strike you dead with a lightning bolt."

Strawhorn chuckled. "You'd fry, too, lady, because I don't intend to let you get very far from me tonight. But hell, you're lucky. If things hadn't got all tangled up back there in town, you'd be dead by now. Durand wanted you shut up. Now you're worth more to us alive. No posse's goin' to get too close to us as long as we got you ladies."

"Are you sure my baby was all right?" Delia asked wretchedly. She had asked the same question several times already.

Durand moved his horse up alongside Benton's and said to the worried young mother, "I assure you, madam, your child was not injured. The townspeople will have found her by now and be taking care of her. I'm sure you'll be back together with her soon."

Delia gave him a despairing look. "You're lying," she said dully. "You're going to kill us. I know you are."

Durand wanted to promise her otherwise, but he couldn't. There was no way of knowing what was going to happen. He hoped that Delia and her unborn child would survive this ordeal, but he cared less about Simone.

She obviously shared that feeling. She looked over at him with hate in her eyes and said, "I'm not surprised you're mixed up with these outlaws, Durand. I never trusted you."

"Oh?" he said. "You trusted your husband, didn't you?"

"Of course!"

"Well," Durand said smoothly, "Andrew was just as much a part of the arrangement with Strawhorn here as I was. He was a thief just like me."

"That's a lie!" Simone said.

Strawhorn moved his hand up her body and let his thumb caress the bottom of her breast. "Nope, Durand's tellin' you the truth, lady. Your husband was in it as deep as any of us. He just had the bad luck to get in front of a bullet."

Simone shuddered and fell silent, gritting her teeth to hold back screams of outrage as Strawhorn continued caressing her.

Durand frowned blackly, thinking about the money that had been left behind in Wind River. Perhaps Strawhorn would split the part of the payroll they had been able to salvage, but even that wouldn't be enough for a proper stake to start over. Durand needed more money. . . .

And he suddenly thought he might know where to get it.

"Where are we?" he asked.

Strawhorn shrugged. "Maybe eight miles northwest of town. I figured we'd push on for a few hours, then hole up for the night somewhere up in the foothills. If that storm comes on in, it'll wash out our tracks and those bastards'll never be able to trail us."

"What about Marshal Tyler?" asked Durand. "He has something of a reputation as a scout and a frontiersman."

Strawhorn snorted contemptuously. "I ain't worried about Tyler. He can chase us from here to kingdom come and not find us."

"I hope you're correct. Do you know where the Diamond S ranch is?"

"The spread started by that Texan?" Strawhorn frowned. "Not exactly. What's that got to do with us?"

"I've done some business with Mr. Sawyer," Durand said. "He and I formed a limited partnership so that he could establish his ranch on some land I had bought from the railroad, and I happen to know that he brought quite a bit of money with him from Texas along with those ludicrous-looking cattle. The funds were for expenses encountered in setting up his new ranch. I imagine he still has most of the money."

Strawhorn looked over at Durand and grinned. Clouds hadn't covered all the sky yet, and there was still enough moonlight to shine on his teeth as he asked, "And you figure to pay this fella Sawyer a visit 'fore we move on?"

"I think we can put those funds to better use than he can, don't you?"

"Damn right. Can you find the place in the dark?"

"Perhaps. If we get close enough, we should be able to see their lights. . . ."

They rode on, Durand hoping now that the storm would move down out of the mountains so that it would cover their tracks — but not until they had reached the Diamond S and left with the money Kermit Sawyer had brought from Texas.

The lightning grew more intense but didn't seem to be moving any closer. Against the frequent glow in the sky from the electrical discharges, Durand spotted the ranges of hills with the bluff in between at the head of the valley where Sawyer's ranch was located. Strawhorn found the trail leading up to the top of the bluff, and just as Durand had thought, when they crested the rise, they were able to see the yellow glow from the windows of Sawyer's cabins.

"We can't ride in there with the women," Strawhorn said when they were only half a mile or so from the ranch headquarters. "They'd give us away in a second." He reined in. "Miz McKay, you're going to get on that spare horse. Benton, take the women and circle around the ranch. We'll meet up with you at the other end of the valley."

"What if the lady tries to run off?" Benton asked.

"Shoot her," Strawhorn said simply. "I'd

rather have two hostages than one, but I reckon we can make do with Miz Hatfield if we have to."

Simone shuddered and kept her eyes downcast. "I won't give you any trouble," she said quietly. She slid down from Strawhorn's horse and moved over to the one he had been leading.

Durand frowned. It wasn't like Simone to be so passive and accommodating. She might be up to something, he decided. Or it might be that everything she had gone through tonight had finally gotten to her, crushing that stubborn, independent nature of hers. After all, until recently she had always had Andrew to protect her and shield her from some of the harsh realities of life. Tonight she had learned that even the man she had loved had been a stranger to her.

When Simone was mounted, Benton took the reins of her horse and moved off into the darkness. Durand watched them go and asked quietly, "Can we trust that man?"

Strawhorn patted the saddlebags where the payroll money was cached. "As long as we got these, we can trust Benton," he said confidently. "He'll meet us at the other end of the valley, just like I told him to."

Durand and Strawhorn rode toward the Diamond S headquarters, the lights gradually drawing closer. It took them a quarter of an hour to reach the cabins and corrals. Durand was no cattleman, but even in the dark, the ranch was taking on the look of a successful operation. It was a shame he wouldn't have the chance to take it over as he had planned, he thought.

A dog was barking as Durand and Strawhorn rode up, and several men came out of the cabins to see what was going on. In the light that spilled through the open doors, Durand recognized one of them as Kermit Sawyer. The old rancher was carrying a rifle, and he called, "Who's out there? Better sing out before I start shootin'!"

"It's William Durand, Mr. Sawyer," Durand replied hurriedly as he rode his horse into the light. "And this is my friend Mr. Strawhorn."

"Durand?" Sawyer sounded surprised. "What are you doin' out here in the middle of the night, and with a storm comin' up at that?"

"Business brings me out here, sir," Durand said smoothly. "I was wondering if we might have a talk with you — in private."

Sawyer lowered the rifle. "I reckon that'd be all right," he said grudgingly. "Light and set a spell. There's a jug inside, if you'd like a drink."

"That would be an excellent idea," Durand said as he dismounted. He had been counting on Sawyer's ingrained notions of western hospitality to get them into the cabin.

"You boys go on back to the bunkhouse," Sawyer told the hands. "It'll be time to turn in soon."

The cowboys said their good nights and did as Sawyer had instructed them. The cattleman tucked the rifle under his arm and jerked his head toward the door of the nearest cabin, indicating that Durand and Strawhorn were to follow him.

The place wasn't fancy, Durand saw as they stepped inside, but it appeared to be comfortable. There was a single room inside the building, with a rug on the floor, some rough-hewn chairs, and a fireplace dominating the front half. In the back was a bunk and a small carved wooden chest. Pegs had been driven into the wall so that clothes and guns could be hung on them. Sawyer put the rifle on a couple of the pegs and then turned back to his visitors. "What can I do for you gents?" he asked.

Then his eyes widened as he saw the gun that had appeared in Strawhorn's hand. "You can give us all the money you got here," the outlaw told him harshly.

"What the hell are you talking about?" demanded Sawyer.

"I'm sorry, sir, but we must ask you to cooperate with us," Durand said quietly. "Mr. Strawhorn and I need money, and I happen to know that you brought a considerable amount with you from Texas. You haven't deposited it in the bank, so I assume you still have it here with you."

"You're crazy, both of you. I don't have any money, and if I did, I wouldn't just hand it over."

Durand listened to Sawyer's angry words, but he also watched the rancher's eyes and saw them shift for a second toward the fireplace. "Please don't lie to us," Durand said. "We don't want to hurt you."

"You can't do a damned thing to me. This is my spread, and if I yell, I'll have forty cowboys in here in no time. Same thing'll happen if you shoot off that gun." Sawyer sneered at them. "I don't know what's goin' on, Durand, but you and this other fella better get off my land pronto."

"It's *my* land," Durand reminded him.

"I don't reckon it'll stay that way much longer. You're on the run for some reason, or you wouldn't have come here lookin' for money." Sawyer grinned. "I've got papers on this ranch and I'd say I'll be takin' over this land 'fore you know it."

Anger churned Durand's insides at the reminder of how his plans had fallen through. He growled, "There can't be that many hiding places in this cabin. Cover him, Deke, while I look around." He turned toward the fireplace.

Sawyer exclaimed, "You son of a bitch!" and leaped forward, unable to control his rage any longer. Strawhorn met him, lashing out with the gun in his hand. The barrel thudded against Sawyer's skull and sent him tumbling to the puncheon floor. Blood leaked from the gash opened up by the gun barrel and ran into the rancher's thick white hair.

"Blast it," Strawhorn grated as he kept the gun trained on the unconscious Sawyer. "What do we do if you can't find that money?"

"I can find it," Durand replied as he went to the fireplace and began testing the large flat stones of which it was built. It took him less than two minutes to find one that was loose, and when he moved it aside, he reached into the cavity that was revealed and took out a good-sized leather pouch. He opened it and saw the wads of greenbacks inside. "This is what we were looking for."

"Damned lucky, if you ask me. Do I kill this old bastard?"

Durand nodded. "But quietly. Use your knife."

Strawhorn holstered his gun and reached for the blade sheathed on his other hip, but before he could draw it and plunge it into Sawyer's body, the clinking of spurs came from outside the door. "Mr. Sawyer," a voice called. "Hate to bother you, boss, but them cattle're gettin' mighty nervous 'cause of all that thunder and lightnin'. What should we do?"

Durand motioned for Strawhorn to put the knife away, then he opened the door and said, "Come in, young man. Mr. Sawyer wants to see you."

The cowboy stepped into the room, holding his hat in his hands. He stopped short when he saw the rancher's senseless form stretched out on the floor with blood on his head. But before he could do anything except gape, Durand had swept up one of the chairs and brought it crashing down on top of his head. The young puncher collapsed as Durand dropped the wreckage of the chair.

"That almost felt good," Durand said with a savage grin. "It's been too long since I did something like that." His expression became more serious. "We've wasted enough time. Let's get out of here."

"I can kill 'em both," Strawhorn offered, reaching for his knife again.

Durand shook his head. "There's no need. I've thought of a way we can keep everyone busy for a long time." Carrying the pouch he had taken from the fireplace, he led the way out of the cabin, leaving the two unconscious men behind him.

Most of the herd Sawyer had brought up with him from Texas had already been pushed out into the valley to run loose and fatten up on the good grass, but several hundred head were still confined in the corrals for one reason or another. Their long horns made clacking sounds as they hit against one another while the cattle stirred restlessly.

As the cowboy had said, they were nervous because of the impending storm. Durand nodded in satisfaction as he looked toward the corrals. He mounted up and motioned for Strawhorn to do likewise. No one seemed to be paying any attention to them.

"Come on," Durand said quietly, then led the way past the corrals. When he was just beyond them, he reined in and turned his horse. As Durand pulled a small pistol from his pocket, Strawhorn laughed softly.

"Damn good idea," the outlaw said. "That'll keep 'em busy for a while." He drew his own gun.

Then both men let out whoops and started firing over the heads of the startled cattle.

The animals bawled frantically and surged against the pole sides of the corrals. The pens had been built securely, but with hundreds of maddened cattle pressing against them all at once, something had to give. The poles began snapping with loud cracks, the noise making the cattle even more frenzied. As the walls of the corrals collapsed the herd surged out and thundered around the cabins in a deadly wave of cow flesh.

Durand and Strawhorn whirled their horses and galloped in the opposite direction as the small stampede poured out of the corrals. A glance back told them that the Diamond S cowboys who had come running out to see what was going on were ducking back into the buildings as quickly as they could. The cabins themselves might collapse under the onslaught; Durand hoped so. Either way, the cowboys would be much too busy to even think about giving chase. By the time anyone could come after them, they would be miles away.

Earlier tonight everything had gone

wrong, but now his luck was turning, Durand sensed. It was only a matter of time until he was as rich as ever. He gave a great booming laugh as he rode, full of godlike power. He might suffer a minor setback or two along the way, but there was no one who could stop him from achieving his destiny. No one.

CHAPTER 16

Cole was tired, bone-tired, as he led the posse back into Wind River with lightning flickering in the distance. The last four days had been frustrating and exhausting and at times dangerous, not to mention unproductive. He was looking forward to sprawling in his bed in the room at Lawton Paine's boardinghouse and not moving for the next eight or ten hours.

But before he could do that, there was an unpleasant chore to take care of. He had to tell the Union Pacific supervisors that the payroll for their crews was gone.

After burying the outlaws who had been killed, the posse had spent the better part of a day trailing the two men who had gotten away with the money. The tracks had finally petered out in a particularly rocky stretch, and search as they might, the men from Wind River had not been able to find them again. Finally, Cole had admitted defeat, as galling as that was for him, and turned back toward town before camping for the night. It had taken them all the next day and part of tonight to get here.

The weather matched his mood, Cole thought as he reined up in front of the marshal's office — dark and threatening. He hipped around in the saddle to face his worn-out companions and said, "I want to thank all of you for sticking with me. I know it was a hard trail, and we didn't get what we went after. But you men gave it your best shot."

"That's not good enough," Michael Hatfield said miserably. "The payroll's gone, and God knows what's going to happen now."

"Amen, Brother Hatfield," rumbled Jeremiah. "God *does* know, and it's not for us to question His judgment."

"Maybe not," Cole said, "but I'd sure like to have more to show for our trouble than what we got. Six dead owlhoots won't save this town."

Hank Parker said, "At least nobody in the posse was killed. That's something to be thankful for."

Cole stared at him. He wasn't used to Parker expressing such sentiments. But what the one-armed saloonkeeper said was true.

They had been damned lucky. There were a few minor wounds among the men, mostly bullet burns from that ambush, and one horse had been killed, forcing a couple of the men to ride double. That was the extent of their casualties. It could have been worse, Cole thought, a lot worse.

"You men can head on home and get some rest," he told them. "Like I said, I'm mighty grateful to you —"

He broke off his thanks as a large group of men came out of one of the saloons down the street. Somebody spotted him and yelled, "There's the marshal! The posse's back!" The men hurried down the street, almost running.

Most of them were railroad workers, Cole figured, anxious to find out if their missing payroll had been returned. He hoped they wouldn't riot and pull the town down around their ears when they found out the money was still gone. If they tried, he would do everything in his power to stop them, but he had seen in the past how futile it usually was for one man to try to stand up to a mob.

"Marshal!" one of the men called excitedly as he ran up to the golden sorrel. Cole recognized him as the track layer called Dooley. "The doc said we was to send ye down to his office if any of us seen ye!"

"Dr. Kent?" Cole asked with a frown. "What does he want with me?" It seemed to him that the work crews were in a little better mood than when he had left, and he had no idea why that would be the case.

"Aye," Dooley said. "He's got yer dep'ty down there, patchin' him up again."

"Billy!" Cole burst out, forgetting about his tiredness. "Billy Casebolt's back?"

"Oh, aye, a lot's happened since ye've been gone, Cole, me boy. We got part of our wages back. Found half o' the lake from that robbery in Durand's hotel room, we did."

Michael yelped, "Mr. Durand? What's he got to do with that payroll money?"

Cole threw his right leg over the saddle and slid down. "Michael, you come with me," he barked. "The rest of you men go home and get some rest. I don't know what's going on here, but I'll tend to it."

He didn't get any arguments from most of the men, although some of them were muttering with curiosity. If they wanted to stay and talk to Dooley and the other railroad workers, that was their business. Cole wanted to get down to Dr. Kent's office and find out what the hell had happened in Wind River while he and the other men were gone.

Michael hurried to catch up to him and match his long strides. The young editor was agitated as he said, "That man made it sound like Mr. Durand had something to do with the train robbery. Otherwise how would he have wound up with part of the money?"

"That's a good question," Cole said. "Maybe Billy and Dr. Kent can give us some answers."

All the lights seemed to be on at the doctor's place and the front room was crowded when Cole and Michael pushed their way into it a few moments later. A childish voice shouted, "Daddy!" Gretchen Hatfield ran across the room, holding up her arms to her father.

Instinctively, Michael bent over and scooped her up, hugging her tightly as he frowned. "Gretchen?" he said. "What are you doing here? Where's your mama?"

"Bad men took her!" Gretchen wailed, and Cole felt himself go cold at the child's words.

He glanced around, saw that the room was filled with townspeople, gamblers, and soiled doves. He spotted Rose Foster and Lawton and Abigail Paine. Across the room Billy Casebolt was sitting up on Kent's examining table while the doctor finished putting some fresh bandages around his torso. A couple of the town's citizens were conspicuous by their absence, Cole suddenly realized — Simone McKay and William Durand.

He stepped across the room and shook the hand Casebolt held out to him. "Are you all right, Billy?" he asked.

"Mr. Casebolt will be fine," Kent answered before the deputy could speak. "He aggravated a previous injury tonight, but other than losing some more blood, he didn't do any further damage to the wound. With rest and proper care, he should make a complete recovery."

"What happened to you?" Cole demanded.

"That fella Strawhorn shot me," replied Casebolt. "Did his best to kill me a couple of times now. Wish I could catch up to him and settle the score."

"Strawhorn?" Cole repeated. "You were supposed to be keeping an eye on him, not getting into a gunfight with him."

Casebolt shook his head. "It wasn't a gunfight. He tried to kill me when I caught him havin' a secret meetin' with Durand. They was plannin' to hold up the train and steal that payroll money."

This was going almost too fast for Cole,

and Michael was obviously just as confused. "Where's my wife?" he asked urgently.

An expression of sympathy and concern appeared on Kent's bearded features. "Durand and Strawhorn and another desperado took her with them, Michael, when they fled from Wind River earlier tonight." He sighed heavily. "They took Mrs. McKay, too."

"Dear Lord," Michael whispered, his voice stunned. "Was Delia all right?"

"She was alive when they left here." Kent shook his head. "I can't speak for the safety of either woman by now."

Cole felt sorry for Michael, who was clearly shaken to the core by this news, but there was no time right now to be patting anybody on the back and telling them things were going to be all right. He said grimly to his deputy, "Billy, you'd better start at the first and tell me everything that's happened around here in the past four days."

Casebolt did, aided by Dr. Kent. Within a few minutes they had laid it out for him as they had pieced it together, the whole story, from the partnership between Durand and Strawhorn, to the accidental discovery by Delia and Gretchen and Simone, to the outlaws' flight from Wind River with the two women as their hostages. "I'm fixin' to get on their trail right now," Casebolt

324

concluded, "just as soon as the doc gives me my shirt back."

"You'll do no such thing," Kent said briskly. "If you do anything except rest, Deputy, you'll be risking your life, and I'm not in the habit of losing patients like that."

"Dr. Kent's right, Billy," Cole told the older man. "You take it easy. You did a damn fine job uncovering all of this, and now you just leave it up to me." His earlier weariness was gone now, forgotten in his desire to see justice catch up to Durand and Strawhorn. "I'll get after them right away."

"I'm going with you," Michael said in a choked voice. "They've got my wife."

Cole was about to tell him no, then he saw how futile that would be. If he had been in Michael's place, no force on earth would have stopped him from going after the fugitives. Michael had a right to come along.

Cole nodded and clapped the young man on the shoulder. "Get yourself a fresh horse," he said. "You'll need one."

Abigail Paine stepped forward and said, "I'll take care of little Gretchen for you, Michael. She can stay with us until you and Delia get back."

"Thank you, Mrs. Paine." Michael hugged the child hard, kissed her, then said, "You be good, Gretchen, you hear? I'm going to get your mama."

The little girl tried to cling to his neck, but Michael handed her over to Abigail, even though Cole could see it pained him to do so. Michael turned to the marshal and nodded his readiness to go.

"You'll be in charge around here until I get back, Billy," Cole told Casebolt, "but take it easy as much as you can."

The deputy promised to do as Cole said, then went on, "You better be careful, Marshal. That Strawhorn's fast, damned fast. And you can't trust Durand."

"I never did," Cole said flatly.

He and Michael strode out of the doctor's office and went back to where they had left their horses. The mounts were worn-out from the long, fruitless chase, and although Cole hated to set off on some other horse, he knew Ulysses had to have some rest. Quickly, he led the sorrel to the livery barn to be unsaddled. Michael followed him.

It didn't take long for both men to get fresh mounts under them. As they rode out of the stable Michael asked, "Are you going to form a new posse?"

Cole shook his head. "The men who went with us are as used up as those horses we left back there. You and me have personal stakes in this, but I can't ask anybody else to go along. There's no way of knowing how long it's going to take, and these folks have lives of their own they need to get on with."

"You won't turn back, though, will you?" Michael asked desperately. "No matter how long it takes?"

"I won't turn back," Cole vowed, "not until those ladies are safe, and Durand and Strawhorn have gotten what's coming to them."

Thunder was rolling and booming to the north as Cole and Michael rode northwest. Cole knew from his talk with Casebolt that Strawhorn and Durand had fled in this direction with their captives. He watched the sky as streaks of lightning played through the gathering clouds. "Can't tell if that storm's coming this way or not," he mused aloud.

"Does it matter if it does?" Michael asked. "You're not really following any tracks, are you? You couldn't see them in the dark."

"That's true enough," Cole said. He was holding his horse to a walk, saving the animal's strength and stamina for later, if he needed it. "What I thought we'd do is stop by Kermit Sawyer's place and find out if anybody there noticed some riders going by earlier in the night. That valley where

Sawyer's got his ranch is the easiest passage through the foothills, and I figure Strawhorn and Durand would take that route if they want to put a lot of miles behind them as fast as they can."

"And if Sawyer or some of his men saw them?"

Cole shrugged. "Then we'll know we're on the right track. We'll spend the rest of the night at the ranch and start out again at first light in the morning. Like you said, we can't track at night." He paused, then added, "Well, actually, some folks can, if there's enough light from the moon and stars. But that's not the case tonight. Too many clouds have blown in. Getting back to your question, I'd just as soon it didn't rain. That'd just make it harder to follow when we *do* pick up their tracks."

Michael nodded and muttered, "I guess there's a lot I don't know about living out here on the frontier."

Cole glanced over at him. "You'll learn," he said. He had grown to like Michael over the past few days. The young newspaperman hadn't complained any more than any of the other townies, and although he wasn't much good during the fight with the outlaws, he hadn't lost his nerve. As Michael himself had said, he was just inexperienced.

Cole hoped the youngster lived long enough to gain that experience.

Even in the darkness, Cole was able to follow the trail that led to Sawyer's Diamond S spread. When he and Michael topped the bluff and started down into the valley, Cole frowned and said, "Look yonder."

"At what?"

"All the lights burning at Sawyer's headquarters. Except for a couple of nighthawks, everybody ought to be asleep by now and the cabins ought to be dark. Maybe they've had some trouble." Cole glanced at the sky to the north and could almost feel electricity crackling in the dry air. "Could be the cattle are restless from this weather and Sawyer's trying to keep them from stampeding again."

As they approached the cabins a voice suddenly challenged them from the shadows, demanding to know who they were. "Marshal Tyler and Michael Hatfield from Wind River," Cole called in return. "What's going on around here?"

"There's been trouble, Marshal," the cowboy who was on guard duty replied, walking his horse out from behind some trees. He was carrying a Winchester across the cantle of his saddle. "Ride on in, but be sure to sing out to let 'em know you're comin'."

"Thanks," Cole said, then heeled his horse into a faster gait. Michael followed.

A few minutes later they were being ushered into Sawyer's cabin by another rifle-carrying ranch hand. Another puncher — Cole recognized him as the one who had brought him and Dr. Kent out here after the cowboy called Sammy had been trampled — was sitting in a chair with his bandaged head drooping forward. "It's all my fault," he was saying.

"I want you to stop that damned foolishness, Lon," Sawyer told him sternly. The old cattleman was sitting on the bed while another man wound a strip of cloth around his head. Both Sawyer and the cowboy called Lon had obviously been clouted by somebody. Sawyer looked up, saw Cole and Michael, and grunted, "It's about time the law got here."

"What happened?" Cole asked.

"That fella Durand was here earlier," Sawyer replied, "along with some hardcase pard of his. That other son of a bitch pistol-whipped me, knocked me out. Then Durand stole the poke I brought up here with me from Texas." He growled, "This country's full o' thieves."

Cole didn't waste time arguing with him. "Did they have two women with them?"

Sawyer frowned. "Women? I didn't see anybody but Durand and that bastard Strawhorn, I think Durand called him. After they laid me out, they did the same for Lon here, then stampeded the cattle we had penned up in the corrals and took off headin' north, as best we can figure. Happened less'n an hour ago."

"They're heading for the mountains," Cole muttered.

"Yeah." The man bandaging Sawyer's head finished, and the cattleman stood up. "But I'm goin' after them. They won't get away."

"You'll have company," Cole said. "Michael and I are trailing them, too."

"What the hell's goin' on, Tyler? I thought Durand was some big important businessman in that town of yours. I even made a deal with him myself."

Cole said, "We don't know the whole story yet, but it looks like Durand was nothing but a crook. He set up Strawhorn to steal a Union Pacific payroll from the train bringing it in. I took a posse out after the robbers, but two of 'em got away. That had to be Strawhorn and another man. They circled back to Wind River to split the loot with Durand, but things didn't work out for them. All three of them nearly got caught, and they had to run." He looked over at Michael. "Durand probably sent your wife and Mrs. McKay around the ranch with that other outlaw to watch them. They'll all meet up again somewhere north of here."

"I've done enough jawin', and listened to enough, too," Sawyer said as he reached for a gunbelt hung from a peg on the wall. "My boys got their hands full keepin' that herd from goin' crazy again, but they can manage without me for a while. I'm goin' after Durand."

"So are we. Might as well ride together."

Sawyer looked stonily at Cole for a few seconds, the old resentments obviously still there. But then he nodded abruptly. "Might as well," he agreed.

The young cowboy called Lon stood up. "I'm going with you, boss," he said.

Sawyer shook his head. "Nope. I know you feel like you got a score to settle with those bastards, Lon, but this is a job for the marshal and me and this other fella."

"Damn it, Mr. Sawyer, one of 'em hit me over the head —"

"I know it. But I promised —"

Lon interrupted, his voice bitter. "I know, you promised my mama you'd look after me. But you knew this trip up here wouldn't be easy. Why in blazes did you bring me along if you knew it was goin' to be dangerous?"

"I've asked myself that same question, boy," snapped Sawyer. "Now, you do as you're told." He finished buckling on the gunbelt, then took down a Winchester from another set of pegs. He picked up his black hat and put it on gingerly, wincing a little as it came down over the bandages around his head. "Come on if you're ridin' with me," he said to Cole and Michael. "We got some owlhoots to catch."

They followed him out of the ranch house. Sawyer obviously intended to take up the trail tonight, storm or no storm. Now that he knew how close they were behind Durand and Strawhorn, Cole was inclined to agree. It wouldn't hurt to push on for part of the night, anyway.

The odds were even now, Cole thought as he and Sawyer and Michael mounted up and rode away from the Diamond S. Michael was a greenhorn, of course, but so was Durand, at least to a certain extent.

Something Sawyer had said came back to Cole suddenly. The rancher had referred to Wind River as "that town of yours." And that was the way Cole thought of it now, he realized. Somehow, without noticing it, he had put his nomadic existence working for the army and the railroad behind him, and now his life was tied up inextricably with the settlement called Wind River.

Despite the corruption that had lurked underneath the surface, he sensed that the town would be a good place to live, a good place to settle down and make a life. The whole idea came as a surprise to him, and his acceptance of it came as a bigger surprise. He knew now that when he had ridden into Wind River tonight, he felt like he was coming home. He looked forward to experiencing that feeling again.

But first there was a chore to do and some scores to settle with William Durand and Deke Strawhorn.

Cole was looking forward to *that,* too.

CHAPTER 17

Simone's body was a mass of pain as she rocked back and forth in the saddle. Strawhorn had not called a halt until well after midnight the night before, and they had all been up and in the saddle before dawn this morning. The lack of sleep and the unaccustomed exertion had taken a toll on Simone, and on Delia Hatfield as well, Simone knew. Delia was still riding with the man called Benton, who seemed to have taken quite a liking to her.

So far neither of the women had been molested; the outlaws had been too tired the night before to do anything except sleep and take turns standing guard. But Simone knew that situation wouldn't last. Eventually, once the fugitives thought they were safely beyond pursuit and could slow down, she and Delia would be attacked.

Before she would allow herself to submit to them, Simone vowed, she would throw herself in a ravine or off the side of a bluff. She just hoped she would have the resolve to carry through on that when the time came.

Strawhorn and Benton kept an eye on their back trail as they led the group deeper into the foothills. The mountains of the Wind River range were still up ahead, seeming to draw closer at a snail's pace due to the deceptive nature of distances in this high, clear air. From time to time Simone looked back, too, hoping to see someone following them, someone who would rescue her and Delia.

The outlaws had a good lead on any posse that might have left Wind River, and a larger group wouldn't be able to travel as fast as the three outlaws and their hostages.

Simone did what she could to slow them down, hanging back on her horse and forcing Strawhorn to ride back and threaten her if she didn't pick up the pace. She knew he was losing patience with her, but she was going to stick to her plan as long as she could. It was the only hope for her and Delia.

There was one other thing to be thankful for — it hadn't rained the night before. The storm had slid out onto the plains to the east, leaving behind only some distant lightning and thunder. Simone was glad she hadn't been soaked by a downpour.

And that meant their tracks hadn't been washed out by the storm, too, and she was glad of that. Somewhere back there, some-one was following them. She sensed it in her bones, and from their attitudes, so did Strawhorn and Benton. Help was on its way.

Simone clung to that hope, clung to it tightly.

Michael Hatfield had gone beyond tired. He and Cole and Sawyer hadn't stopped until very late, and Michael had gotten only a couple hours of sleep. Cole let him take the last watch so that at least he could sleep straight through before taking his turn at standing guard, but that hadn't helped much. The long days of riding had hardened Michael's body somewhat. His aching muscles still cried out in protest at every jolt of the horse's hooves, though.

He didn't waste time and energy feeling sorry for himself. No matter how exhausted he was, the situation had to be worse for Delia, and his thoughts were all of her. He wished with all his heart that they hadn't parted angrily.

If only he could get her back safely, he promised himself, then he would give in to her demands and take her and Gretchen back to Cincinnati. But that was a big if, and Michael knew it.

At least it hadn't rained the night before. This morning, as the sun rose, Cole had picked up the tracks of four horses, one of them carrying double judging from the impressions left by its hooves. That was an encouraging sign; it meant that both women were still alive, even if they were also still prisoners.

Today the air was clear and clean and the sun cast a warm yellow glow as it rose higher in the blue sky. Cole was able to follow the tracks with little trouble, and he kept his companions and himself moving at a grueling pace.

They had already closed up some of the gap, Cole had declared earlier. Michael prayed the marshal was right and kept riding.

Right now that was all he could do.

Strawhorn reined in sharply. "Son of a bitch!" He was peering back to the south. Pointing, he asked Benton, "You see what I see?"

The other outlaw pulled his horse to a stop and turned around to stare at their back trail. About a mile behind them, three figures on horseback were silhouetted for a moment at the top of a ridge. The riders disappeared a second later.

"I saw 'em," Benton said grimly. "But there ain't nothin' sayin' they're after us, Deke. Could be somebody else ridin' through these hills. Trappers, maybe."

"Most of the beaver in these parts have been trapped out for twenty years or more." Strawhorn's voice was taut and angry. "I'd be willin' to bet one of those bastards is that damned marshal from Wind River."

Simone's heart leaped at Strawhorn's bitter declaration. From the first, she had known that the only real chance she and Delia had for survival lay in Cole Tyler. The frontiersman was probably the only man in Wind River with the savvy and toughness to track down the outlaws and rescue the prisoners. She hoped Strawhorn was right about the identity of the pursuers. She looked over at Delia, hoping to see some spark in the eyes of the other woman, but Delia still had her head down. Her shoulders slumped in despair.

Durand was sweating under the increasingly hot sun. He mopped moisture from his face with what had once been a fine silk handkerchief and asked nervously, "What do we do now?"

"We saw them, but there's a chance they

didn't see us," Strawhorn replied. "They must've damn near rode those horses into the ground to catch up to us. They ain't goin' to get discouraged and turn back. We'll have to deal with 'em sooner or later, and I want to pick the spot for the show-down."

"Then we push on?" Durand asked.

"We push on" — Strawhorn nodded — "but as soon as we find a good place to fort up, we'll fix a little surprise for Tyler and whoever he's got with him." A savage grin pulled Strawhorn's lips back. "This'll be one ambush that son of a bitch won't get out of."

This time Simone prayed he was wrong.

Cole felt like something was crawling up his spine. That was a sure sign of impending trouble, but he was damned if he could see where it was going to come from. His keen eyes had been searching the landscape in front of them all morning, but he hadn't caught even a glimpse of their quarry.

Durand and Strawhorn were up there somewhere, Cole knew, along with the prisoners and that other hardcase. The tracks were clear enough — four horses, one carrying double. Cole judged the fugitives were still almost an hour ahead of him and

Michael and Sawyer.

At the moment the trail was leading through a valley that twisted around among steep-sided, heavily timbered foothills. A narrow creek flowed through the valley as well, a ribbon of water lined with spruce and aspen and cottonwood. At one point, the tracks entered the creek, and Cole was afraid that Strawhorn was trying to throw off any pursuit by riding in the shallow stream and possibly even doubling back.

The tracks emerged, however, on the far side of the creek and continued on in roughly the same direction. Cole reined up and studied them, frowning.

"What's the matter?" Michael asked as he brought his mount to a stop alongside Cole's. Sawyer did likewise.

Cole shook his head. "Don't know. Something just feels wrong about this. Strawhorn had a chance to hide his trail for a while, and he didn't take it. That doesn't seem like him."

"Maybe he ain't thinkin' straight," Sawyer grunted. "From what you told me, he's been on the run for days now, first tryin' to get back to Wind River with that loot, then tryin' to get away from there. Could be he's tired."

"I sure am," Michael put in wearily.

"Strawhorn may be tired, but I don't think that would muddle him any," Cole said. "There's got to be a reason why he rode straight across that stream, but damned if I can figure out what it is."

He stared up the valley. The creek was to their left now, and the wooded slope to the right turned into a rocky, rugged-looking ridge about five hundred yards ahead. Cole's eyes scanned the face of the ridge but didn't see anything except some good-sized boulders that had tumbled down sometime in the past. The trail didn't veer toward the ridge but ran fairly straight beside the creek.

Cole gave a little shake of his head and shrugged. "Let's go," he said. "We won't catch up to 'em just sitting here."

He rode forward, trailed by Michael and Sawyer, but although he watched the tracks left by the outlaws, something kept drawing his eyes toward the rocky bluff. His frown deepened as he tried to figure out what was making his instincts react that way. Nothing about the trail had really changed, he told himself as they drew even with the point where the wooded hill gave way to the more rugged slope. There were still four horses ahead of them, one of the four still carrying more weight than the other three.

Cole hauled back on his mount's reins, a warning sounding in his mind as he realized what was wrong with the tracks. His eyes darted to the rocky bluff. The midday sunlight glinted on something in a cluster of boulders about fifty yards up the slope.

"Come on!" Cole shouted as he jerked his horse toward a grove of trees not far from the base of the bluff and kicked the animal into a gallop. He hoped Michael and Sawyer followed his lead, but there was no time to wait and see. As he leaned forward something buzzed past his ear and he heard the distant crack of a rifle.

Strawhorn had set up another ambush for him, and he had nearly stumbled right into it. If they had been riding alongside the creek, they would have been picked off like targets in a shooting gallery.

Puffs of powder smoke floated up from the rocks where the outlaws were hidden. Even though Cole hadn't seen them yet, he was sure the ambushers were Durand, Strawhorn, and the other hardcase. He pulled his horse to a skidding, sliding stop as he reached the trees and flung himself out of the saddle, pausing only long enough to jerk the Winchester free from its sheath before ducking behind one of the trees. A bullet chewed bark from the trunk about two feet above his head.

Michael and Sawyer had reached the trees safely as well. Cole saw. The Texan dismounted and sought cover as smoothly as Cole had, but Michael was slower and more awkward. Slugs kicked up dust around his feet as he clambered down from his horse. "Get down, Michael!" Cole called to him.

The young newspaperman threw himself headlong behind one of the trees, rolling over a couple of times to put the trunk between him and the rocks where the bushwhackers were holed up. He had had the presence of mind to hold on to his rifle, but it wasn't going to do him much good, pinned down like he was. He lay on his back, wincing as bullets plowed up dirt less than a foot away on either side of him.

"Don't move!" Cole told him. "Wait until Sawyer and I give you some covering fire, then get up on your feet again! Now!"

He thrust the barrel of his Winchester around the trunk of the tree and opened up with it, pouring lead toward the rocks but aiming deliberately low to avoid any chance of hitting one of the prisoners. He hoped Sawyer had the sense to do the same. The rapid fire from Cole and Sawyer made the shots from the bluff die away for a moment, and during the lull, Michael scrambled to his feet and pressed his body to the tree trunk. "I'm all right now!" he shouted to Cole.

Cole and Sawyer ducked behind their trees again to reload the rifles. Cole had plenty of shells in the loops of his gunbelt and in a small pouch just back of the sheathed knife on his left hip, but he didn't know how Sawyer was fixed for ammunition.

What they had here was a standoff, he thought as he studied the situation. He and Michael and Sawyer were spaced out in the trees about ten yards apart, and they could cover the whole face of the bluff with their fire. But they had to be careful for fear of hitting the two women, and the ambushers had them pinned down here behind the trees. This was as tricky a problem as Cole had run up against in a long time.

Sawyer leaned back a little to call past Michael, "How'd you know they were up there? The trail led alongside that creek!"

"My gut told me something was wrong," Cole replied, "but it took me a few minutes after we crossed the creek to figure out what it was. There were still the tracks of four horses, one of them carrying more than the other three just like before, but none of the tracks were as deep as they were on the other side of the creek. Two of the men dismounted in the creek, along with the women, while the third man led the horses on out of sight. The two men and the women walked downstream a ways before getting out and circling around to the bluff, where they met the fella with the horses. The plan was to lead us right in front of the rocks where they were hidden so they could pick us off. Once I figured it out, I got lucky enough to spot the sun shining on a rifle barrel up there and knew the trap was about to close."

The explanation was punctuated by continuing gunfire from the boulders where the outlaws were hidden, as well as the thud of bullets into the tree trunks. Even though they were pinned down, there had been no choice but to seek cover here. If they had fled the other way, back across the creek, it would have taken too long to get out of rifle range, and the ambushers could still have picked them off. Commanding the high ground as they did, Strawhorn and his companions had all the advantage.

But maybe there was a way to turn that around, Cole thought.

"Somebody's got to get above them and behind them on that slope," he said to Michael and Sawyer. "One of them must be guarding the women back behind those rocks while the other two take potshots at us. If we could get rid of that guard and get Mrs. Hatfield and Mrs. McKay to safety, then we'd have the other two in a cross fire."

"Not a bad plan," grunted Sawyer, "but how do you figure somebody's goin' to get behind 'em without gettin' shot?"

"Well, there is that problem," Cole admitted.

"I'll go," Michael said abruptly.

Cole exclaimed, "Wait a minute. You can't —"

He was too late. Michael was already sprinting out from behind the tree where he had taken cover. He dashed past Sawyer's position and through the grove of trees.

"Damn it, Michael!" Cole shouted. More shots were coming from the bluff as the bushwhackers concentrated their fire on Michael. Cole swung around the tree and went to a knee, firing as fast as he could toward the boulders, trying to give the young man at least a fighting chance. Sawyer was doing the same thing.

Michael emerged from the cover of the trees and started across a wide, grassy stretch. Suddenly he let out a cry and pitched forward, rolling over and over. He fell with the limp, nerveless sprawl of a man who had been fatally wounded, and as he came to a stop all Cole could see of him was one booted, motionless foot.

"Damn it," Cole grated. Michael hadn't had a chance, and now he was lying out there badly wounded or maybe even dead. And the odds against Cole and Sawyer had just risen that much more.

"Boy was brave but stupid," Sawyer called over to Cole. "Should've let us give him some covering fire first. You can do that while I give it a try."

"So that you can get yourself killed, too? Forget it, Sawyer, it was a bad idea. Maybe we can wait 'em out —"

Cole ducked as the shots from the bush-whackers swung back toward the trees and started chipping away at the bark again. One of those bullets was going to get lucky sooner or later and find him or Sawyer, and then the odds would get even worse for the survivor. He wished he had tumbled to the trick at the creek a little sooner so that he would have had time to work out a better plan.

He glanced again toward the spot where Michael had fallen, wondering if Delia Hatfield had seen her husband's sacrifice. Cole's eyes suddenly narrowed in surprise.

Michael's foot wasn't where it had been a

few moments earlier.

Cole felt a leap of hope inside and warned himself not to get carried away. Michael might have drawn his leg up out of sight in the tall grass as he writhed in the throes of death. But there was another possible explanation. The young man might have pretended to be mortally wounded and could even now be working his way slowly through the grass toward the bluff.

He searched the grass, looking for some telltale movement, since if he could follow Michael's progress by the waving of the stalks, so could the outlaws in those boulders. There was a breeze blowing down the valley, though, so Cole couldn't tell if the stirring he saw in the grass was caused by Michael or by the vagrant wind.

"Sawyer!" he called. "Can you see Michael anymore?"

The cattleman peered toward the spot where Michael had gone down, then looked over at Cole and shook his head. "He's not there anymore. You reckon he wasn't hurt as bad as it looked like?"

"I think maybe he wasn't wounded at all," Cole replied, knowing his voice wouldn't carry to the rocks, especially over the sound of the shots. "I think he's headed for that bluff. It's going to take him some time to get there, though, because he'll have to go slow."

For the first time since Cole had known him, Sawyer grinned. Granted, it was sort of an ugly expression, but it was still a grin, Cole thought. "We'll just have to keep those bastards busy for a while," the Texan called.

Cole levered his Winchester, edged the barrel around the trunk, and squeezed off a shot toward the boulders. He hoped he was right about Michael. He hoped, too, that the young man wouldn't get impatient and give away the game too early. They would lose whatever advantage they might have gained if Strawhorn and the others realized Michael was still alive before he managed to get behind them.

Over the next three quarters of an hour, Cole and Sawyer settled down into a routine, alternating shots and spacing them out so as to conserve ammunition but still keep the bushwhackers occupied.

Cole watched the open ground between the trees and the bluff, and he watched the face of the ridge itself, looking for any sign of Michael. His frustration grew as time passed and the young newspaperman didn't put in an appearance. Maybe he'd been wrong about what Michael was planning, Cole thought. Maybe Michael was still lying there in the grass, dead and just out of sight.

That thought was going through his head as he spotted a flicker of motion on the face of the bluff, about seventy-five yards to the right of the boulders where Strawhorn and Durand had forted up. Cole stared hard, waiting for something to move again, and was rewarded a couple of minutes later by the sight of Michael edging from one chunk of rock to another, staying out of sight as much as possible.

"He's up there," Cole called quietly to Sawyer. "Look to the right of those boulders."

"I see him," Sawyer grunted. "Think he can sneak up on those hardcases without them noticin' him?"

"They're not looking for any trouble from that direction. All we can do is hope," Cole said.

Hope . . . and keep throwing slugs to distract Strawhorn and Durand and the other outlaw until Michael was in position to strike. Michael wouldn't have thought it possible that his heart could pound so hard. With each beat it seemed as if it was going to tear itself right out of his chest. He had to stop every few feet and force himself to take several deep breaths in an effort to calm down. His nerves were stretched so tightly that it took all his willpower to keep himself from leaping up and charging the men who were holding his wife prisoner.

He had no idea where he had gotten the idea to fake being shot and then crawl through the tall grass toward the bluff. It had simply come to him, and he had acted on it before his fear could convince him to abandon the notion.

He had angled well away from the trees, crawling ever so slowly so as not to give away his position, raising his head just enough from time to time to make sure where he was. When he reached the bluff, he had started climbing, knowing that he had to get above the outlaws before he could work his way behind them.

It was working. He was less than fifty yards to the side of the boulders now, and he could look down and see Durand and Strawhorn crouching behind one of the big rocks as they peppered the trees with rifle fire. Farther up the slope, behind another boulder, were Delia and Simone McKay and a lean, dark man who was holding a revolver on them. None of them was looking in his direction, and Michael hoped that situation held true for the next few minutes.

He estimated that when he arrived behind the man who was standing guard over the prisoners, he would be about a dozen feet up the slope from the outlaw. He could drop the man with his rifle. It would be an easy shot. Durand and Strawhorn would be so surprised that he could probably shoot them, too, before they even turned around.

Michael asked himself if he could squeeze the trigger. He had never killed a man before, never even shot at a man. During that other ambush, when he had been riding with the posse, he hadn't even managed to get off a shot. Now he was planning to cold-bloodedly gun down one man and maybe two others.

But the lives of Delia and their unborn child were at stake now. That made all the difference. Michael told himself he could do whatever was necessary to save them.

He moved closer and then a little closer, carefully placing each of his feet so they wouldn't slip. Just a little farther, he told himself, a little farther . . .

That was when a rock shifted under his foot without warning and he started to slide down the face of the bluff. He caught his balance and stopped sliding, but the rifle slipped from his fingers and clattered down toward the startled outlaw, who was spinning around to see who was behind him.

No time to recover the rifle, Michael realized. Without thinking about it, he pushed himself away from the slope and threw himself into the air, diving down toward the gunman with an incoherent shout. The man was twisting around to meet this new threat, the revolver in his hand lifting and roaring as smoke blossomed from its muzzle almost in Michael's face as he hurtled down.

Cole saw Michael drop the rifle, then fall or jump, heard the young man's yell and the crack of the pistol. "Charge em!" Cole shouted to Sawyer as he came out from behind the tree and raced toward the cluster of boulders. He hoped that Michael's sudden appearance would distract the other two long enough for him and Sawyer to reach the rocks. One way or another, the standoff was over.

Simone McKay was as surprised as she had ever been in her life as Michael Hatfield hurtled down the face of the bluff and smashed into Benton, driving the owlhoot to the ground. She was afraid Benton had shot Michael at point-blank range, but the young man seemed unhurt as he started slamming frenzied punches into Benton's face. Michael was still shouting crazily, obvi-

354

ously fighting on instinct and anger.

She heard cries of alarm from Durand and Strawhorn. Strawhorn yelled, "Give Benton a hand, damn it!" Simone saw Durand's bulky figure racing around the boulder behind which she and Delia had been kept.

Her eyes fastened on something else then. Benton had dropped his gun when Michael landed on him, and the pistol was lying almost at her feet. She bent and scooped it up, her finger going through the trigger guard and her thumb looping over the hammer. Andrew had made sure she knew how to shoot a gun before moving her out here to the frontier, and although this Colt was heavier than the smaller pistols she was used to, the walnut grips of the gun felt good against her palm as she lifted the weapon and swung toward Durand.

He slid to a stop, holding his own rifle down low as he tried to see what was going on back here. His eyes widened as he saw Simone pointing the gun at him, steadying it now with both hands. He tried to bring the rifle up, but he was much too late.

"This is for Andrew," Simone said as she drew back the hammer. Then she pressed the trigger.

The pistol boomed and tried to come up, but she fought down the recoil as the first slug slammed into Durand's chest, driving him back against the rock. She cocked and fired again and again, a cloud of smoke drifting from the barrel and obscuring the sight of Durand bouncing off the boulder with each shot, his chest turning into a red ruin.

When she finally lowered the gun, she saw him fall to his knees, then slump forward to land on his side. He twisted his head so that he could look up at her. He managed to say, "I didn't —" and then blood gushed from his mouth, drowning anything else he was trying to say. The last thing he saw as death glazed his eyes was Simone McKay staring at him, a dazed expression on her face.

She stumbled back suddenly and let the empty gun fall from her hands as she shook her head. She tore her gaze away from Durand's body and saw that Delia had run out of the rocks and was making her way to safety down the slope. At least she must have thought she was safe, because her husband was still pounding away at Benton, whose struggles were weakening in the face of Michael's berserk rage.

But then Simone saw Deke Strawhorn step up onto a smaller rock and heard him yell, "Come back here, damn you!" Strawhorn's rifle came up to his shoulder, and Simone could look past him to see that he had his sights lined up on Delia's back.

"Strawhorn!" a voice shouted, and Simone recognized it as Cole Tyler's.

Cole saw Strawhorn's white hat rising as the man leaped onto one of the boulders and then aimed his rifle at the fleeing Delia Hatfield. As he shouted the outlaw's name Cole stopped and went to one knee to steady himself. The smooth stock of the Winchester nestled against his cheek as he settled the sights on Strawhorn's chest. A few yards away Kermit Sawyer was aiming at the gunman, too.

Strawhorn must have heard Cole's yell, because he swung around sharply, trying to bring his rifle to bear on the two men in front of the bluff. He actually got off the first shot, but it was a wild, hurried effort.

Cole fired, and a split second later so did Sawyer.

Both bullets bored into Strawhorn's chest, lifting him up and back off the boulder. His arms and legs flew out wildly as he seemed to sink in slow motion to the earth. An instant later he slammed into the ground on his back, already dead as he landed beside Durand's body, almost at the feet of Simone McKay.

That was the scene that greeted Cole when he bounded into the rocks a moment later. He had left Sawyer behind to grab Delia and stop her wild flight before she hurt herself. He had levered another shell into the Winchester's chamber as he ran up to the boulders, and he kept the rifle trained on Strawhorn as he went over to the sprawled body. Glancing at Simone, he asked, "Are you all right?"

She nodded jerkily. "I am now."

Strawhorn was dead, no doubt about it, and so was Durand. A few yards away a panting and shaken Michael Hatfield was still sitting astride the man he had battered into unconsciousness. Cole said, "What about you, Michael?"

"Wh-what?" Michael looked up, his hair disheveled, his face dirty and sweaty.

"Are you hurt?" Cole demanded.

Michael shook his head. "No, I . . . I'm all right. But . . . oh, God, where's Delia?"

"Take it easy, Hatfield," Sawyer called from down the slope as he led the shaking Delia toward the rocks. "Your wife's all right, too, just scared out of her wits. Why don't you come hug her and tell her everything's goin' to be all right, boy?"

Michael got to his feet and hurried down to meet them, folding Delia into his embrace

358

and holding her tightly. While Michael was doing that Cole finally lowered his rifle and heaved a weary sigh.

"It's over," Simone said. "It's finally over, and Andrew has been avenged."

Cole gestured at Durand. "You kill him?"

"Of course," Simone said. She sounded a little surprised at the question. "Wouldn't you have?"

Cole thought about Durand's treachery and Andrew McKay's murder, about how Billy Casebolt had almost been killed, about how close all of them had come to death because of Durand's ruthless greed.

"Yeah," Cole said. "I damn sure would have."

CHAPTER 18

It was another big day for Wind River. The roundhouse had been completed, and the first east-bound train would be pulling out shortly. Cole Tyler and Billy Casebolt strolled down the boardwalk toward the station, intending to see the train off. Casebolt was mending nicely from his wound, although the bandages around his midsection still made him walk a little stiffly.

Cole didn't expect to see Simone McKay at the depot today for the big send-off, or at least he hoped he wouldn't. Ever since the end of the ordeal with Durand and Strawhorn a few days earlier, Simone had kept pretty much to herself, moving back into the big house on the western edge of town.

Cole figured it would take her a while to get over everything that had happened, but sooner or later Simone would have to face up to her new responsibilities. He had taken it on himself to wade through all of Durand's paperwork, and the partnership agreements were clear enough. Durand had no relatives listed, so with one exception his assets reverted to the heir of his former partner.

Simone now owned practically the whole damned town.

The exception was the Diamond S, which was now Kermit Sawyer's free and clear. The way things had worked out, Simone was a rich woman, and Sawyer was well on his way to being the most important cattleman in the territory. Too bad folks had had to die for all that to come about, Cole thought. But the blame for that lay with Durand and Strawhorn — and Andrew McKay, because he had been part of the original plan to loot the territory by using Strawhorn's gang. McKay and Durand had intended to play both ends against the middle, and they had paid for their plotting.

Overall, Wind River was a lot happier place these days, what with the return of the rest of the Union Pacific payroll. Work was going ahead on the rails west of town, and the threat of a riot by the Irish laborers had evaporated. As marshal, now all Cole had to worry about were the usual problems: crooked gamblers, thieves, saloon brawlers, murderers . . .

Cole and Casebolt weren't the only ones on their way to the station. As they neared the newspaper office Michael Hatfield emerged, shrugging into his coat. He greeted them with a smile. "Hello, Marshal, Deputy Casebolt. Are you heading down to the depot?"

"That's right," Cole replied.

"So am I. This is a big story — the first train heading back east. Not as big as when the very first locomotive rolled into the station a while back, of course. That was quite a day."

"Yeah," Cole said dryly, remembering how the celebration had turned into a brawl and how he had found himself drawn inexorably into the affairs of the town called Wind River. "Quite a day."

"How's your wife doin', Michael?" Casebolt asked.

"She's fine. Dr. Kent examined her and said she and the baby are all right. He was worried that all that horseback riding would have caused problems with Delia's condition, but we were lucky."

"Hope you don't mind me sayin' so, but after everything that happened, I sort of figured she might be on that train headin' east."

"So did I," the young man said. "But Delia has surprised me. She moved back home from the hotel, and she says now she wants to stay here. I think it changed her opinion of me when I jumped down on top of that outlaw. Maybe she thinks now that I *can* take care of her and the children, even if the frontier is still wild." He smiled sheepishly as he fell in step beside Cole and Billy. "What I haven't told her is that I fell as much as I jumped, and I was lucky I landed on top of Benton without getting shot."

"You handled yourself all right," Cole told him. "You'll do fine out here, Michael, and I'm glad you and the missus are working things out."

"I hope we are," Michael said fervently. "I guess I'll just have to wait and see what happens."

"That's all anybody can do."

They arrived at the train station a few minutes later and found the platform fairly crowded, although it was nothing like that first day. Passengers were boarding the single passenger car while the engine steamed and rumbled at the head of the train. Cole spotted Dr. Judson Kent standing at one end of the platform and started toward him, leaving Michael and Casebolt talking to each other. As he approached the physician he saw that Kent hadn't noticed him yet but was instead watching intently as someone boarded the train. Cole glanced over and frowned. Kent was watching a gaudily dressed young woman who looked vaguely familiar. She looked back at the doctor for a second before she disappeared into the passenger car, and Cole recognized her as one of the soiled doves who worked the saloons.

What the hell was Kent's connection with a woman like that? Cole wondered. But he kept the thought to himself. He had come to respect and like Kent, and he wasn't going to pry into the man's personal business.

" 'Morning, Doctor," Cole said as he came up to the Englishman.

"Hello, Marshal," Kent replied, taking his eyes away from the train. "Are you here on business, or just celebrating the departure of the first train for the East?"

Cole said dryly, "I wouldn't call it celebrating. Just keeping an eye on things, I guess." He looked around the platform. "I was halfway expecting to see Mrs. McKay here with a bunch of trunks."

"You thought she would leave Wind River?" Kent sounded surprised by the idea.

Cole shrugged. "I figured it was possible after everything that happened. Got to be lots of bad memories here for the lady."

"True, true," murmured Kent. "But I think you underestimate Simone's strength. She does not like to allow anything to defeat her."

"Yep, I saw what she did to Durand. But I reckon she had a right if anybody did, considering how Durand killed her husband to get McKay out of the way and take over the whole town."

"If that's what happened," Kent said, then grimaced as if the words had come out of his mouth without his consent.

Cole looked sharply at him. "What's that mean? Mrs. McKay and Delia Hatfield both told us the things Durand and Strawhorn said about Andrew McKay being in on the plan from the first. Durand had plenty of motive for getting rid of him. What else could have happened, unless it really was a stray shot that killed McKay?"

"What else indeed?" Kent said with another glance at the train.

This was going beyond the realm of personal business and getting into something that he had a legitimate interest in as marshal, Cole thought. "You'd better tell me what's going on here, Judson," he said quietly. "I saw you looking at that young woman getting on the train a few minutes ago. Does she have something to do with this?"

"I honestly do not know," Kent replied, "but I've been doing a great deal of thinking about the matter. That woman is named Becky Lewis, and she is one of the, ah . . ."

"I know what she is," Cole said.

"Step over here to the corner of the platform where we can have some privacy," Kent said, "and I'll tell you the story as I know it, Marshal."

Cole followed the physician and listened intently as Kent explained to him about Becky Lewis's visit to his office and the condition in which she found herself. "I've decided to send her away so that she can make a new life for herself elsewhere, and thank God she agreed," the doctor concluded. "Simone was gracious enough to provide the funds so that Miss Lewis can do exactly that."

"You told her that her husband was maybe the daddy of that girl's baby?"

Kent nodded. "She took it very well, especially considering everything else that has happened recently to her. Simone McKay is, above all else, a lady, my friend. She was quite sympathetic toward Miss Lewis."

"Well, I reckon that's nice of her, all right, but what's all this got to do with McKay's murder?" asked Cole.

"I discovered inadvertently that the young woman was not completely truthful with me. She knew she was pregnant before she came to see me, and it's quite likely she even confronted Andrew McKay and demanded money from him. He refused. In fact, he laughed at her. Miss Lewis felt wronged — and she has quite a temper, I'm told."

Cole frowned in thought for a few seconds as he considered what Kent had told him, then his eyes widened abruptly in surprise. "You think this Lewis gal . . . Was she here on the platform the day McKay was killed?"

Kent's features were grim as he replied, "I've asked around in the saloons and determined that she was seen here before that brawl broke out. After the fighting began, no one noticed her anymore because they were all busy trying to break someone's head open or avoid having their own broken."

"Then, damn it, she could have been the one —" Cole started toward the train.

Kent stopped him with a firm hand on his arm. "Let her go, Cole," he said quietly. "You'll not accomplish a thing by bringing her back and forcing the truth out of her."

"But if she killed McKay —"

"Simone executed William Durand for killing her husband," Kent insisted. "She pulled the trigger of that gun and took his life. I for one do not care for the idea of telling her that she may have killed Durand for nothing. Although Lord knows the man deserved killing for other reasons," he added with a snort of contempt.

"Yeah, I reckon there's that to consider," Cole said grudgingly. "I don't much like it, though."

"Nor do I. Sometimes, however, it's better to do nothing and to let everyone involved forget. For Simone's sake . . ."

Cole nodded. "The train's about to pull out. I don't want to delay it."

Kent smiled. "Thank you, Cole."

The locomotive's whistle shrilled, signaling its departure. With steam billowing from the stack, the drivers began to work, turning the wheels and sending the train rolling down the tracks out of Wind River. Along with everyone else on the platform, Cole watched it leaving, but only he and Kent knew that it might be carrying Andrew McKay's murderer with it.

Or it might not, he thought. Kent was right; they might not ever know the truth, so it was best just to let things stand as they were.

Besides, he had other things to worry about. Wind River was still full of railroad workers and saloonkeepers and gamblers and wild cowboys. He and Sawyer had worked together temporarily to rescue Simone and Delia Hatfield, but it was clear the Texan still didn't much like Cole, and with Sawyer's growing power and influence, that could lead to problems in the future. Plus there was always the threat that the Sioux and the Shoshone might not continue to abide by the treaties they had signed with Washington, even though the Shoshone had helped save Billy Casebolt's life. All in all, Cole thought, it was going to be a long time before Wind River was truly civilized, and while he was the marshal, he was going to have his hands full. . . .

"Marshal," Billy Casebolt said urgently, breaking into Cole's reverie, "somebody just came runnin' up and told me there's fixin' to be a killin' in Hank Parker's saloon. Reckon we better do somethin' about it?"

Cole swung around, reaching down to make sure his revolver was loose in its holster. "That's what they pay us for," he said with a faint grin as he led the way off the platform. With Casebolt trailing him, he

369

headed for the downtown area at a fast walk, then broke into a run as he heard the crashes and angry shouts of another brawl erupting.

Yep, Wind River was a long way from civilized, all right. And right now that was just how Cole Tyler liked it.

ABOUT THE AUTHORS

Lifelong Texans, **James Reasoner** and **L.J. Washburn** have been husband and wife, and professional writers for more than thirty years. In that time, they have authored several hundred novels and short stories in numerous genres.

James is best known for his Westerns, historical novels, and war novels. He is also the author of two mystery novels that have achieved cult classic status, TEXAS WIND and DUST DEVILS. Writing under his own name and various pseudonyms, his novels have garnered praise from Publishers Weekly, Booklist, and the Los Angeles Times, as well as appearing on the New York Times and USA Today bestseller lists. He recently won the Peacemaker award for his novel Redemption, Kansas. His website is www.jamesreasoner.com

Livia J. (L.J.) Washburn has been writing professionally for over 30 years. Washburn received the Private Eye Writers of America award and the American Mystery award for the first Lucas Hallam mystery, WILD NIGHT. Her story "Panhandle Freight" a Hallam story, in The Traditional West anthology, was nominated for a Peacemaker award. Her website is www.liviajwashburn .com

They live in the small Texas town they grew up in.

Websites: www.jamesreasoner.com

www.liviajwashburn.com